Trickster

JAMES W. HALL

For Evelyn, my love, my rock.

"Time passes. Memory fades, memory adjusts, memory conforms to what we think we remember."

Joan Didion, Blue Nights

ONE

THORN HAD JUST FINISHED TYING off his skiff to the dock cleats when the girl appeared in his yard. The girl who would force him to reconsider every moment of the last twenty years.

It had been a gloomy summer with an unceasing string of tropical storms lined up from Africa to the Keys like a succession of armadas steaming off to war.

Between the rainfall and relentless wind, the fishing business had been dead through July and August—not a single buyer for his custom merchandise appeared at his dock, and now his tackle box, brimming over with freshly tied flies, was shut and gathering summer dust.

At first, to pass the vacant hours, he experimented with new designs, scraps of fur he'd scavenged from roadkill, squirrels, possums, and a host of unidentifiable pelts. He added snips of osprey and owl feathers he collected from his yard and others that washed up on the shoreline.

Odd jobs around the house distracted him for a while. Resetting the old Chicago bricks in the pathway to the dock. Sawing some pressure treated two by fours to replace a patch of dry rot on the railing of the upstairs deck—a job he halted until he could run down to Shell Lumber for the right galvanized nails.

To fill more squally days he settled into a chair to reread some old favorite sea stories from his shelves. But one by one he managed only a few pages before setting each aside. Books had never failed him before. Never once had the prose of a favorite author turned to blurry mush as his eyes traveled the lines of text.

Normally he would have taken breaks to drive down US 1 to Sugarman's PI office. Shoot the shit, catch up on island news or Sugar's latest case, plan an evening out to one of the local joints, Snappers, Lorelei, Sundowners. But Sugar was off on a cross-country trek with his twin daughters, a pre-college last hurrah before they headed off to Tallahassee.

Their postcards arrived once a week.

For Thorn's amusement, the girls selected cards featuring the most freakish roadside attractions they stumbled on: The World's Largest Ball of Paint in backwoods Georgia, a life-sized Triceratops splashed with dayglo colors, a chainsaw the size of an eighteen-wheeler, a six-story elephant looming over an Alabama tourist shop, a pod of blue whales swimming across an empty field in Tennessee advertising nothing but hillbilly eccentricity. Each postcard had the same scrawled message, "Having boatloads of fun, wish you were here, love you, Thorn."

Each gave him a twinge of pleasure and afterward, he stashed the postcards in a drawer of his rolltop and returned to them when he needed a boost.

All his guide buddies had fled the island for summer fishing gigs. A few were snagging salmon in Alaska, one was taking well-heeled parties to the rivers of Mongolia in search of Taimen, the monster-trout, and a couple had gone up to Ucluelet, British Columbia and Lake Ontario, looking for walleyes, big bass, and hammer-handle pike. No silly postcards from those hard-boiled hombres.

He hated to admit it, but he was lonely. As a confirmed hermit, he prided himself on being immune to loneliness. But this long, empty summer was exposing his hubris.

Even the local Key Largo nightlife had gone sour. The bar music was too loud, the laughter too raucous and it only took a few seconds for the ladies who wandered over to chat with Thorn to recoil at the flinty light in his eyes or his surly smile.

He was rotten company even for himself.

The only positive in those weeks of stormy weather was that the building project next door was dormant. Just twenty yards beyond the hardwood hammock where a dense stand of tamarind, West Indian mahogany, gumbo-limbo, boxwood, cocoplum, and a dozen other native trees and shrubs lined the northern border of his property and had given Thorn decades of privacy from the next-door neighbor, a development had been okayed by the Monroe County Commission. A Margaritaville Bar and Grille was planned for the adjoining six acres—seating capacity two hundred, rum drinks and late-night reggae, and a marina to accommodate boat traffic and jet skis. Thorn's worst nightmare.

He'd showed up at the zoning board meetings along with a few dozen other locals and they'd aired their grievances and made their righteous arguments and the board members had listened without comment. It was a lost cause. One more in a long string of lost causes in the Florida Keys where one side was fueled by a passion to preserve their ramshackle sanctuary, the other side fueled by barrels of cash. After the decision, a collection of local environmental groups hired an attorney to fight the development, but Thorn had seen that approach fail too many times to hold out hope. He'd been toying with the idea of selling his land and drifting down the Keys. Search out a spot so secluded even Jimmy Buffett couldn't find it.

It was a Thursday in late August, another thunderstorm with pelting rain and lightning stretching from Key Largo out to the western horizon, showing no sign of moving away. Thorn decided to hell with it, he'd filled his tacklebox to the brim with new flies and run out of inspiration. So, stormy weather be damned, he was going fishing.

In his flats boat, he plowed across the white caps of Blackwater Sound, headed through the Boggies, and slammed his way through the heavy chop past Nest Key, through Lake Key Pass, and across a stretch of bumpy open bay until he worked his way carefully through the channel at Crocodile Dragover and cruised into the relative calm of Madeira Bay.

His rain gear hadn't kept him dry so he stripped it off, then said what the hell and stripped off his soggy shirt and his drenched shorts, and stood naked in the rain in this hidden cove listening to the thunder rumble and growl like a savage beast roaming the heavens with yellow bolts of lightning firing from his fingertips.

He took a long look around, reminded why he treasured this wild spatter of mangrove islands and sandbars and seagrass, long-legged egrets and herons marking the ever-changing flats. Out here, he was inextricably mingled with the elements. There was no Thorn. His breath was the wind, his skin was the rain, his thoughts, his loneliness were the water and the light and the fish lurking below the surface waiting for the right bait to draw them out.

He tied a recent creation to his line, a crab fly made of olive-colored yarn from a sweater his mother knitted for Thorn when he was ten. For years, Thorn had been unraveling that sweater, using the strands of wool in dozens of different flies.

To form the bulk of the crab's body, he'd fuzzed up a couple of strands, scoring them with a dull knife blade, then he had attached the wool and two bead chain eyes to the number four hook, and tied on four black legs he'd fashioned from the rubber cover of an electrical cord he'd slitted into long stems.

Down on the muddy bottom, a redfish, tarpon or even a bonefish would not be counting the legs to see that Thorn's crab was missing four, or notice that the crab's bead chain eyes were on the wrong end of the body.

Balanced barefoot in the rocking skiff, in that deluge and wind, while concentrating on the tension in his line, the telltale riffles of water, alert to the slightest tug, Thorn felt a quiet elation. A challenging test of his patience, his watchfulness. All that noise and movement and chaos making it hard to keep a keen eye for any subtle cloudiness in the water where a fish was debating, wavering, tensing for a strike.

He picked a spot, cast and waited, gave the line a nip or two to tweak his wooly crab across the bottom, and when he'd waited long enough without a nibble, he hauled in his crab, chose another spot, measured the trajectory of the wind, the shifting current, and cast again and plonked it down for another presentation.

Whatever skills Thorn possessed, he'd earned on days like this. His senses trip-wired to the rod in his hand, the belly in the line, the shadows inside the shadows, the tricky light made by a steady stream of thunderbolts. He had no special powers, only these simple ones. These finely tuned senses, this determined patience and vigilance.

Around noon, he was about to put away his gear and call it a day, when he saw a small puff of silt near his bait. He waited. His fingers alive for the slightest tension, watching for the split-second move of the ghostly creature. If he twitched the line too early, it would scare away the fish, too late he would miss it entirely. Once the bait was in the fish's mouth, setting the hook too quick or too slow would lose him. The smarter the fish, the more perfect the timing had to be.

His arms relaxed and limber but taut.

Before it hit the wooly crab the fish must have accelerated from zero to sixty in a half second, slamming the bait, taking the hook, and Thorn stayed in tune with its pace, kept the line slack for a second, then two seconds before wrenching the line, feeling a deep jolt in his shoulders.

It was a brawny fish, though in the muddy water Thorn couldn't be sure what species. Of the thirty thousand types of fish that existed, only a dozen or so who haunted these waters were this fast and strong.

The fight was brutal, Thorn working hard to keep the stubborn fish from disappearing into the mangrove roots and breaking off the line. It took fifteen to twenty minutes, his shoulders starting to ache, arms sore, the rain coming down hard the whole time, but finally Thorn won back enough line to bring the fish close, and brought it to the surface, a big silvery bonefish.

Had to go around fourteen pounds, close to a world record specimen for the light tackle he was using. He drew the bone from the water, jimmied the hook from its gristly lip and slipped the exhausted creature back in the water, moved it back and forth to revive it, spoke a grateful word and gave it a small push, and watched it flash its silver fins in a last defiant gesture and disappear.

When it was gone, Thorn stood for a while and watched the ripples it left behind. Then he stored his gear, dressed in his sopping clothes, and cruised home through the downpour, lonely no more.

He tied off the skiff's lines to the dock cleats and was stepping onto the weathered wood when a car drove up his gravel drive.

A Rolls Royce. He wasn't sure of the model, a Silver Cloud, perhaps. But clearly a Rolls of a distant era, pearl blue with cream fenders, a bulging, ungainly vehicle.

When the car stopped, a girl exited the rear door, and the car turned slowly and headed out his drive to the Overseas Highway where the Thursday traffic roared like agitated surf—a steady stream of Harleys, RVs, rental cars, and the usual slew of Miami weekenders hauling ass to their getaway homes.

Thorn stepped closer for a better look and got a glimpse of the license. A Florida vanity plate: **TRKSTR**

The girl in his yard was a teenager, sixteen, seventeen. The black hair hanging loose to the middle of her back was curly with lustrous ringlets. She sauntered directly to the front of Thorn's house, crossing the property with the lazy swagger of a creature with no natural enemies.

In her right hand, she gripped a cell phone, in her left she held a small duffel. She halted in the scraggly grass and gazed out at Blackwater Sound, at Thorn's dock, his old Chris Craft cruiser and his flats boat, and when the kid met his eyes, she shook her head with something like disdain.

She wore faded blue jeans torn at the knees, and a white long-sleeved T-shirt that draped loose around her body, hiding her shape. Her basketball high-tops were black, the laces undone and trailing through the grass.

As Thorn crossed the yard to intercept her, the dark clouds parted, and for the first time in weeks, the sun materialized and almost instantly, the mushy ground began to fog the air with humidity as dense and airless as woodsmoke.

A believer in weather omens, Thorn took that sudden return of the sun as an encouraging sign. How wrong he was.

The girl watched Thorn approach with cool disinterest.

"May I help you?"

"Maybe, maybe not," she said. "But I guess we'll see, won't we?"

The message on her T-shirt looked like it had been scrawled in Magic Marker.

What the fuck are you staring at?

The phrase appeared below a rip in the cloth that exposed her considerable cleavage.

"Okay, what do you need?"

"What do you have to offer?" the kid said with a sly smile.

Thorn didn't bother with a comeback.

She chuckled and said, "So, I take it you're Thorn?"

"That's my name. And yours?"

"How's Stetson strike you?"

"Stetson." Thorn paused, fetching for the name among his friends' kids, drawing a blank.

"You know, like the hat. Kind cowboys wear. Cowboys like you."

"What makes you think that?"

Stetson nodded toward the dock, the water, Thorn's boats.

"A quick look around, evaluating what I see."

"A skiff and a prehistoric cruiser, that makes me a cowboy?"

"You don't like the label? Consider it an insult?"

"Do I know you? Have we met?"

"Not in person, no."

"What's that mean?"

"Something for you to figure out."

"Let's cut the crap. Who are you, what're you doing here?"

"You look a little flushed. Got a blood pressure issue?"

"Come on, kid. Are you lost?'

"Isn't everybody? Aren't you?"

"I'm not going to ask again. What do you want?"

"I believe I was expecting somebody you're not. That's my first impression, but I'm willing to be convinced otherwise."

Thorn took a leisurely breath. Irritated but intrigued.

In the midday sun, the girl's skin had the tint and silkiness of butterscotch pudding.

"This game we're playing, give me the rules so I can compete."

"Games are for children."

"Okay, let's try this. Who was driving the Rolls? Why'd they bring you here?"

"You're not real smart, are you?"

"Depends," Thorn said, "what scale you're using."

She snorted with scorn.

"Sure. So, you know about boats, navigating by the stars, nautical bullshit. But nothing that matters."

"Might matter if you were lost at sea."

"There it is again. You've got a thing about being lost, don't you?"

Thorn stooped a few inches to peer directly into the girl's eyes.

"Are we going to keep playing smartass ping pong, or you going to tell me what the hell you're doing here?"

The girl smiled. Pale lavender eyes with lashes so long a flutter might make wind chimes tinkle. She was going to break hearts if she hadn't already.

"Oh, no. Have I pissed off the cowboy?"

"That what you're trying to do?"

The girl groaned her impatience and ambled off toward the shore with a loose-limbed cockiness that struck Thorn as more performance than genuine. He caught up to her as she was halfway out the dock.

"What the hell is that thing?"

She pointed at the piling where a metal hook extended two feet over the water.

"An artifact from a bygone era when fishermen used to hang up their catch."

"Their dead fish, you mean. Displaying their manhood, their substitute cocks."

"That sounds about right."

She looked at him, studying his eyes for several seconds.

"Now that I've had a good look," the girl said, "I don't think you could manage it."

"Manage what?"

"Seeing you up close, seeing all this." She motioned at his boats then turned and dismissed his house and land with a backhanded wave. "I think you're an imposter. You've got that tight ass look, more worrier than warrior."

"So that's what you're looking for, a warrior? Gun for hire?"

She settled her gaze on him, and the quiet ache in her eyes softened his exasperation.

"You hungry, kid? I could use some lunch."

Stetson was studying Thorn's flats boat.

"Like what?"

Thorn said, "Fish sandwich, fries. Take the skiff to Buzzard's Roost."

"The two of us in that boat?"

"Best fish sandwich in the Keys."

"That's your big idea?" Stetson said. "Shoot the shit, get to know each other. Win me over with French fries."

"I'm buying," Thorn said.

Her chuckle was derisive as was the shake of her head.

"Sure, whatever. Give it your best shot."

TWO

THORN CHANGED OUT OF HIS damp clothes, swapping one pair of shorts and T-shirt for another, then met Stetson at the dock.

Under the brightening sky, Blackwater Sound was as flat and polished as a silver tray. Its surface marred only by a single windsurfer, a distant jet ski, and a sloop on its lazy way south into the mouth of Dusenbury Creek. A rare moment when no other powerboats but his own were churning up the bay.

Perched on the narrow bench seat with her back against the center console, Stetson faced into the breeze. Her raven hair streamed around the sides of the fiberglass and whipped across Thorn's hands on the wheel, tickling his fingers. An oddly intimate sensation that gave him a momentary shiver of unease.

He didn't know how to read the girl's posture. Her rigid back, her motionless head. Not so much as a glance at the boy her age flashing past on a jet ski, whooping into the wind, or the three dolphins that rolled in their starboard wake for a few hundred yards before those supple creatures curled away for more important missions. She might have been terrified or bored. It could have been her first boat ride or one more in a long string.

Thorn cut his speed, idled through Adams Cut, and on the far end, entering Largo Sound, he flattened the throttle and rose back on plane, swung into the mouth of North Sound Creek, then skimmed through the mangrove canals to Rattlesnake Key, and finally Garden Cove.

An easy thirty-minute trip. Over the years he'd navigated these channels with friends and lovers, but mostly alone, covering the same course in every weather and at every hour of the day and night. Back in that tangle of waterways, he'd explored each nameless creek and cove, pushed his way through snarls of branches to reach lagoons where he'd caught countless fish, drifted for hours studying the flights of spoonbills and cooper hawks and ospreys going about their business.

But he'd never made the trip with such strange cargo.

When they docked, the restaurant was packed and noisy, but Carla Sheets spotted Thorn, signaled him to follow her and she whisked away the dishes of a departing party and settled Thorn and Stetson in a premier spot with a view down the narrow canal toward the Atlantic beyond. Long ago Carla and Thorn had been classmates at Coral Shores High, dated a few times though nothing serious. Stayed cordial over the years.

"Who's your friend, Thorn?"

Carla smiled at Stetson, but the girl kept her head down and said, "Not friends. Not even close."

Carla gave Thorn a 'what's-with-her' shrug.

"We're working on her manners," Thorn said. "Got a way to go."

"Menu," Stetson said.

"Right away, ma'am."

She sent Thorn a sympathetic eye roll. Though he tried to steer clear of local gossip, he knew Carla's teenage daughter was building a substantial file with the Monroe County Sheriff's department. Petty stuff so far, but a bad trajectory.

Carla brought menus and Stetson sighed and flipped hers open, scanned it for a few moments and slapped it shut, and slid it aside.

"Conch fritters, yellowtail, grouper, mahi, fried, grilled, blackened, same fish, same preps. Day after day after day."

"Which means you live in the Keys."

"Brilliant deduction."

"Well, the good news is, those fish were swimming an hour ago."

"Like I said, same old shit."

"Your mother makes you meatloaf, mashed potatoes, green bean casseroles?"

"I have no parents."

"Sorry to hear that."

"You don't either. Yours are dead."

That threw an extra beat into Thorn's pulse. He measured a breath, took a moment to let the heat in his cheeks cool, then said, "That's right. They're dead."

"Drunk driver forced them off the road. They drowned in Lake Surprise, just up the road from here. They were bringing you home from the hospital, day you were born. When the car hit the water, baby Thorn was thrown onto the shelf of the back window, saved from the rising water like Moses in the bullrushes."

"Where the hell did you hear that?"

"I didn't hear it. I read the stupid book. Though it wasn't Lake Surprise, or even Florida. But it's still you. It's your story."

"What book are we talking about?"

She grinned and shook her head.

"Oh, man, you're a major disappointment. North isn't this dumb."

"North?"

"In the book. The hero. North."

"You're going to have to sketch it in better for this dim-witted old guy."

"Just so you know," Stetson said, "I'm not your long-lost daughter, okay? We're not related in any way. Got it? So, cross that off your list of guesses."

Carla appeared at Thorn's shoulder.

"Decide?" she said. "Hogfish is super fresh. Mahi too."

Thorn ordered a grilled hogfish sandwich. Stetson settled for a house salad with blackened shrimp, balsamic on the side. When Carla was gone, Thorn studied the kid, settling on a different tack, non-threatening questions.

"How old are you?"

"Seventeen."

"You go to school?"

"When I feel like it."

"How often is that?"

"Not very."

"Coral Shores?"

She snorted her contempt.

"Home school."

"Who does the teaching?"

"I do," she said.

She looked away from Thorn, watching a rental pontoon boat full of landlubbers thump hard against a piling, the woman behind the wheel yipped and lurched away, foisting off the docking duties to a guy with gold chains looped around his neck. The Seventies living on.

"So, when you graduate, you plan on college?"

"I'm done with school. I'm ready to start my education."

It was an echo of a Mark Twain line if Thorn remembered right, which made the girl a bookish type or else suggested she lived among literate folks.

"And you, Thorn. You tried college but didn't make it through one semester. Got homesick for your flip-flops."

"You know a lot about me. Why's that?"

"Figure it out. Isn't that what you do? Play detective."

"Is that your real name? Stetson."

"You want to pick another, feel free. Do I look like a Bonnie to you? Grace?"

"Is this some kind of prank?" he said.

"I don't know. Is it?"

"This is tiresome."

Thorn ate a few bites of his sandwich, watching an old-timer in an aluminum skiff idling out the canal with a yellow lab beside him.

"What'd you say?"

Thorn continued to eat. Carla was right, the hogfish was damn fresh. He wasn't trying to provoke Stetson, if that was truly her name. Thorn had simply reached the final innings of this annoying game. At first, a duel of wits with a teenager was mildly diverting, a quirky story he'd share with Sugarman later. More entertaining than another day of make-work.

"I'm tiresome? Look at me. Is that what you called me? You? A guy with one friend in the world. Your only hobby is seducing the next piece of ass, then moving to the next. A guy caught in such a sad fucking loop, it's a wonder you can find a reason to get up in the morning. Same day as yesterday, same day as tomorrow. Now that's tiresome."

Thorn finished his sandwich, waited till Stetson had speared all the lettuce and shrimp she wanted and pushed her plate away. He caught Carla's eye and scribbled in the air.

She nodded. Gave him another pained look of commiseration. Fucking teenagers.

On the way back to Blackwater Sound, Thorn considered dumping the kid on one of the mangrove islands, let her practice her survival skills overnight, return at dawn and see if she was ready to talk. But he fought the impulse and made it back to his dock, got the lines fast, the bumpers in place, and without a word, he headed to the house.

"Oh, yeah, the silent treatment," Stetson said. "Very grown-up. Very mature."

With Stetson hovering behind, Thorn climbed the stairs and stopped at the doorway.

"I don't remember inviting you inside my house."

Stetson snapped a salute, her cellphone in the hand at her forehead, duffel in the other.

"Permission to come aboard, Captain. I promise to be slightly less tiresome."

Thorn considered his options for a moment, then held the screen door open and waved the kid inside.

She marched to Thorn's worktable, touched a finger to the custom vise.

"So, these are the famous bonefish flies."

Stetson set down her bag and flipped open the lid of the tackle box and bent to examine the contents.

"People pay you for these?"

"A meager amount."

"Your customers, they can't tie their own?"

"Most can."

"Why buy yours? Some kind of charity? Keeping poor Thorn afloat."

"Apparently they bring some people luck. Or so they say."

"I don't get it. What's the point?"

"Point of what?"

"All that work to catch a damn fish you're just going to let go."

"That *is* the point. The work."

"You can't eat bonefish."

"That's right."

"Which means you're just torturing it for perverse kicks."

"Bonefish are wary creatures. Catching one makes it a little smarter, more careful."

"What bullshit. It's torture, plain and simple. Hurting them for fun."

"Fish aren't mammals. Pain isn't an issue."

"If they have eyeballs, they're not plants." She huffed. "What's this supposed to be?"

She held up one of Thorn's latest patterns.

"I'm calling it shrimpzilla. The spun possum hair at the head pushes water, and that makes the tail wiggle. It has a single mono weed guard."

"Doesn't look like a shrimp."

"You're not a bonefish."

"Why not use a real shrimp?"

"Too easy."

"What's the goal, catch the fish or fake it out?"

"Both," Thorn said.

"This whole fishing thing, it's fucking sad. Those fish are your sacrificial lambs. They suffer so you can feel all manly. Throw a bunch of money at your flashy boats and rods and reels and all the swag that goes in your tackle box, and what's it for? Hours in the sun looking for a ripple, tail sticking out of the water, a trail of mud on the flats, whatever. You hook the unlucky bastard, dumb enough to fall for your fake shrimp, he fights for his life, scared shitless, all of it so you can hold him up for a photo and dump him back in the water. It's nothing but macho porn."

Thorn nodded.

"I see your point."

That shut up the kid for a minute. She looked around the open living room as if searching for more evidence against Thorn.

"There's a lot of that going around," she said. "Sacrificial lambs."

"In what way?"

"Never mind. Thanks anyway. You're not what you're cracked up to be."

"So, what're you planning to do? Call your chauffeur to drive you home?"

She sighed, did a theatrical eye roll.

"Look, if you're not going to explain how I can help, then you need to go. Your parents are probably worried. And I've pretty much had my fill of you."

"Whatever."

She said it with that dismissive teenage insolence that Sugar's daughters sometimes used. Phony indifference.

"Where's the bathroom in this dump? I got to pee."

After a second of hesitation, Thorn directed her to the john and when the door shut, he squatted beside the worktable, unzipped the kid's duffel, and dug through its contents. It was stuffed with clothes and toiletries. He dug deeper, searching for any ID, running his hands along the bottom of the duffel, poking along the sides. On one end, his fingers snagged a zippered pocket. He opened it, fished out a Ziploc bag filled with tiny black disks smaller than shirt buttons. He took one out, studied it for a moment. Nothing he'd ever seen before. Good bit heavier than a button. With a twinge of suspicion, he slipped the disk into his pocket.

He tucked the bag back in the compartment and closed the duffel. From his worktable, he picked up Stetson's cell phone, walked out to the deck, and made the call. Told the dispatcher he had a teenage trespasser who wouldn't leave, wouldn't reveal her identity. Somebody in a fancy car dumped her hours ago and hadn't returned. Probably a runaway. He'd tried to win her over, but she resisted everything, and he was out of options.

He went back inside and as Stetson exited the bathroom, he slipped the cell back on the worktable and busied himself with straightening his tools until the kid was by his side.

"Jesus, your bathroom's way too clean, toilet shiny, smells like Clorox. What're you, some kind of neat freak? Bet you fold your underwear, iron your socks."

"I don't own an iron," he said, "or socks."

"Yeah, yeah, good old North. Living the Spartan life beside his Walden Pond."

"What book are you talking about? This guy, North. His parents' car wreck."

"North, Thorn. It's an anagram. You need me to define that for you?"

As he was about to answer, out in his yard a siren whooped once.

"Aw, shit. What the hell did you do, Thorn?"

"Helping you get back home."

"Going to get me killed."

"You serious? Talk to me, Stetson. Be straight. Do it quick."

"Never mind. You made your choice. I'll deal with it."

He searched her face but saw no sign of fear, only the same tough audacity she'd shown from the start. For the last few hours, he'd tried and failed to separate truth from fiction in the things she said, until now he was no longer certain of the girl's mental health.

He went out to the deck and watched the deputy exit his patrol car and climb the stairs.

"That was one hell of a response time," Thorn said.

The deputy looked puzzled. His nameplate said: Minks.

"I just called it in two minutes ago."

"You're complaining I was quick?"

"Just surprised is all."

"I was passing by. Where's Stetson?"

"That's her name, yeah, but I don't remember mentioning it to dispatch."

"Where is she? She here or not?"

Thorn could see her slouching in the chair, eyes turned upward, glowering at the exposed beams. Resigned to the inevitable.

"You were sent, right?"

"I took the frigging call," Minks said. "You're that guy Thorn, aren't you?"

"I am."

Deputy Minks gave Thorn a weary look. He was a bulky guy, fifty pounds heavier than Thorn. Hair cut flat as a putting-green, shaved on the sides.

Thorn happened to know that Minks was new to the Monroe County Sheriff's department, transferred down from Miami PD a couple of months ago. Sugarman had heard the scuttlebutt and mentioned him in passing a few weeks back. His Miami record had somehow been expunged, so he was officially clean, but word had it that Minks was known to prey on the homeless and hookers he encountered on the Miami streets. Breaking ribs and fingers, exchanging get-out-of-jail cards for blowjobs.

"I got the license plate of the Rolls if that helps get her home. T-R-K-S-T-R. You want to write that down, or can you remember it?"

"I'll try extra hard to remember, okay?"

They were standing out on the open deck. Behind them, Blackwater Sound had turned noisy with weekend traffic including the ever-present parasail, two customers waving down at the poor earthbound fools.

"Look, the girl, I don't know who she is or what she wants. I tried to get her to open up but looks like the quickest way to get this kid home is for you guys to take over. Put the fear of god in her."

"I heard about you," Minks said. "Local fuckup, nose for trouble."

"We all have reputations, don't we?"

"What's that supposed to mean?"

Minks' eyes hardened, and his chin jutted, a look he probably used to intimidate law-abiding citizens. Didn't do much for Thorn.

"All right, smartass, move out of my way, let me do my fucking job."

Thorn stepped back and Minks opened the screen door and entered the house.

"Hey, Stetson," Minks called. "Come here, girl. I'm here to take you home."

THREE

AFTER MINKS LEFT WITH THE girl, Thorn sat out on the deck, stared out at Blackwater Sound, and reviewed the morning, running through his exchanges with Stetson, searching for any clues to her identity he'd missed. He sat and worked it through for maybe an hour. All he had at the end of it was the same few morsels. She was most likely a Keys kid with a bookish background, there was some character named North from a book that Thorn apparently reminded her of, and Stetson's parents were dead. But maybe all of it was a lie. Hard to tell. But all that stuff about his own background, his parents' car sailing into Lake Surprise, that was what he kept circling back to.

He was getting up to stretch his legs when another patrol car pulled into his drive.

Thorn walked downstairs as Officer Max Silverstein was unfolding from the driver's seat. Max had been a football star at Coral Shores, a couple of years before Thorn's era. He was a tall guy with long ropey muscles. End sweeps were his signature play. Deceptively strong, Max regularly flattened linebackers twice his size.

They shook hands and Max got right to it.

"I understand you've got a girl, a teen, she's trespassing, won't leave."

"Minks took her away more than an hour ago."

"Deputy Minks?"

Thorn explained about Stetson, the Rolls, the vanity plate, how he'd spent a few hours trying to wheedle some information from her. Got nothing except smartass.

"Minks recognized that plate. It mean anything to you?"

"Can't say it does."

"Minks knew the kid's name, but I don't remember mentioning it to dispatch. He got here no more than a minute after I called it in. Whole thing didn't seem right, but I let it slide."

"Minks is a big-time jerk. I can confirm that."

"I should've stopped him. Or called the department to check. It felt way off."

"Don't sweat it. You might've said her name to dispatch and forgot. Minks hears the call on the radio, he's driving by, so he responds. Didn't know it was me catching the 63. That's 'Criminal Trespass' for you civilians. I was on another call, a domestic clusterfuck. That's why it took so long."

"I don't like this," Thorn said. "Something's wrong."

"Whoa, now. I know how fond you are of messy situations, but you need to cool your jets. When I get to the station, I'll check on the girl. Probably a harmless mix-up. I'll call you, let you know what's cooking."

"No phone."

"Yeah, yeah. So, how is it you stay in touch with the world?"

"I try not to."

"Okay, look, so happens I live a couple of miles up the road, Canal Street, behind the Lazy Lobster, end of my shift, I pass by here. I'll swing in, let you know what's up face to face."

"I'd appreciate that. If for some reason I'm not here, would you leave a note? Door's always unlocked."

A few minutes after Silverstein left, unable to let it slide, Thorn started up his VW and headed down to Islamorada, picking the only loose thread he could think of. The one nagging him most.

Hooked on Books was in a strip shopping center at Mile Marker 81, the last bookstore still operating in the Upper Keys. Not long ago there'd been five local bookshops, mostly catering to tourists looking for Keys' history books, or glossy volumes on local birds and fish. The stores were also well-stocked with bestsellers and shelves full of Florida comic novels with garish covers and goofy serial killers.

Maybe they were out there, but Thorn had gone up against more than his share and hadn't met a goofy killer yet.

Crammed into the strip mall with the bookstore was a discount jeweler, a T-shirt shop, and a sandal warehouse. Thorn was mostly a library guy, but over the years he'd frequented Hooked on Books to buy birthday gifts for Sugarman's daughters and an occasional hardback copy for friends who admitted they'd never read Patrick Smith's *A Land Remembered*.

The middle-aged fellow behind the counter wore a Sundowners' T-shirt and had a mahogany tan and sun-burnt hair, the look of a local. The man set aside the magazine he was paging through and asked if he could help find something.

"I know this is weird. But I'm looking for a book with a character named North."

"Hell, I've heard weirder."

Thorn introduced himself and the guy said his name was Julius.

"That character's name is all I have to go on. Somebody I know made a big deal out of the book. I'd really like to track it down."

"Everything in the store is alphabetical," Julius said. "By author's last name."

"This is a character in the book, not the author."

"Doesn't ring a bell," Julius said. "But then I'm not much of a reader."

"You work in a bookstore."

"Yeah, it can be a drawback. But the owner's usually here and most people know what they're looking for. If it was me, I'd try Googling it. Put *North* together with *novel* or some other search terms. That's probably the best way."

"I don't have a computer," Thorn said.

"A smartphone would work."

Thorn shook his head.

Then he lifted his chin directing Julius's attention to the computer on the checkout desk.

"Sure," Julius said. "I could give it a shot."

The entrance bell rang, and two elderly women entered the store and marched to the back wall where the used paperbacks were shelved.

Julius brought the computer alive, typed in a few words then sighed.

Typed some more and sighed some more.

"Can't find anything?" Thorn said.

"Just the opposite. Two million hits. Take you a week to scroll through these."

"Well, thanks anyway."

"Tried narrowing the search. 'Fictional character, North.' 'Character in a novel, North.' Must be a very popular name for novel characters. You got another phrase I could use?"

"Try 'North, parents died in car crash.'"

"Car crash?"

Thorn shrugged.

"Just something my friend mentioned about one of the books."

Julius typed some more.

"Same thing. A few hundred thousand. Don't see anything about novels. You want to come around the counter and scroll through?"

"That's okay. I believe you."

The two ladies had appeared next to Thorn, each of them holding a stack of well-worn paperbacks.

"Be just a second," Julius said.

The lady in front grunted.

"All right, all right." Julius reached out and took the stack of books from the first lady and started ringing them up. "Tell you what, Thorn. Boss is doing an early happy hour at Morada Bay. Sandy Richards. She's the owner. Used to be a publishing kingpin in Manhattan. Big leagues. Ask her about this North fellow, if anybody knows, she's the one, better than Google. Tall, red hair. Can't miss her, she'll be the rowdiest one at the bar."

The tall, red-haired woman sat on a pink stool at the end of the bar. At the other end, three guys guffawed over some whispered joke. The woman sipped her margarita, then dabbed her tongue at the salt on the rim. She turned a page in the hardback book that lay on the bar in front of her. Nothing the least bit rowdy about her.

Thorn drifted over and asked if the stool beside her was taken.

She lifted an eyebrow at him and said, "Appears to be vacant."

When he'd settled in and ordered a Red Stripe and had a long sip, he turned to her and said, "Julius told me you might be able to help me with something."

"He called, said you were coming."

"Did he tell you what it was about?"

"North Danielson."

"Oh, so the guy has a last name."

"I take it you're not a reader, Mr. Thorn?"

"Not much modern stuff. Naval stories, adventure yarns, some non-fiction. So yeah, I'd call myself a reader. Though I can't remember ever bringing a book to a bar."

She dog-eared a page, closed the book, and gave him her full attention.

"I like to keep a hardback close by when I'm drinking in public," she said, "in case I need to clobber some asshole."

"I don't believe I've ever been hit by a book before. Not that I can remember."

"With the right book, a good whack can short circuit the memory."

Sandy Richards had cherry-red hair, just long enough to comb, and a dusting of freckles across her forehead. Her eyes were a lucid blue, eyebrows thick. The bridge of her nose was crimped as if she'd dented it when young and had never bothered having it straightened. There was something knowing and faintly ironic in her well-structured face. A worldly calm. She was older than Thorn, but hard to tell by how much. Maybe five years, maybe ten.

Thorn took another sip of his beer, set it down, and said, "So this North Danielson, what can you tell me about him?"

"Been a while since I read one, but I'll tell you what I remember."

She licked more salt from the rim, took a healthy swig, and exhaled. Looked around at the Thursday sunset crowd taking their places in the Adirondack chairs scattered on the expanse of white beach. A nice beach, better than most, but like all the others nearby, it was fake. The authentic shoreline in the Keys was rocky or lined with mangroves. That sand was probably scraped up in the Bahamas. But the sunset crowd didn't seem to mind. And Thorn no longer let such deceits aggravate him. It was Florida, after all, a paradise of artifice.

"I believe there's fourteen or fifteen of them so far," Sandy said. "First couple were pretty good, twenty years ago. Fast-moving, with a dash of poetry. Those first ones were surprise bestsellers. Made the author a shit-ton of cash right out of the gate. The rest in the series, the writing has gone steadily downhill. Schlock. But they still sell. Name recognition."

"Crime novels," Thorn said. "North is the hero."

"That's right."

"Can you tell me anything about him?"

"Anti-hero is more like it. Simple guy, bit of a smart ass in the Raymond Chandler mode. Not a cop or PI, lawyer, or journalist. He's a moody loner living a primitive life in Cape Cod in a beachfront house he inherited from some relative. No bank account, no savings. He gets by selling scrimshaw to local art galleries. So, there's this sensitive artistic side to the guy that apparently appeals to the ladies in the books, but he's basically a rough and ready brawler. No martial arts training. He's average size, not some six foot five and muscle bound jock. Just a tough, unconventional guy. People bring him their problems."

"He solves cases."

"Solves, yes, you could call it that, but he's no Sherlock. He can be a little dense. He blunders into things. Impulsive, unpredictable. He has his scruples but basically, he's a vigilante who knocks over all the hornet nests in his way to bring down the bad guys."

Thorn finished his Red Stripe in one long swallow and lifted a finger to the bartender who'd been watching the two of them.

"Refill?" he asked her.

"No, I'll just suck the life out of these ice cubes. Got to drive back up the road in a bit."

The bartender brought his beer and set down a plate of conch fritters.

"Help yourself," Sandy said. "I have a standing order for these."

"Thanks, but I had a late lunch."

In the mirror behind the bar, Thorn watched her eat. Nothing dainty about it. He suspected if he hadn't been sitting beside her, she would've wolfed down the whole plate in less than a minute.

"You seem to know a lot of details about this North fellow."

"My company published the first few books. I wasn't the editor, but I read them. Ordinarily, I wouldn't have bothered, but they made big money, got good reviews, I thought I should know what the fuss was about. Three books with my house, then the author moved across the street for a bigger payday."

"Across the street?"

"Another publisher."

The guys at the end of the bar clinked beer glasses and toasted something Thorn couldn't make out.

Sandy said, "The business has changed. Back then there was still competition, a dozen publishers fighting for the best writers. Not anymore. It's only three big boys now, there's no street to cross. There's a few dozen small presses in the minor leagues, but they pay shit. No way to bump up your advance. Everything is computerized, which means every publisher knows every book's sales figures, so authors are paid exactly what their last book earned, not a penny more. Good reviews, good writing, it doesn't figure in the equation. It's strictly corporate number crunching. One reason I decided to retire."

She looked at Thorn.

"Sorry," she said. "I'm boring you with publishing horseshit."

"Back to North," he said. "Did his parents happen to die in a car crash?"

"So, you *do* know the books."

"Is that a yes?"

"It's been years since I read that first one, *Under A Moonless Sky*, but yeah, I seem to recall a car crash. I believe North was a newborn coming home from the hospital. Drunk driver drove the family off the road, car sailed into a lake or a pond, parents drowned, baby North survived. Not even a day old and already an orphan. A mythic opening."

Thorn nodded. It took a few seconds, but finally he managed to draw a decent breath. Thorn had been that newborn, losing his parents in that exact same manner, though he'd never considered any of it mythic. Sugarman knew the complete story, but Thorn couldn't recall sharing it with anyone else and he was confident Sugar hadn't either.

"Looks like I'm going to have to sit down and read one," Thorn said.

"We don't carry them in the store. People around here seem to prefer their crime stories set in Florida."

"I'll check the library," Thorn said.

"Well, I have a few of those early ones at home. Happy to loan you whatever you'd like. I'll leave them at the store, and you could pick them up when it suits you, or if you're in a hurry, you could follow me home. I'm up in Tavernier, oceanside."

"I guess I am in kind of a hurry."

"Can I ask why you're so fixated on these books?"

He shook his head.

"Personal matter," he said. "I don't mean to be impolite."

"Well, that's very mysterious."

"Do you know the author personally?"

"Met her a few times at the office, her editor showing her around."

"What's her name?"

"Katarina Mayfield is her nom de plume. I don't recall her real one. Woodburn, Wood something or other. An odd name."

"You know if she has children?"

She closed her eyes and tipped her head upward, searching her memory.

"I think there might be a daughter. Probably a teen by now. Maybe an only child, I'm not sure about that."

"Would you happen to know if the daughter's name is Stetson?"

She picked up the last fritter, bit it in half, then dipped it in the cocktail sauce and slipped it into her mouth. Wiped the grease off her fingers on the paper napkin.

"Now that name I do remember. Such an unusual choice for a girl. Yes, Stetson. I think I remember mother and daughter were estranged. But I'm not sure I have that right. Could be another writer. So don't quote me on that part."

The bartender drifted down and asked if anyone wanted more. Sandy didn't and Thorn declined as well. He asked for the check.

"So yes, if you're willing, I'd like to borrow a couple of books."

"This is all very curious. Of course, you can borrow as many as you like, but I'm dying to know why the hell you're so eager."

"I'll fill you in, I promise, soon as I know for certain."

FOUR

JOHNNY JOE MINKS WAS COUNTING the twenties. Not that he didn't trust the guy. The man had always been a hundred percent reliable with his payments. Crisp new twenties every time. Never fifties or hundreds, just twenties. Do a job, bingo, a neat stack of twenties inside a plain envelope shows up inside his mailbox.

Minks stacked the bills because he liked feeling that paper in his hands. The touch of it, the crinkly fresh greenbacks, the smell, the tingle as he lay one new twenty on another, lined them up, Andrew Jackson looking out, all prissy and proper. Stacking them, neatening the stack, feeling those precise, perfectly sliced edges.

At that exact moment, the sun penetrated the smudgy window, shining right on the table, lighting up all that cash. Felt symbolic. A new day, a bright promise, the heavens smiling.

He stopped at a thousand and looked out at the doublewide across the asphalt strip that was known as Main Street in the trailer park. Old man Cooper was sitting out there in his rusty golf cart with aerials on each corner so he could fly his Miami Dolphin pennants—sitting in the sun in his ratty wife-beater and Bermudas. The guy was a ridiculous fan of a ridiculous team that hadn't had a decent season in fifty years.

Minks hated losers. And Breezy Palms Trailer Park was lousy with them. He'd hated the place the minute he set foot in it, but it met his needs, a crash pad where nobody gave a shit who he was. His neighbors were either drunks or so dazed by old age they didn't recognize him from one day to the next.

Minks kept an apartment twenty minutes up the road, an address where his mail went, his bills and shit. Far as the official world was concerned, that's where he lived. Minks knew there'd be a day when someone would come looking for him. There always had been that day and given his tendency toward felonious misconduct there always would be.

So, he lived in one place, kept the other as a ruse. After paying the sky-high rent for the dummy apartment, this shabby trailer was all he could afford on his cop's salary.

Blame that on the damn Miami Cubans, jacking up real estate prices in Key Largo. They'd bought half the houses on the island and were trying to buy the other half, hiking rents, tearing down cheap two-bedroom bungalows and replacing them with gaudy three-story monsters, cramming houses butt to jowls into every inch of the island.

Breezy Palms was the last trailer park still standing in the Upper Keys after Mildred or Marty or whatever the hell the last hurricane's name was. Minks hated the Keys. Hated all the water, the boats, the weekend partiers, the endless traffic streaming to Key West, kamikaze motorcycles flashing in and out between the campers and rental convertibles.

Minks hated just about everything about the Keys. The fucking humidity, the funky bars, and waterside restaurants where the white bread Canadians and Minnesotans went to soak up the atmosphere. Minks hated funky, hated Minnesota and Canada. All the things he hated made for a long list. Longer than he cared to consider.

With that five grand added to his nest egg, Florida could kiss his hairy ass goodbye.

His plan was to drive west, and when the money ran low, he'd use his sanitized resume to find police work in some Podunk town in Montana, Colorado, Idaho. He was pumped about the trip, driving those straight, empty roads past all that purple mountain majesty, waving grains of wheat, if that's how the song went.

Head west, take the southern route, hit New Orleans, down a few shots of a fine bourbon on Bourbon Street, hook up with a hooker or two. He'd heard there were good ones there. Russians, Latvians, those were his favorite. Proud broads, tough and tall. He liked bringing those bitches down a few notches, a quick knockaround, turn their legs to jelly. No blood or broken teeth, just leave a few bruises like yellow-blue souvenirs of Johnny Joe Minks.

He got back to counting. Another neat stack of twenties. Later he'd rubber band them, stuff them in the Subaru. A few thousand under the mat in his trunk, around the spare. Wedge some under the seats. Use all the cubby holes.

"New Orleans," he said. "Way down south in Dixie."

Uncle Jack stared at him. Sitting there on the tabletop. Ragged scars all over his tomcat head. Tuxedo cat with white spats, white vest, glossy black everywhere else, dressed like a dandy, but that cat was a headfirst motherfucker, taking on all comers around the trailer park after dark when he went out looking for trouble. Iguanas, possums, raccoons, other toms.

The cat didn't belong to anybody, but a few months back Uncle Jack and Minks bonded. He believed it was their shared love of battle.

Sometimes the cat even spoke to him, short sentences, one syllable words like dashed off texts. Johnny Joe knew the words were all in his head, but then, shit, what wasn't? The cat talked. Not much, and only when he had good reason. But he did, the fucker spoke English. Used better grammar than most of the assholes Minks dealt with day to day.

Uncle Jack reached out a paw and touched a stack of twenties. Like that damn cat understood the power in those bills. And he wanted to soak up its potency for the night ahead.

Minks watched as Uncle Jack kept his paw against the stack, then that tomcat turned his head and fixed his green eyes on Johnny Joe's and gave the stack a tiny push that sent the twenties fanning across the tabletop.

"Damn, Uncle. Look at the mess you made."

The cat drew his paw back and licked it for a few seconds then settled back into his casual perch, fixing his eyes on Minks.

"Knock it down," Uncle Jack said, "makes you boss."

See. Right there. English.

Uncle Jack rose, turned, and jumped from the table. He flicked his tail back and forth as he walked across the linoleum over to where the girl sat in the back room. To check on her, Minks had to push his kitchen chair a foot from the table and tip it back.

She was watching Uncle Jack's approach. Minks had stripped her to her bra and lacy panties. Fine-looking body on the young lady, some serious breasts and a teeny waist, shapely ass. When he undressed her, he'd been sorely tempted to go farther, but he knew better than to play around with this one.

She was glossy with sweat and had a lump on her jaw where Minks had to reason with her. That thick black hair with all those pretty curls had gotten snarled and clumpy.

He'd positioned her in the ratty recliner, Zip-tied her wrists behind her back. And her head was pinned tight against the headrest, held there by a couple of yards of fishing line he'd crisscrossed over her face and lashed to the headrest. Simple.

The fishing line was an emergency choice. He'd brought her back to the trailer and only then realized he was out of fucking duct tape. Fishing line was his creative solution. If it cut her a little that was her own damn fault.

When she struggled against the monofilament, it bit deep into her flesh. There was blood seeping from around her lips from when she'd smart-talked him. That girl had a wiseass mouth. But in the last few minutes, she'd quieted down. Glaring at him. Eyes on fire.

He'd told her, try screaming one time, that'll be the last noise you ever make.

Not that any of his neighbors would care, hell, if the deaf bastards could even hear it.

That old tomcat, Uncle Jack, stared up at the girl for a second or two, then sprang into her lap, licked up a few smears of blood on her silk panties, kneaded her crotch for a minute, then curled into a ball and went to sleep, resting up for the battles to come.

Minks got back to stacking the bills while a deep purr came from the back room.

Stetson had volunteered for the job. Selling her dad on her eagerness to join the family business. Pleading with him to give her a chance to show what she could do.

She'd heard him discussing the task with one of his flunkies and the hair rose on her neck. This was her chance.

A simple mission. Go to Thorn's house, replace a few duds. A basic assignment. The guy was gullible, an easy mark. That's how her dad described him.

Get in, distract him, do the job, get out. It should only take five minutes.

Once inside his house, pretend she saw someone offshore splashing around, drowning, and while Mr. Boy Scout was running down there to help, Stetson would do her work.

In and out, back to the highway, Facundo picks her up and brings her home.

"I can do it," she told him. "I won't let you down."

He handed her the Ziploc bag and said, "Better not."

Stetson's enthusiasm was a fraud. Scamming her dad so she could meet Thorn, size him up, see if he might be the pit bull she needed. Since her father was so fixated on the guy, Stetson was expecting someone formidable. A kick-ass hero. That's what she'd picked up from hearing bits and pieces of her father's conversations over the last few years, Thorn-this, Thorn-that. Somebody to reckon with.

But in person, Thorn was an instant disappointment. Such a simpleton. She'd been hoping for North's equal. Valiant, fearless, a well-muscled, ex-Marine, martial arts expert.

Of course, it was silly to think anyone could live up to North. She'd read every book her mother wrote, read most of them several times, saturated herself in North's world, his calm strength, his Zen-focus, his unwavering honesty, his willingness to take any risk to right wrongs and save the lives of the endangered. Sure, she knew North was fiction. She knew he was idealized. But she also believed that such men did exist outside the covers of books. She needed them to exist. And she needed to find one to help her do what she could not do alone.

So the minute she saw Thorn, his shaggy hair and brooding vibe, she couldn't help herself. She was so disheartened she'd started giving him shit, and eventually, he got testy back, and she lost her focus.

Christ, she'd even gone to lunch with the guy. Once she'd seen who he really was, she should've done her job and bailed. Look elsewhere for her white knight.

And to make matters more fucked up, her dad probably knew exactly what went down. He had eyes and ears everywhere. Up and down the Keys. Probably a spy at Buzzard's Roost. Some were trying to curry favor, others were on his payroll. What the hell was she thinking? She'd have to manage some fast talking to get out of this one.

"You're a lowlife scum-sucking pig," Stetson said, her voice muffled by the binding.

He scooted his chair back to see her, and he winked.

It hurt her to talk, the fishing line cutting deeper with every word.

"How'd you get like this?"

"Get like what?" he asked.

"Depraved."

"Depraved, hell, no. I'm hundred percent red-blooded normal."

"Kidnap a teenage girl, strip her, tie her up with fishing line. That's depraved shit."

"If you say so."

"How'd it happen? Parents abuse you, big brother come into your bed at night?"

"Listen to you, analyzing me, going to fix all my neuroses."

"You made a mistake, shit-for-brains. I'm not some skanky runaway you can sell to a sex trafficker."

"Oh, I don't know," Minks said. "You're a little skanky around the edges. But no, I got other ideas for you. More profitable."

"My people will track you down and split you into little pieces."

The asshole chuckled.

"You're fucked," she said. "You've stepped into poisonous quicksand."

Every syllable hurt. But she couldn't stop herself. Never could control her mouth.

"You don't know who I am, do you? You got no idea."

He kept counting the cash, stacking it.

"Your only chance is to cut me loose. Hope they don't find me like this."

Blood was dripping off her chin. Cat's raspy tongue licking it off her thighs.

"My father is going to eat you alive, slimeball. Gobble up your spleen."

Minks chuckled, looked over at her.

"Your father?" he said and chuckled again. "Who you think paid me all this cash?"

FIVE

THORN FOLLOWED SANDY RICHARDS' SILVER Jaguar north on the Overseas Highway to a cluster of low-rise condos on the oceanside in Tavernier. Million-dollar ocean views, a marina, a long dock. Gumbo limbos, mahogany, and Jamaican dogwoods created a solid canopy over the winding walkways.

Walker's Pointe had been built when Thorn was just a boy. Back then there'd been a fuss about the development violating the pristine land, followed by legal suits and public hearings, until finally, to quiet the outrage, the seller wrote a provision into the deed requiring all future owners of the land to preserve the native trees and flowering shrubs in perpetuity.

What had once seemed a quaint and naïve agreement had made Walker's Pointe one of the premier residences in the Upper Keys. A safe haven for wildlife and migrating birds, and a rare patch of shady land in the midst of the bulldozed and sparsely landscaped properties that surrounded it.

"You chose your home well," Thorn said as they walked together from the parking lot.

"It's my dad's place. He's lived here since it was built."

"Then I probably know him," Thorn said. "Small town."

"I'm not sure anybody knows him anymore."

Thorn didn't ask, and she didn't explain.

Sandy held the front door open and gestured him inside.

Across the living room, a bald man with a fringe of ginger hair stood at the picture window. The view of the Atlantic was framed by two arching coconut palms.

"That goddamn osprey has been screaming all afternoon like a five-alarm fire. Up in its nest on that light pole, noisy ass bird, trying to scare away a red-shouldered hawk in the oak over there. That's what I do, just stand here watching the goddamn birds, that's my complete day while you're gone. All I've got left."

"I've brought a guest, Dad."

The old man turned from the glass doors and peered at Thorn, frowned, and said, "Joe Bay, twenty-eight years ago, middle of January, just after sun-up."

It took Thorn a few beats to place the old man.

"Yeah, right. Northwest corner of the bay, a dogleg to the left, little pond up there. I scared off a school of tarpon you were into."

"Those were world-record fish, and they didn't return. All because of you."

"I thought it was my secret spot," Thorn said.

"But you were fucking-well wrong, weren't you?"

"Yes, sir. I fucking-well was."

"Well, good," Sandy said. "I'm glad we've got that out of the way."

That fishing hole was a mile off Joe Bay, up a maze of creeks to a tiny lagoon teeming with snook, tarpon, permit, lemon shark, and yellowtail snapper. It was a hard-won discovery Thorn had made after battling his way through tangles of mangroves and cobwebs and fallen limbs. Going back that second time, he'd been crestfallen to find this man casting his line in that lonesome spot he'd thought was all his own.

After a brief and grouchy exchange, Thorn retreated, puttering back the way he came, and he'd reluctantly scratched it off his list. Nowadays, all of Joe Bay was off limits to motorized craft. Only kayakers and canoers were allowed. A win for the fish. A sad day for Thorn, though he grudgingly supported the closure. Another necessary step to preserve what was left of the pristine backcountry from the hordes who'd been despoiling it for decades.

"Captain Harry, good to see you again after all these years."

"Can't say the same," the old man replied.

"Dad can hold a grudge longer than any man alive."

"You here to seduce my daughter?"

"He's here to borrow a book, Dad. That's all."

"Book, my ass. Don't believe it. This is Mr. Hot Sheets Thorn in case he hasn't introduced himself."

"That's one nickname I haven't heard."

"Fucked me up in Joe Bay, now he's come around to have his way with my daughter."

"I apologize," Sandy said. "I should have warned you. His memory is still firing on all cylinders, but some anger issues cropped up since his last stroke."

"I got good reason to be angry," Captain Harry said. "Plenty of good reasons."

"The books you're interested in are in here. We'll be right back, Dad."

"Pulse or no pulse, this guy will screw anything. Don't turn your back on the fucker."

Sandy led Thorn into the next room. Brightened by skylights and transom windows, the floor to ceiling bookshelves were glossy white and packed with hardbacks. Neatly ordered, a rainbow of spines radiant in the afternoon sunlight. There was a single chair and a reading lamp that sat on a marble-topped end table with heavy scrolled legs, furniture more suited to an elegant Victorian drawing room than a tropical condo.

"Besides the books, that table is the only thing I brought from New York," Sandy said, touching the white marble. "I know it doesn't fit. But what the hell. It's just me and Dad. If *Architectural Digest* happens to call, I'll stash it somewhere while they take their photos."

"It's a beautiful room," Thorn said.

"Well, the light's good. Even on all these cloudy days we've been having."

"It has been dreary, hasn't it?"

Thorn moved to the shelves that covered one wall.

"Listen to us," Sandy said. "Talking about the weather like a couple of awkward teens."

"It's that hot sheets thing," Thorn said.

"That's just Dad being Dad. If you were the Pope himself, he would've said the same."

Thorn scanned the shelves, the awkward silence fading.

"The books you're interested in. Here they are."

Sandy trailed her fingers across a row of bright red spines embossed with gold letters. They lined a shelf just below eye level.

"They're organized from her first to the fifth or sixth. That's when I gave up on her. Though she doesn't actually write them anymore."

"She retired?"

"No, no. The books still come out twice a year. Her name's still on them, but other writers do the work."

"She's still alive?"

"Far as I know. She lives on the Cape, but I believe she has a home down here, too. Key West probably. Actually, five or six homes scattered around, so I've heard. One in France, I think. Or maybe Spain."

"It can work like that? An author pays someone else to write their books. Isn't that cheating?"

"If you want to crank them out fast, that's how it's done. These days she pulls down four or five mil a book, five hundred of that will go to the hack writer, she pockets the rest."

"That's some kind of name recognition," he said.

"Oh, yes. She's up there with Stephen King, Grisham, Patterson, J.K. Rowling. I'm surprised you've never heard of her."

"Like I said, my taste is more last century, or the one before. Sea stories, yarns."

"Good reliable authors, sure, I get it. I have some I come back to over and over. Comfort food."

Sandy plucked a book from the shelf and handed it to him.

"This is the first one. The car crash book you mentioned. Take as many as you like."

Thorn held the book and fanned through the pages.

"Katarina Mayfield," he said, turning the book over, taking in the author photo that filled the back.

A sudden electrified jolt rippled through him.

Her wavy brown hair shone in the studio lights, large, dark eyes, lips slightly parted as if she were about to speak his name, a faint smile, amused by this photoshoot, a small-town girl's scorn of hoopla.

"Oh, wait," Sandy said. "I just remembered her real name."

Thorn said, "Kathy Spottswood."

"Wow. Then you do know her."

Thorn stepped closer to the window, tipped the book so her photo caught the full light.

"A long time ago." He looked out at the purpling sky. "A lover's kiss that lingers across the ghostly years."

"What's that? A poem?"

"Like a poem, I guess. A line from a song she used to sing."

"Katarina Mayfield was a singer?"

SIX

It was Sugarman who met Kathy Spottswood first. Back when he was a cop, he stopped her for doing eighty in a fifty zone. It was well after midnight in the summer slow season, the roads empty. She was on her way home after a late-night gig, not endangering anyone but herself.

They chatted on the roadside while his blue light whirled. She talked her way out of that ticket. One of her skills, a silver tongue, charm the birds from the trees, the bees from the blossoms. Sugarman was instantly swept away. Kathy invited him to come to her show at Snappers, one of the better local seafood joints. She played there on the weekends, singing solo, backed up by her acoustic guitar.

After he'd seen her perform several times, Sugar invited Thorn along. Sugarman was married, and though his marriage was unraveling, it wasn't in Sugar's nature to cheat, though he was surely tempted by Kathy. Maybe Thorn was Sugar's offering to this goddess of song. Thorn never asked him about that. Didn't really want to know. Didn't want to suggest that Sugar had pimped her. And later on, he didn't want to do anything that might muddy those luscious hours with Kathy Spottswood.

On stage she radiated a sly, erotic charm, nothing showy or vulgar, but that voice had depth and range, part opera star, part throaty roadhouse spitfire. Her lyrics were a rapturous poetry with an earthy country edge. Sugar described her songs as one part Joni Mitchell, a dollop of Dolly, and a healthy dose of Lena Horne's "Stormy Weather." When it came to musical expertise, Thorn wasn't in Sugar's league, but he'd never heard a singer that hooked him so fast and deep.

And he wasn't alone. That night the rest of the audience loved her too. Drinking men set down their beers and listened. The talkers shut up. Lovebirds swooned. The old couples laced their fingers together and smiled.

Kathy Spottswood wore a knee-length scarlet dress that glittered as if coated in crushed diamonds. It was cut low and revealed just enough of her breasts to lure the eye while remaining refined. Her hair was a lush cinnamon brown and fluttered against her bare shoulders in the ocean breeze. Her eyes were coffee dark, a heady brew. They seemed mirthful even when she wasn't smiling.

When her last set was done, she came to the table and sat down beside Sugarman, gave him a quick kiss on the cheek. Sugar was a handsome man whose Scandinavian mother passed on to him her long lashes and delicate cheekbones, and his Rasta father gave him the rawboned physique of a soccer star who could sprint for hours without breaking a sweat. His skin tone split the difference between those two cultures, a silky caramel with an extra spoonful of cream.

From any distance, Sugar and Kathy made a fetching couple.

Kathy politely brushed off Thorn's compliments about her singing. And to the people who stopped by their table to give the kind of breathless praise she must have heard hundreds of times before, she was gracious and welcoming, a reaction that seemed more patient than such intrusions might have deserved.

He noticed the untanned depression on the ring finger of her left hand. When she caught Thorn staring down at that hand displayed on the table-top, she smiled at him with a cock of her head which he took to mean the missing ring was not a burning issue.

As the last few tables on the outside deck emptied and the canned rock music on the speakers went silent, Sugarman stood, said it was past his bedtime. He looked back and forth between Thorn and Kathy as though waiting for them to stand.

When they didn't, he said, "You okay to drive, Thorn?"

"Just a couple of beers," he said. "I'm good."

"And you, Kathy. You need help getting your equipment into the car?"

"I'll manage, but thanks, Sugar."

He waited a few more seconds, appraising them, then sighed in quiet assent, and told them goodnight.

"I feel like I already know you." Those were Kathy's first words to him alone, as the staff cleared away the last of the dinner plates and silverware. "Sugar goes on and on about you."

"And hearing about me, it didn't scare you off?"

"I'm braver than I look."

"You saw me looking at your ring finger."

"Separated for a month, divorce should be final in a few weeks. My lawyer is aiming for the first of July, a month, maybe a little longer. So far, it's been less than amicable. Married for two years which was a year and eleven months too many. Is that enough?"

"Still, it takes a while for that groove in your finger to return to normal."

"Oh," she said. "A metaphor. The rare man who can manage two meanings at once."

She was quiet for a moment, looking down at her wine glass.

"Sugarman said you're not seeing anyone."

"True," Thorn said. "Been living the monastic life the last year or so."

"What do you consider monastic?"

"Other than Sugar, the only company I've had is a family of lizards that rent space under my couch."

"Lovely."

"They do a lot of pushups, more than I can manage, showing off. Cocky little guys."

"I believe those are mating dances, not intended for you."

She had a final sip of her Chardonnay.

"Someday I'd like to meet your lizards. Not tonight. I'm not that forward."

But it was that night. And she was just forward enough to make it so.

On his deck, under the blazing stars, they chatted for hours, an easy banter, and around dawn when the stars began to disappear, they glided to the bedroom and finished their conversation silently.

For the next two weeks, she wrote her songs out in the sun on his deck. He watched her from his fly-tying table, watched the breezes lift her hair and swirl it across her face as she tried out new chords on her guitar and sang quiet melodies, words he couldn't hear. Writing nothing down, committing it all to memory, just as Thorn was committing everything about her to his.

Their hours in the bedroom were spirited and harmonious, and finding what pleased her and what did the same for him was accomplished with wordless nudges and tugs and gentle guiding hands. His own body had never felt so malleable. They fit together like well-worn puzzle pieces, every new position, every groan and shudder and gasp felt both fresh, and a revival of some long-forgotten elation.

On weekends, late in the afternoon she left to perform at Snappers and returned right afterward. She asked him not to come along, saying his presence would make her too self-conscious. Thorn made room in his closet for some of her clothes. An odd mix of sparkling outfits and her everyday faded denim shorts and running shoes and modest tops that were not quite billowy enough to hide her magnificent body.

In late June, after three weeks together, Kathy took a long-planned, two-week vacation from the stage. Thorn proposed a cruise to the Bahamas, do some island-hopping, fish, lounge in the sun, stay well clear of the cruise ship ports, maybe hit up a few of the thatched roof bars he knew on Eleuthera and Little San Salvador Island.

Kathy was delighted by the idea. In preparation, he spent a week polishing the brightwork and tuning up the engine of his Chris-Craft Express Cruiser that was moored at the far end of his dock. The *Heart Pounder* was a thirty-footer that still burbled along on its original Chevy V-8. It was his once-a-week custom to spend at least a half day on the boat's routine maintenance. The vessel had been in his family since the middle of the last century, so there was nothing onerous about keeping the old girl shipshape. He considered it his ancestral duty.

On their passage across the Gulfstream, the seas were calm, no tropical activity off the African coast which meant at least another few weeks without a hurricane gathering strength. They caught a mess of yellowtail off Red Bay and Kathy showed him a recipe that involved avocados and lime and chili powder, all of which she'd brought along. They swam, they read, they talked in the moonlight and their lovemaking was set off by the smallest glancing touch or sidelong look.

In the evening of their second week, anchored off Spanish Wells on the northern tip of Eleuthera, after splitting a bottle of red wine, Thorn said, "You haven't mentioned him once. Haven't even told me his name."

The sky was dense with starlight that had traveled longer than the history of planet Earth to reach them. Kathy stared up at the dazzling whirlpools of light and sighed.

"Osvaldo Baltazar Garcia," she said, the name flat and neutral on her tongue.

"Cuban?"

"Very."

"Meaning what, he was controlling?"

"Controlling would be the kindest way to put it."

"He hit you."

"Only once."

"That's when you left."

"As soon as I could."

"Does he know where you are, that you've been living with me?"

She looked away. She'd returned to earth, a hard landing.

"I don't speak to him. Only through the lawyers."

"But he knows about us. Is that what you think?"

"He has ways. He's powerful and wealthy. If he wanted to know, yes, he could find out. About you, about us, anything he wanted to know."

"What does he do, his work?"

"He plays at real estate, but he has money that slipped out of Cuba just in time. Rum, gambling, nightclubs."

"If you don't want to talk about this…"

"I don't mind," she said. "It all feels like it happened to someone else. A person I vaguely knew, somebody I left behind like a snake sheds its skin."

"Is he a bad man?"

"As bad as a man can be."

"But somehow he charmed you."

"That's part of what makes him so bad."

They were silent for a while watching the fiery pulses in the sky. The billion-year-old beams bombarding Earth with signals no human had yet decoded.

"Do you believe in free will, Thorn?"

"What's the other choice?"

"I'm serious."

"If I said yes, would it change things between us?"

"It's not a trick question. For me, I believe there's something we can't see or know that has some effect on our destiny. Something I can't really explain, something that ties all this together, makes it coherent. An underlying principle at least. Not a god you need to pray to or anything like that. Just something more than chaos. And we're part of it, some tiny part, but still a part."

Thorn was silent, fetching for a response worthy of the moment.

"I sound like a madwoman."

"Not at all. Looking up at all those galaxies, sure, we want it to make sense. I agree with the underlying principle, physics, math, some kind of science we haven't discovered yet. But I don't think anything's controlling our personal destinies. If we fuck up, get sick, run our car into a wall or win the lottery, it's bad choices, bad luck or good luck."

She was silent, digesting his words with a few faint nods.

"Okay," he said. "So, is any of that a deal-breaker?"

She shook her head.

"No. I'm with you. We invent our moral codes, we either live up to them or we don't. It's an unimaginably colossal universe, but essentially humans are on our own."

"Well, when you put it that way, sounds pretty bleak."

A swell from far off in the darkness rocked the boat gently. Thorn was trying to think of something witty to break the uneasy silence when she said,

"All right. I told you mine, now I want to hear your story."

"I don't have a story."

"Of course, you do. Everybody does. Sugar told me a little, a few scraps."

"What did he tell you?"

"Your parents, how they died. Rushing to get their baby boy home from the mainland hospital within twenty-four hours so you'd officially be a Conch. A bit of Keys folklore. And the car crash."

"Anything else?"

"Just that you've had some scrapes with the law. Helping your friends, doing whatever it took to make things right."

"He give you details of any of those scrapes?"

"Not really. But he's proud of you. Honored to have you as a friend. That's how I knew you were okay. Sugarman vouched."

"And was he right?"

She hummed to herself, a few teasing notes.

"Maybe ever so slightly better than okay."

Thorn supposed he told her the rest of that story. The crash that killed his parents. The drunken driver who'd been speeding straight into their headlights and had forced them to fly off the road and sink into Lake Surprise. Maybe he'd even hinted at the rest of it, how Thorn had waited eighteen years before taking his revenge against that driver, waiting until he was a grown man with a pig-headed notion of justice. Maybe he told her about that drunk driver's daughter who tracked Thorn down just as he had tracked down her father. And he might have told her what came after that and after that.

The years had washed away the rest of that night under the stars. All he remembered for certain was that Kathy Spottswood listened to every word and when he finished, she said, "Can I use that?"

"Use what?"

"I'm tired of songwriting. I've been trying short stories. I've finished a few, but I want to do more."

"Your songs are great."

"But they're not enough. I feel cramped creatively. I can't really stretch out and howl."

"Well, I'm sure you'd be great at howling."

"I have to do more than songs. But at this point, I don't have the courage to tackle my own life. Yours is so colorful, so dramatic. Would you be willing to let me try to capture your story? But no pressure. I'll understand if you say no."

Thorn couldn't remember exactly how he replied. But given the fact he'd fallen in love with Kathy Spottswood, feelings that were more intense than any he'd felt in years, he'd probably said, sure, she was more than welcome to use Thorn any way she wanted.

Two weeks later, back in Key Largo, on a night bright with moonlight, Kathy shook Thorn awake from a bottomless sleep and whispered, "Someone's here."

It was more than someone.

There were three of them, four if you counted Osvaldo who stood in the bedroom doorway and watched while Kathy screamed, and the three men barged in and swarmed Thorn and unleashed a series of highly efficient punches and kicks until Thorn staggered against a dresser. In the full moon light, Thorn got a good look at his attackers. All three had the long tresses and sharp-angled features of the Adonis heartthrobs ornamenting the covers of romance novels. Two had well-groomed beards, one was clean-shaven, all of them were built from the same physical mold, well-muscled athletes with the reflexes of black belts in some unpronounceable martial art.

Thorn took a couple of swings at the assholes before a devastating punch landed on his jaw and he sank to his knees, blood half-blinding him, and another kick to his gut sent him sprawling, face up, panting and twisting his head to retch on the floor beside his bed.

Just conscious enough to hear Osvaldo say, "This woman is my wife. I do not forget or forgive. If I ever see your motherfucking face again, I will not be as merciful as tonight."

His face in shadows, his wavy hair silvered by moonlight, Osvaldo wrenched Kathy's arm, hauling her naked from the room. When they were gone, the three men resumed the beating until finally, Thorn dissolved into mist, rising to the ceiling, floating there while his carcass lay on the bedroom floor struggling to breathe.

He spent the next day in Mariner's Hospital with a grade 3 concussion, two broken ribs. Left eye swollen shut. A molar gone. So many stitches it doubled his lifetime total, and he'd already been stitched plenty. For years he'd stuck his nose in places it was not welcome. But he'd always been able to fight back, block enough punches to hold his own. He'd never been assaulted by such cold, methodical men, clearly experts in the business of breaking bones and convincing the unconvincible.

Thorn and Sugarman spent the rest of the summer trying to locate Kathy Spottswood and Osvaldo Baltazar Garcia. Sugar used every database the Monroe County Sheriff's Department provided. Doing his part, Thorn hobbled into Snappers and questioned Harold Deneen, the owner, and a friend for years. All Harold could offer was Kathy's rental address which Thorn already knew. It was a one-bedroom apartment downstairs below a waterfront home on Stillwright Point. The apartment had been stripped bare, not a single item of Kathy's left behind. They'd done the same with Thorn's house. While he was lying unconscious, they'd swept up all her clothes, her toiletries. Leaving behind no sign she'd ever been present.

Osvaldo Baltazar Garcia had no local address. No sign of him in Miami or anywhere else in Florida. Frank Sheffield, long-time friends with Sugarman and Thorn, was the Special Agent in Charge of the Miami field office of the FBI, and as a personal favor, Frank ran a search on Osvaldo and managed to locate a man by that name in Northern California. But that Osvaldo Baltazar Garcia had died the year before of natural causes leaving behind no known relatives.

Frank said, "The guy you're looking for, as far as the federal government is concerned, he doesn't exist."

For a wealthy man who supposedly dabbled in real estate, Osvaldo managed to keep his name off deeds and tax rolls, maybe shrouding himself behind a series of shell companies that were hidden inside one another like nesting dolls. Or more likely, that name was simply an alias he used to hide his true identity, even from his wife, Kathy Spottswood. A ghost of a man who left Thorn with a battered body and a wound deep in his chest that never quite healed.

After leaving Sandy Richards' condo, Thorn drove home with five of Kathy Spottwood's novels riding shotgun. Every minute or two, he reached over to touch their shiny covers, resting his hand on the pile of books as if to feel some lingering vibration from his long-ago lover.

Back at his house, he found a handwritten note from Deputy Max Silverstein thumbtacked to the front door:

Stetson made it home. Her old man called the sheriff to say he was grateful. Even promised a hefty donation to the -Police Benevolent Association. So you did the right thing, Thorn, and for once nothing bad came of it. Congrats.

SEVEN

MINKS WAS SO ENGROSSED WITH counting and stacking the bills, he wasn't paying close attention to Stetson. Every few minutes he'd inch his chair back to check on her, but the intervals between the checking had grown longer.

In the meantime, she'd started contorting her face. Systematically squeezing her cheeks, gritting her teeth, and writhing her jaw, grimacing, squinching her eyes wide open and shutting them hard and all of it seemed to be working. Slowly wriggling a few strands of fishing line toward her mouth.

Minks, the moron, had made a single continuous wrap around her face and knotted it to the headrest of the moldy recliner. If she could chew through a single strand, she was pretty sure with a little more wriggling she could loosen the whole thing.

Then it was only her hands that were bound. She could rise and make her escape. There was a bathroom off to her left. A window next to the toilet. Screened, but the window was open. An escape hatch.

That's what Stetson was visualizing as she twisted her face, blocking out the pain and trickles of blood as even her smallest efforts made the fishing line slice deeper.

But she pressed on, tilting her head to the right, strands stinging her cheeks and chin and finally one of those strands slipped past her lips.

She tongued it into her mouth, bit down. Chewed.

It was harder to sever than she'd thought, but she sucked it deeper which tore into the corners of her mouth. When she finally got it between her molars, she gnawed at the fucker, kept working it until she felt a twist of filament against her tongue, the strand unraveling. She ground harder.

A few seconds later she stopped.

A car or truck had pulled up out front of the trailer.

No one was coming to rescue her, she was pretty damn sure of that. But hell if she was going to wait around to find out.

In one grinding bite, she broke through the fishing line. Stoked by a feverish rage she shook her head back and forth to loosen the bondage. After several agonizing seconds she was free and on her feet, moving toward the bathroom, toward that window next to the toilet.

With her hands bound behind her back, she had to use her foot to close the toilet lid, then she stepped up on it. From that position, the windowsill was waist high. The screen was rusty, a ragged tear on one side.

She studied the angles, gamed out the physics, then chose what seemed her best shot.

She bent her knees, crouched, and launched herself head-first into the screen.

Minks looked up at the rumble of engine noise outside.

A white Escalade with dark-tinted windows pulled up just outside his trailer, parking so close to the front door, its big wheels crushed the two bougainvillea bushes beside his sidewalk.

A tall, sturdy man got out of the passenger door and the driver came around the front of the big SUV, also rangy and over six feet. Both had thick, dark hair, one curly and hanging past his shoulders, and the other one with his mane twisted up into a bun that sat on top of his head. They had matching two-day beard scruff and each of them wore white guayaberas with lacy stitching down the front. Like uniforms of some hellish team. A third guy, a half foot shorter than the other two joined them. <u>Pablo</u> was the little guy's name.

Man-bun opened the back door and the silver-haired man got out. He had on a black T-shirt and tight jeans. Trim, handsome, tall. Osvaldo was his name, but everyone called him Trickster. At their first meeting Minks had asked one of his goons about the alias.

The thug told Minks a fairy tale about how Osvaldo was supposedly a sorcerer, a man with such magical gifts he could make strong men swoon to their knees with nothing more than a wave of his hand.

Even after Minks met him twice more, he'd seen no sign of anything unearthly about the guy. Good head of hair, but otherwise, far as he could tell, Osvaldo was just another sleek, swaggering Cuban gangster.

Uncle Jack jumped back onto the table and looked out the window.

"Killers," the cat said. "Bad news."

"Not necessarily," said Minks. "It's my boss and a couple of his boys. That's all."

"Not the plan," Uncle Jack said. "Run for your life."

"So, the plan changed. I'm flexible. No sweat. *Tranquilo*, dude."

Uncle Jack jumped to the floor and padded over to the doorway, sat down to one side like he might be preparing to trip the first one through.

"Be cool," Minks said.

Maybe he was talking to the cat, maybe to himself. Hell, maybe the cat never spoke at all, and it was only one side of Minks' wild-ass brain talking to the other crazy-ass side. Who the fuck knew?

When man-bun opened the screen, the tomcat shot out the opening and raced away.

The first one into the room was the boss of this crew. Victor was his name. Pablo came next, little guy, smartass smile. Then Jorge, beard scruff, the man-bun. These three were at the top of the hooligan scale, Osvaldo's personal body men. Gym rats who specialized in gouging eyes and snapping finger bones.

Victor glanced at Minks and didn't say anything, then took a careful look around the room and spoke in Spanish to little Pablo. Pablo passed along what Minks assumed was the all-clear signal to their boss and a few seconds later, Trickster entered the trailer.

No friendly hello, just, "Where is she? My daughter."

Minks motioned to the back room.

"Tied her up in the recliner. She's a little worse for wear. Bitch tried to bite me."

"Count the money," Osvaldo said to Victor. "Make sure it's all there."

"Wait, what?" Minks stood up, blocking the table and the neat stacks of bills.

Victor put a hand on Minks' shoulder and heaved him aside.

"Well, fuck me with a limber dick," Minks said. "Money was never mine, was it? Whole time this was a bait and switch. Get me doing the dirty work, then you come grab the cash."

"Count it," Osvaldo told his goon. "And Jorge, go get the girl."

Jorge marched into the back room and returned a few seconds later and said, "She's not there. Went out the bathroom window. Screen's busted."

"She was here a second ago," Minks said. "I was watching her. You drove up, it distracted me. Not my fault, hombre."

Osvaldo told Jorge and Pablo to go find the girl. She couldn't have gone far.

He turned to Minks, right hand brushing against his belt and sneaking under his shirttail. In a flick of his wrist, the gleaming blade appeared in his right hand. Some customized device, half knife, half straight razor

Minks stepped back, bumped against Victor's chest.

"Wait a minute. Whoa, hold on, I can find her, get her back. Give me a chance, I know my way around the trailer park, all the hidey holes."

"You had your chance," Osvaldo said.

Minks had never seen the tattoo on Trickster's right forearm. One of those tribal tats like the boxing champ had on his face. Only this one was a fish. Minks didn't know fish, so he was about to ask what kind it was, make friendly conversation, develop a connection.

But no, while Minks had his eyes on the tattoo, Trickster's hand whisked through the air so quick Minks just caught a blur, the blade coming too fast for any creature on the planet to block it.

The slice across his throat was deep, and so well-aimed Minks felt zero pain, just the warm flood of what must have been blood trickling down his chest.

So, the stories were true, the man was magically fast.

The silver hair, the handsome face, all of it went hazy as Minks dropped to the floor.

His last thoughts were of the cat. Minks should've listened to that damn Uncle Jack, taken his advice, gotten the hell out of there while there was still a fleeting chance.

In bra and panties, and bleeding from the slashes on her face, Stetson didn't know which way to run—toward the highway, maybe a hundred yards east, or deeper into the trailer park, west toward the bay. The obvious choice was the highway, wave down a passing car. So obvious it was almost certain they'd search that way first.

Still debating, she slipped along the back of Minks' trailer, past a window, ducking below, then halting because she'd caught a glimpse of silver hair, thick and wavy.

She edged to one side of the window, peeked past the checked curtain, and saw her father facing off with Minks. Minks was talking fast as her dad moved a half-step closer, then his hand flashed past Minks' throat. Minks sagged to his knees, toppled forward, face slamming the floor. She ducked her eyes as the linoleum darkened with blood.

Locked in place, she fought to breathe. Everything she'd long believed was confirmed.

"Hey, you okay, girl?"

A gray-haired lady in a flowered shirt stood in the doorway of the next trailer.

"No," Stetson hissed. "I'm not."

"I'm Mabel. Just made a batch of lemonade. You look like you could use a sip."

Osvaldo's men split up to search the grounds, one jogging out to the highway, the other hustling to the bayside of the trailer park. Osvaldo stayed in Minks' trailer and gathered the cash, packing it into an aluminum briefcase that he stashed in the Caddy.

When his men returned empty-handed, Osvaldo ordered them to go trailer by trailer, break doors down if they had to, rough up anybody who resisted until they found his girl.

Try not to kill anyone, but if they had to, do it quietly. And don't fail him.

The water was cool and smelled of mildew. There was just enough room to keep her head above the waterline. It was Mabel's idea after they'd seen her father's henchmen hammering on the doors of nearby trailers, barging inside. Mabel's was next in line.

"They're after you, right?" she'd asked.

"They are."

"They do that to your face?"

Stetson nodded.

"Fucking men," Mabel said. "Okay, then, let's move."

She'd led Stetson out to her back deck and unsnapped the cover of the hot tub and peeled it back. Stetson slid into the musty water and Mabel snapped it closed again.

"Best I can do," she'd said. "Stay low on that far side. Be calm, girl. We'll make it."

Now Stetson smoothed out her breathing. She concentrated on the rumble of air-conditioning units and the distant blare of an outboard on the bay, a bird nearby running through its calls. And then there was a man's voice inside the trailer.

Mabel sounded calm, saying, "Sure, help yourself. Would you like a glass of lemonade, it's fresh? Made it from scratch."

She felt the floor of the trailer shudder, heard doors slam, a man grunting as he stomped room by room. Then she heard the sliding glass door scraping across its track and felt the quake of his steps on the wooden deck.

"What's this?" It was Pablo, one of her father's bodyguards.

Mabel said, "A hot tub. You get old like me, you need to soothe the joints."

Stetson drew a breath and heard the snaps rip open.

Pablo peeled back a corner of the cover and looked in. She saw the shadow of his face on the surface. He splashed an angry hand through the water sending ripples that tickled her cheeks.

Pablo cursed and grunted and drew away and stomped back across the deck.

She waited till she heard the front door slam before she let out her breath.

A few seconds later, Mabel was back, unsnapping the rest of the cover and opening it.

"I'll fetch you a towel, then put some antiseptic on that face, honey. You're a bloody mess."

"Thank you," Stetson said. "Thank you."

"No need for that. There must be one hell of a story here. That man gave off some evil fumes. His poor mother, I can't even imagine how sad she must be at how her boy turned out."

While Stetson dried off, Mabel Sager took a ramble around the trailer park, circling it three times, walking every street, saying hello to her friends, hearing several reports about the men who'd muscled into their trailers. She listened and clucked her tongue but didn't give away a thing she knew. She kept poking around until she was confident the men searching for Stetson had departed.

"I need to go," Stetson told her when Mabel returned.

"Well, not in bra and panties. Even in the Keys that might get you in a speck of trouble."

Mabel led Stetson into the guest bedroom and rolled open the closet door.

"My daughter, Hilton, she was about your size. Not as shapely, but something in here should fit."

Stetson asked her where Hilton was now.

"Three years dead. Girl was hooked on so many drugs I couldn't keep track. Wasn't anybody could lure her away from them. God knows I tried everything a mother could, anything and everything county, state, and feds provided, private detox, group therapy, AA, but nothing was as tempting as the next snort or jab of the needle. Till one jab too many."

"I'm sorry," Stetson said.

"Unless you got a repulsion to a dead girl's clothes, something in that closet should do the trick."

She settled on a pair of jeans, an olive green T-shirt, and an Atlanta Braves baseball hat. Over the top of the T-shirt, she chose a Buffalo Bills hooded sweatshirt for better concealment. The sweatshirt was white with a blue buffalo rearing back to butt heads with some unseen combatant. Seemed appropriate.

Mabel's daughter had a large collection of running shoes and sandals all of which were too small but mixed in with those were a man's Nikes that fit just fine.

"Got those kicks from her boyfriend. Jake was his name. Boy tried like hell to rescue her, just like the rest of us did. He's married now, got a kid on the way. That could've been Hilton, and that would've been my grandkid, but no, all that's finished."

"I better go."

"You don't want to tell me why those men were after you, that's fine."

"I think you're safer this way."

"That Minks, he was a devil. Never had a good word for anyone."

Stetson considered telling Mabel that the devil was dead, but decided it was better to let that emerge in its own way.

As Stetson was about to leave, Mabel reached out and tucked a wad of folded bills into the pocket of the jeans.

"I can't take that."

"It's a loan," Mabel said. "When you're safe and back to normal, I expect you to show up at my door and return it with interest. Ten percent."

Stetson tried to hand it back, but Mabel dodged out of range.

"Don't insult me," Mabel said. "And those cuts on your face, don't worry about those, they'll heal fine. Just takes time. Like everything. Just takes time."

"I'm lucky I found you."

"And one more thing. Kind of men you're dealing with, you'll likely need it."

The canister of pepper spray was pink. Stetson didn't hesitate. She took it and tucked it in the back pocket of her jeans.

Then she hugged Mabel and left, pulling the hood up, heading to the highway, eyes roaming the adjacent streets for her father's White Escalade, though she knew it was only one of many cars in his fleet, and that by now there'd be more of his men cruising the nearby neighborhoods in search of her.

She knew where she needed to go. Miles away. Hell of a hike. But she was ablaze with so much anger, she believed she could slog all the way to Canada if she had to.

She was a mile north of the trailer park, walking along the bike path, facing into oncoming traffic, head ducked, hood pulled all the way up, when a black Tahoe, swerved across two lanes of traffic, horns blaring at its reckless move.

It bumped across the curb and blocked Stetson's way, passenger door flying open.

She dodged to her left, hurdled a hedge, and sprinted down a narrow asphalt lane with modest one-story houses on either side. She could hear the slap of feet behind her, a man chuffing, gaining on her. She cut to her right and vaulted over a chain-link fence into someone's backyard where a pit bull was sleeping in a patch of shade. It sprang up, loped after Stetson but she was already over the back fence and into someone's yard on the adjacent street.

She heard the dog begin to growl, a throaty forbidding sound, and the howl of the man who'd been chasing her. She didn't wait to hear more.

She plunged into a thicket of buttonwood and thatch palms, pushing deeper until a snarl of bougainvillea thorns snagged her sweatshirt and clawed at her flesh. Disentangling herself, she emerged into an open field, and tore off the sweatshirt, slung it aside. Hoping her pursuer would be misled by the green T-shirt and the Braves baseball cap.

She jogged toward a cluster of people, about a dozen of them, each with a leashed dog, the group bunched around a woman who was leading them one by one through obedience drills. Sit, down, stay.

As she slowed to a walk, the leader of the group noticed Stetson and gave her a welcoming nod. The rest of the class, mostly senior citizens with smallish canines, were too focused on their pets to pay her much attention.

For the next half hour, Stetson hovered at the rear of the group and cast uneasy looks back toward the neighborhood she'd cut through. When the class was done and the group began to disperse toward a sandy parking area, Stetson latched onto a man in his sixties with a King Charles Spaniel that had done quite well with sit and down but had not been able to stay when the owner moved more than a few feet away.

"I've always wanted a Cavalier," Stetson said.

"Harvey's my fifth," he said. "Everybody raves about how cuddly they are, and my others were great lap sitters, but old Harvey here, he'd rather climb onto the back of a couch and stare out the window like he's waiting for his bus."

"I'm Stetson."

"Rory," the man answered.

"Rory and Harvey."

They walked in silence till they reached his car in the lot. A red Tesla.

He slipped Harvey into a Sherpa bag on the rear seat and turned to Stetson.

"Need a ride somewhere? I'm going north, back to Ocean Reef."

"Matter of fact," she said. "That would be terrific. Up near Pennekamp is where I'm headed."

"What happened to your face?"

"Long story," she said.

"I'll drive slow, give you plenty of time to tell it. I'm a doctor, well I was. I'm retired."

He bent close to her cheeks, inspecting the wounds from the fishing line.

"Never seen cuts quite like those before."

"Maybe I'll walk," she said.

"Okay, okay. I won't pry. Tell me whatever you're comfortable telling."

Rory Peterson had been a GP in Miami for forty years, retired now. Stetson asked him a string of questions as they drove north on the Overseas Highway, keeping the spotlight off herself, and Doctor Rory was happy enough to rattle on about his two children who were also doctors and lived in

California, and his three grandchildren, two boys and a girl.

Stetson kept glancing at the rearview, on the lookout for one of her father's SUVs. All clear for miles, until she was finally beginning to relax. But as they passed the entrance for the Publix shopping center, she saw a black Escalade advancing fast in the outside lane.

When it was three car lengths behind them, the Escalade veered into their lane and quickly closed the gap until it was only a few feet from their bumper.

"Listen," Stetson said, cutting Dr. Rory off in the middle of a story about his grandson's soccer skills. "Let me out here."

"Right here?"

"Now," she said. "Pull over, do it now."

They were almost to the Yellow Bait House when he slowed and cut onto the shoulder.

Stetson thanked him and he tried to ask her what was going on, was she in trouble, but she hopped out without a word, slammed the door, and sprinted behind the bait shop and onto Michelle Drive. Fifty yards down the street, she realized her mistake. It was a neighborhood of cul-de-sacs. Every street branching off Michelle dead-ended in two blocks.

Too late to double back to the highway. She halted, indecisive, looking left and right down the short streets, seeing no neighbors outside, no traffic, no Mabel to help her this time.

She looked back toward the highway and there it was, the black Escalade inching down the middle of Michelle Drive, closing in.

The passenger door opened, and Jorge jumped down to the street. Out of the driver's side back door, Pablo hopped out. White guayaberas, jeans, running shoes. Not going to lose her this time. She knew she couldn't outrun these two. She was out of tricks. Or maybe not.

"Hey, *chica*, your *papi* wants to talk to you. Don't be afraid, girl. You know us."

Yeah, she knew them all right.

She waited. Standing in the center of the street, until they were fifteen, twenty feet away then she began to walk toward Pablo, the shorter of the two, letting her shoulders slump like she was giving herself up.

Victor, who was at the wheel, shut off the engine, grinning at her like the ruthless butthole he was. She closed in on Pablo as Jorge came around the back of the SUV to assist.

"You're a fast runner," Pablo said. "You got away from me."

Everyone was cool, glad the game was over. Treating Stetson like a willful child.

From her rear pocket, she palmed Mabel's pink canister, and as Pablo turned to say something to Jorge, she sprayed his face and stepped close to douse Jorge, too, holding the trigger down till the cylinder began to sputter. With both of them coughing and clawing at their eyes, she shouldered past Jorge and sprinted toward the highway.

Twenty feet from the bike path that ran along the edge of US 1, she lurched to a stop.

The hand gripping her shoulder spun her around and Victor grabbed the front of her T-shirt and shook her hard, then slapped her with his free hand.

"Stop fucking around, princess. Time to go back to your palace."

Stetson stopped fighting. Resigned to her fate, all her scrappiness used up. She sat in the rear seat of the SUV, silent during the drive down to Islamorada. At the marina behind the Postcard Inn, she let Victor steer her out the dock. Silently she climbed aboard the Bertram 50 Express, went below deck to the master stateroom, and stretched out atop the bedspread. Victor stood in the doorway and watched her lying limp.

"Trickster's pissed," he said.

"Fuck off. It's none of your goddamn business."

"Just filling you in. Known the man before you were born, never saw him this *furioso*."

"Big deal. So, what's he going to do, slice my throat?"

"Told me to sharpen my machete, so yeah, maybe that's what it's for. Your throat."

EIGHT

THE HERO OF THE NOVEL was North. No last name. A loner with only a single close friend, an African American named Berryman. Berryman was a private detective in the town of Bourne on Cape Cod. North made a trifling income selling his nautical carvings to local tourist shops and he lived simply in a partially restored barn he'd inherited from a distant relative. His back deck had an unobstructed view of the bay and a narrow sandy beach that was his alone. A skilled carpenter, North was refurbishing his home while preserving its rustic origins.

He was something of a lady's man, engaging in a string of brief affairs with an array of islanders, from waitresses to an heiress or two. To those who didn't know him well, he seemed brusque. But he had a softer, poetic side which he kept hidden from all but Berryman and a few singular ladies who earned his trust and were allowed to see past his gruff exterior.

Thorn stopped halfway through the novel, put the book on the side table, stood and stretched, and walked around his living room to turn on a couple of table lamps and gather his wits. The flicker of light across the hardwood floor was in synch with the wobble of his pulse.

Kathy Spottswood had taken the barest outline of Thorn's life story and fleshed it out with remarkable realism. She'd given North and Berryman the same unshakeable bond that Thorn and Sugar had built over a lifetime. Her prose was simple and unadorned, and the plot moved quickly from the car crash that killed North's parents on the day of his birth to a scene eighteen years later when teenaged North hitched a ride into Boston to track down the intoxicated driver who had steered his speeding sedan into his parents' headlights and forced them off a narrow causeway into the black and frigid waters of Buzzard's Bay.

Newborn North survived that crash exactly as Thorn had survived his own. Tossed into the back window ledge, just a few inches above the waterline. The version of North's story was a perfect match for Thorn's. Kathy had embroidered here and there with interior monologues, giving voice to North's moral ambivalence about avenging the death of his parents.

Though she'd changed the setting, there were still a host of similarities between North's rugged way of life in New England and Thorn's hardscrabble existence in the Florida Keys.

In reinventing Thorn, she'd given the fictional North a stubborn isolationist personality that reflected his Yankee roots, a trait he and Thorn shared. Thorn guessed it was possible they shared ancestors as well, since so many of Florida's early settlers were New England transplants, bringing to the Keys their simple cottages of clapboard siding, their tongue and groove furniture, their hardy practicality, and a fearless love of the sea.

In the pages he'd read, there was also a notable sub-plot involving a tract of pristine land targeted for development which North's adoptive mother and the environmental group she led were determined to protect. All of that was a carbon copy of Thorn's own adoptive mother, Kate Truman, who had spearheaded a similar band of conservationists.

As he turned the pages, he found the novel mirroring his own history with such haunting accuracy and detail, it felt as if he were reliving those harrowing days—transported to that period when he had committed acts that would indelibly stain his conscience and shadow him for the rest of his years.

He went out onto the deck, leaned against the railing, and gazed out at Blackwater Sound, at the distant blinking of the channel markers, and the red and green sidelights of passing boats.

He thought of Kathy Spottswood, how she'd launched her writing career by chronicling Thorn's formative years, making his story into a crime thriller brimming with bad guys. Long ago Thorn had given her permission to use his personal history as she saw fit, and by god, she'd fashioned his story into a narrative rich with passion and suspense, and she'd discovered in those incidents a heft and meaning that Thorn had been too self-absorbed to see as he lived through them. She was a gifted storyteller, and it was no surprise the book was a success.

A beam of headlights swung across the darkened trees on the northern border of his acreage. A car crunched down his gravel drive. A late-night intruder breaking the wistful spell.

First the Rolls Royce, then two police cruisers, now this. Four cars in one day, more visitors than his total for the summer. Maybe it was time to install a front gate as North had done to keep away trespassers.

Thorn walked to the side of the deck and peered down into the shadows as the car came to a halt and the door squeaked open and the interior light revealed the only guest that Thorn might have welcomed at such a moment.

"You're back," he called down.

Sugarman crossed the drive and mounted the stairs.

They embraced and Thorn led his friend into the house. Sugar was wearing jeans and a crisp white short-sleeved shirt with a string tie, a triangle of turquoise at his throat.

"A string tie, what happened, you get converted by Texans?"

"I prefer *bolo*," Sugar said. "From the Zuni culture. Very big in Santa Fe. You'd like Santa Fe. Full of weirdos and outcasts, your kind of place."

In the full light, Sugar halted, stepped back and took a measured look at Thorn, and said, "Oh, god, what shit have you stepped in now?"

"I want to hear about your trip."

"That can wait," Sugar said. "You first. What the hell's happened?"

It took the next hour to recount the day's events, the Rolls, its vanity plate, Stetson, her pissy manner, the mysterious man named North she kept mentioning, the story of Thorn's parents' death which Stetson knew in unsettling detail. Deputy Minks taking her away. Then Thorn's drive down to Hooked on Books, meeting Sandy Richards, and discovering the novels that made Kathy Spottswood a bestselling author, returning home to find the note on his door from Deputy Max Silverstein, and finally a quick summary of the book of Kathy's he'd been reading that evening.

When he was done and a long moment of silence had passed, Sugarman got up from his chair, walked over to the stack of books Sandy Richards had loaned Thorn. He picked one up, examined the cover, riffled the pages, then turned it over and studied Kathy's publicity photo on the back.

"If I hadn't pulled her over for speeding," Sugar said.

"Yeah, we wouldn't be having this conversation."

"She'd never have met you, heard your colorful past, and maybe she wouldn't have become a writer."

"I don't know about that," he said. "She was determined. She would've found a way."

"Can I borrow one of these?"

"Help yourself. That one you're holding, it's the second in the series, the follow-up to the one I'm reading."

Sugarman wandered the room with the book in his hand, examining the cover, running his fingertips over the embossed lettering, then turning the book over and staring at Kathy's photo again. Shaking his head.

"So, come on, Sugar, it's your turn. At least give me the highlights of your trip."

After a sigh of resignation, Sugar provided a quick summary of their cross-country journey, visits to national parks and historical landmarks, museums, and monuments while every mile he battled with the twins to put down their phones and relish the sights.

"I got a kick out of the postcards," Thorn said when Sugar was finished.

"That's about the only thing that got them excited, the daffy, bonkers stuff they could photograph and post on Instagram. There's a ton of people making careers out of ridiculing Florida's lunacy, but man, there's some crazy shit in Alabama and the Ozarks and all over the southwest that makes Florida wackiness look downright humdrum."

"I'd like to hear more about the trip, more of the nitty-gritty details."

"How about when I've got it all down in my journal, I'll let you read that."

Sugar was religious about keeping his journal up to date. Thorn had never seen it, but Sugar talked about it now and then, how he used the diary to offload the pressures of his job and his emotional struggles with his ex-wife. Thorn suspected the journal was Sugar's practice session for writing a book, maybe an autobiography.

It was almost midnight when Sugar left with the second of Kathy's novels. They planned to meet for lunch tomorrow and try to make sense of the situation.

Later, lying in bed, staring at the dark ceiling, Thorn replayed the day's events, trying to pinpoint what was making him so tense. Stetson had returned home safely. That was what mattered. And Kathy Spottswood was flourishing in a profession she'd longed to join twenty years ago. All good. But why had Stetson shown up at Thorn's to begin with? Clearly, she was taking his measure for some mission. And he'd failed to pass the test. She was cocky, a wiseass. Not the demeanor of a girl in danger.

He drifted into a shallow sleep and was wakened sometime later by the murmur of an idling outboard engine near his shoreline. By the time he'd dragged himself out of bed and stumbled out to the deck, the engine noise had moved out in the darkness of Blackwater Sound, the boat's running lights switched off.

What sleep he managed afterward was ragged and of no value. Just before dawn he roused himself and went through his morning routines so fuzzy-headed not even a full pot of coffee could clear the fog. Mug in hand, he was headed outside to the deck to watch the brightening sky scatter shades of pink across the massing clouds when he saw the shape of a man sitting in one of his Adirondack chairs, his legs stretched out, feet propped on the rail. He had wide shoulders and wore a baseball cap.

Thorn swung around and returned to the bedroom. Years ago, he had disposed of his only handgun, tossing it along with its grim karma into the depths of the Florida Bay. Aside from his fists, his only personal protection was a Louisville Slugger. He kept it tucked beside his bed in case Osvaldo Baltazar Garcia and his associates made a return visit.

Bat in hand he drew open the screen door, avoided the creaky plank, and stepped onto the deck. Gripping the narrowed handle, he inched toward the intruder, bringing the bat to his shoulder.

"I finished the book." Sugarman turned, saw the bat. "Sorry, man. Didn't realize you were so jumpy. Would've called, but you know, kind of hard with you not having a phone."

Thorn eased into the other chair, lay the bat on the deck at his feet.

"You finished the book?"

"*Dead Low Tide.* Yeah, I finished it. First page to last."

"What, you a speed-reader now?"

"Stayed up all night, haven't slept since I left here."

"It was that good?"

"The book, yeah, solid prose, a few flights of poetry, but it was the subject matter that kept me awake."

"Which was?"

"You, man. It was all about you. Though your name is North. You live on Cape Cod. But otherwise, she nailed you. And I'm in there, too, a flattering portrayal."

"Yeah, I know. In the first one, too, both of us."

"No, hombre, this is different. You gave her the material for that first novel. Your parents' car crash. Eighteen years later, how you tracked down the drunk driver up in Miami. Found him still driving while plastered. You got your revenge. You told her most of that. But not this stuff. These are things you and I were into well after Kathy got dragged out of here, after Osvaldo's rat-bastards beat the shit out of you. This is private stuff that happened a year or more after she disappeared, so she had no way of knowing. Details about Darcy Richards' murder, the tilapia, that whole story. She had all the facts. Stuff nobody could've known but you and me."

"How?"

"I don't know, Thorn. I never told a soul any of it, and I assume you didn't either. It wasn't in the newspapers. It wasn't a police matter or public information."

"The fish farm stuff? That's in there?"

"Yeah, all of it. Every damn thing, breeding the tilapia for the red color, all that money. I mean, yeah, she switched locations to Cape Cod, changed names, got a few things wrong, but I'd say it's eighty, ninety percent identical to what actually happened."

"Jesus."

"And there's another thing."

Thorn sighed, looking out at the clouds, the pink leaching away fast.

"That license plate on the Rolls that brought Stetson."

"Yeah? What about it?"

"It was some letters, right?"

"T-R-K-S-T-R. Why?"

"Because there's a character in *Dead Low Tide* who's manipulating events, screwing around with North, tripping him up, putting him in danger a couple of times. Changing the course of the story."

"Just tell me, Sugar."

"This character, you don't see him, he's not on stage, there's no description of him. He shows up in just a paragraph here and there, his actions, that's all. Nothing about his thoughts. Those paragraphs are always in italics. He doesn't have a normal name. Bill, Joe, Johnny, anything like that. The narrator calls the guy *Trickster*."

"Jesus Christ. Controlling events?"

"Not controlling exactly. The guy comes out of thin air, he'll make a noise to distract North for a few seconds, and that lets a bad guy escape, simple stuff like that, subtle things North would never notice. But they affect the story's outcome bigtime."

"I don't get it. I need an example."

"Okay. It was a long time ago, but you remember when that creep was shooting through your floor, this floor. You and Sylvie were inside here, dodging the slugs, climbing up on the stove to protect yourselves."

"Little hard to forget that."

"And when he stopped shooting, you chased after him. But never saw him for sure. Never really verified it was him shooting."

"It was Roy Murtha. Gangster, former Mafia hitman. Old guy."

"Yeah, but what if it wasn't Murtha?"

"What're you talking about?"

"What if somebody else fired those shots?"

"Whoa. You're saying all this is in *Dead Low Tide*?"

"A lot of it, well, most of it. A dozen shots coming through North's floor. He's got a batshit crazy girl in there with him, spitting image of our friend, Sylvie. After the shooting is done, North runs downstairs chasing the shooter."

"But Murtha is gone."

Sugarman said, "What if it was Trickster who fired those shots?"

"That's in the book?"

"It is. Trickster, sending North off in the wrong direction. After an innocent man."

"Christ."

"Yeah, if what's in the book is true, Murtha wasn't trying to kill you. Trickster was."

Thorn walked out to the edge of the deck, leaned against the railing, trying to absorb the possibility that a man might've been a shadowy presence in his life for years. Corrupting Thorn's decisions, changing white to black, guilty to innocent.

He turned back to Sugarman.

"What the hell is going on here?"

"Hell if I know. But at the very least it seems like Kathy Spottswood has been following your exploits very closely. And mine too apparently."

An easterly gust ruffled his hair. Thorn swept a few strands out of his eyes and looked out at Blackwater Sound at the early morning boat traffic bumping across the chop. And saw something white flapping like a flag of surrender from the top of one of his dock pilings.

"Oh, man. Now what?"

Thorn rose and hustled down the stairs, jogged across the yard. Sugarman caught up with him at the dock.

"What is it?" Sugar asked.

Thorn reached up and pulled the white T-shirt off the hook where a few hundred fish had been displayed over the decades.

Gripping it by the shoulders, he held it up, studied the front for a moment, then turned it so Sugarman could see the scribbled lettering.

What the fuck are you staring at?

"Stetson's," Thorn said. "She was wearing it yesterday."

"Is that blood?"

He pointed at a scarlet spatter near the rip in the material.

Thorn sighed and said, "Last night, boat noise woke me up. It was idling close to shore. That must've been when it happened."

"Jesus, what kind of hall of mirrors is this?"

"What we need to do is make sure Stetson is really safe. After that, locate Kathy Spottswood, find out how the hell she's managed to rip-off our private lives."

"This feels like a trap, Thorn. Bait in a trap."

"What choice do we have? Find Stetson, find Kathy, make sure they're okay."

"Don't forget," Sugarman said, "we spent a couple of months trying to track down Osvaldo and got nowhere."

"This is different. Kathy's a public figure now. There's got to be a way."

On the dock, they strategized for a while until they settled on a plan for the day ahead. Sugarman would drop by the sheriff's office and try to make sure Stetson did in fact get home safely. And Thorn had an idea about uncovering Kathy Spottswood's current whereabouts.

As Thorn was turning away, impatient to get dressed and head off, Sugar halted him with a hand on his shoulder and said, "Since we're splitting up, could you do me a favor?"

"Name it."

"Take this." He dug a cell phone from his pants pocket. "It's a cheapy I bought just for you. My cell number's in the directory. Press #1 and I answer. When this is all resolved you can trash it. But for now, until we sort this out, I think we need to stay in touch."

He held out the phone, his eyes stern, jaw set. Sugarman was so principled, so rooted in moral certitude, he'd never been troubled by the chaotic, free-for-all of the modern world. Having two tech savvy teenage girls helped, but even before they were born, Sugar had stayed up-to-date, fully fluent in the lingo of the moment, an expert with the latest gadgets, surfing every new wave with effortless grace.

In that respect, he was Thorn's opposite. He had only one true north star, an archaic notion of independence. Relying on anyone, or anything, especially some hand-held electronic device galled him to the core.

"I've made it all these years just fine without one."

"This feels ominous, Thorn. Someone's invaded your private life. And mine."

The blare of a passing jet ski drew Thorn's eyes to the bay. He watched the rider head toward the giant wake of a passing yacht and slam through that wall of water, sending salt spray high in the air like the fizz of champagne, a celebratory toast to indestructible youth.

"Goddamn it," Thorn said. "Ominous, yeah, it is starting to feel that way."

And he took the phone.

NINE

"TUG THAT CURTAIN ASIDE," JULIUS, the clerk at Hooked on Books, told Thorn. Julius motioned toward the rear of the store. "Sandy spends most of the day hiding out in the stock room. Not much of a people person."

"My kind of lady."

Sandy Richards had her bare feet propped up on a stack of book cartons. She was leafing through a magazine with an emaciated fashion model on the cover.

Sandy wore a pair of white linen shorts and a lavender top. Her legs were tanned to a sleek golden sheen. Big hoop earrings glittered against her neck. Seeing Thorn, she tilted up her reading glasses, propped them against her forehead.

"Knock, knock. Can I bother you again?"

"Mr. Thorn, back so soon?" She set the magazine aside and stood.

She stepped close, ducked in, and gave him one of those cheek-to-cheek greetings that Thorn had never mastered. As she drew away, he got a whiff of jasmine with a faint undertone of something smoky. Closer to marijuana than tobacco.

"More questions?" she asked.

"If you've got a minute."

"As you might have noticed, the book selling biz is a bit sluggish at the moment."

"Late August in the Keys," he said. "Everything's sluggish."

"I'm discovering that. Down here if you don't make a killing between Thanksgiving and Easter, you're pretty much fucked. Pardon my Polish."

She gestured to a burgundy director's chair and Thorn sat.

"So, what brings you to my humble establishment?"

"Well, for one thing, I'm about halfway through *Under a Moonless Sky*."

"And?"

"It's good. Kathy's an excellent writer."

"First novel, best novel. Not the thing any writer wants to hear, but more often than not it's true. All the naïve energy is flowing like sap in the spring."

"I was hoping you could help me track her down. Her current whereabouts."

She tipped her head to one side, peered at him for a moment, then broke into a smile.

"Oh, my. Is the famous author a past love?"

Thorn didn't answer but could feel his face harden, giving away the truth.

"Golly, gosh. I've always been a sucker for a good love story."

She called out to Julius, told him to hold her calls.

"What calls?" he asked.

"You know what I mean, kiddo. Privacy."

She drew the curtain tight across the doorway and took her seat again.

"Yesterday you mentioned Kathy's editor. Could you call her, get an address?"

"Whoa, there. First, I'm going to need a few juicy details. The why and when and what. I want action, romance. How'd you two get involved, how long did it last, how'd it end?"

Thorn rose from his chair, looked at the curtain, had a strong impulse to push it aside and get the hell out of there. Pissed at her glibness, feeling a flush of blood in his cheeks. But damn it, he didn't have a Plan B.

"Okay, yeah, there was a romance," he said. "It was a long time ago before she started writing novels. But this is about something else entirely. I'm not trying to track down a lost love. This is serious. Lives might be at stake. That's all I can tell you."

"Oh." Her smile melted away. "Why the hell didn't you say that upfront?"

Thorn returned to the chair.

"All righty then," Sandy said. "Kathy's editor, the one I knew, that was ten, twelve years ago. With all the turnover, there's probably been four or five generations of editors by now."

"Her latest one then."

"I could make a few calls, try to track her down, but you should understand if a writer demands privacy, that's a dead end. A major author like Kathy, if she doesn't want her personal info known, it'll be next to impossible to find out where she is. At least from anyone at her publishing house."

"Could you try?"

Sandy took her cell phone out the back door into the alley where the reception was better. She was outside for ten or fifteen minutes. Thorn paced around the stockroom, looked at stacks of books with gaudy covers and silly titles, the Florida writers. He'd tried a few of them but had never made it past the first few chapters. Too many alligators and pythons and billfish in outlandish situations for his taste. He had nothing against sophomore humor, but he preferred his novels to grapple with more plausible matters.

He had just settled back in the director's chair when Sandy came back in. She shook her head.

"No dice. Kathy Spottswood likes her privacy. And her publisher isn't about to betray such a moneymaker."

"All right. What about the person she pays to write the books? That person must know how to contact her."

She looked at him with a sly squint.

"Are you a detective in your spare time, Mr. Thorn? A little like North, perhaps."

"North is larger than life. As you can see, I'm not."

"Are you a dangerous man, Thorn? Am I in danger right now by helping you?"

Thorn sighed and shook his head.

"You're in a lot more danger driving home on US 1."

"Well, damn it all. I could use a little danger in my life."

"Come on," he said. "The person who writes her books. Could that work?"

"Well, Mr. One-Track-Mind, I believe there have been several writers over the years. I don't know who's doing the work now."

"But there's a way to find out?" he asked. "I mean isn't their name on the cover?"

"Some are, some aren't. But wait a minute. Just how urgent is this? These lives at stake, are we talking today, tomorrow, what?"

"Right now, this minute," he said, getting acid in his voice.

Sandy rose and walked over to a cubbyhole where her desk was lodged.

She sat, rolled the chair close, opened a laptop, and began typing. She worked at it for several minutes, keyboard, trackpad, then she stopped and leaned back in the seat.

"The current writer for Kathy's books is named Rocco Budd. But that name doesn't show up on ordinary Internet searches, so I'm going to make another call. Can you wait?"

What else could he say but yes?

Again, she took her cell out into the alley. After ten minutes of tapping his foot, Thorn cracked open one of the Florida novels, read until the first python came out of a toilet, then he put the book back on the stack and just sat and stared at a promotional poster for the latest Oprah Book Club pick.

It was almost thirty minutes before Sandy reappeared.

"I have a son," she said. "Marcus is his name. He's almost thirty now, so I should let him live his life, make his own choices. But I can't seem to do that. He's been in and out of jail for petty theft, stealing to buy drugs. Heroin is his thing these days. I've had to bail him out a half dozen times. He moves around a lot, from one end of the country to the other."

"I'm sorry," Thorn said. "That's rough. But how…"

She raised a hand to silence him.

"Give me a second, I'm getting to it. A few years ago, I found a man in Philadelphia, a white-hat hacker who specializes in tracking down missing persons. He's managed to ferret out Marcus's whereabouts half a dozen times after I've lost contact with him. Homeless shelters, jails, street clinics. Omaha, Houston, Santa Fe, coast to coast.

"I spoke to him just now, my hacker, told him your situation, what you needed to know. Told him it was urgent. He put me on hold, did his rabbit out of a hat magic, and voila, our friend Rocco Budd uses Instacart."

"I'm sorry. What's that?"

"Ah, yes, I keep forgetting you're not plugged into the modern world. Instacart is an online service for ordering groceries. Like so much else these days, Instacart keeps customer names and addresses and credit card info on file, held in a database. The name Rocco Budd doesn't show up on voting rolls or tax or real estate rolls, none of the usual places. But he orders his food through Instacart, and there he is, living on a street in Delray Beach, Florida. A few hours up the road."

"You ever heard of this guy?"

"My hacker sent me his bio. Three crime novels, nothing special, your standard mid-list writer."

Thorn asked her what mid-list was.

"Halfway between the top of the heap and the bottom. Not long ago mid-listers could have decent careers if they got good reviews or an editor took a shine to them, hoping they'd break out one day. Not anymore. If the sales aren't playing nice with the company algorithms right away, boom, the ejection seat fires, hey, it's been fun, have a nice trip back to Earth and try not to break your legs when you land."

"Rocco Budd," Thorn said.

"You want his cell, or should I print out a map?"

"Both," Thorn said.

"Does this mean I'm your sidekick, now?"

Thorn chuckled.

"It's a start," he said.

To Sugarman it felt like sitting outside the vice principal's office, next in line for a paddling. The straight-back wooden chair he occupied was one of six identical seats in the waiting room outside Captain Ron Sprunt's office. Not meant to be comfortable.

Sprunt ran the district 7 sub-station out of the Roth Building in Tavernier. Back in his policing days, Sugar had been close friends with Rick Roth who at the time was the Monroe County Sheriff. Roth had been a humble and dedicated public servant so beloved by the community there'd been no debate about renaming the substation in his honor when Rick died.

Captain Sprunt was a different animal. Gruff and blatantly political, Sprunt had his eye on more lucrative prizes than police work and everyone in the department knew it, which was why the morale had deteriorated so badly. A lot of Sugarman's old pals on the force had moved on to other police departments around the state or retired early to escape the rotten atmosphere.

Today when Sugarman arrived, he'd signed the visitor's log and said hello to Jinny Strickland who was stationed behind an imposing desk outside Sprunt's door. For decades Jinny sat behind that same desk, serving under several different regimes. Back in Sugarman's era, Jinny had been an easy-going island girl with a quick smile and a raunchy joke for every occasion. But today she barely managed a curt nod before returning to her keyboard.

Sugar had been sitting there for an hour and he'd watched Jinny call out the names of six others who went one by one into the sheriff's office, half of them arriving well after Sugar. All had exited Sprunt's office considerably more downcast than when they'd entered.

Sugarman shifted the paper grocery bag off his lap and set it on the floor beside him. Concerned his sweaty palms would soak through the paper and contaminate Stetson Spottswood's bloody T-shirt.

It was possible the T-shirt had evidentiary value. Maybe it wasn't related to the commission of a crime, only something malicious. He'd brought it along as leverage, to prove he had a legitimate interest in Stetson's case, though he'd been hoping his tenure as a deputy would suffice to let him into the loop. His primary objective for this morning's visit was to get the tick-tock on Deputy Minks' delivery of Stetson to her father and to pick up any info he could about Kathy Spottswood or Osvaldo Baltazar Garcia.

That task was complicated by Sugarman's status as a private investigator, a profession held in low regard, if not downright contempt, by Sprunt. But the even greater challenge was Sugarman's widely known friendship with Thorn whose indifference to the rule of law had brought him into so many clashes with the sheriff's office over the years that anyone even remotely connected with Thorn was considered unsavory if not downright criminally inclined.

After Jinny's cool greeting and the long wait, he was getting the sense that his demerits outweighed whatever laurels he'd accumulated in his decade of police work with Monroe County. But even though the odds were against him, he wasn't about to leave. It wasn't in his nature to quit.

At noon, an hour and a half after arriving, Sugarman watched a young man in shorts and a Morada Bay T-shirt enter the waiting room. He was carrying a plastic bag that left the aroma of garlic, coconut, and French fries in its slipstream. Jinny waved the kid into Sprunt's office.

When the delivery guy exited, Sugarman asked Jinny if it would be much longer.

"Can't say."

"He knows it's me, right?"

"He does."

"I don't have the plague," Sugar said.

"I know you don't."

"This isn't like you, Jinny."

"I'm sorry, Sugar. Things aren't like they were."

Sugar nodded.

"Plus, I've got four months left till my thirty is done," she said. "And two grandbabies and another on the way. Turns out I'm their sole means of support."

"I get it."

She lowered her voice to just above a whisper, saying, "I'm sorry. I really am. He's not a good man."

"Maybe you could take a bathroom break. Disappear for five minutes. That's all I need. His door isn't locked, is it?'"

Jinny looked at him for several moments and sighed.

"He'll throw you out," she said.

"Five minutes," Sugar said. "And I bet those grandbabies are beautiful."

"Oh, they are."

Jinny rose, rolled her eyes at Sugarman's bullheadedness, and left the room.

"What took you so long?" Sprunt said when Sugarman stepped into his office. "I make you wait a couple of hours, and you just keep sitting. Doesn't show much fervor or initiative."

He was using a knife and fork to carve up a snapper fillet smothered in salsa.

"Oh, I'm full of fervor."

"I know why you're here and it won't do any good."

"I'll bite. Why am I here?"

"Trying to intervene on behalf of your fucked-up friend, Thorn."

Sugarman settled the grocery bag on the floor beside him.

"You're a couple of steps ahead of me," Sugarman said.

"My friend, I was born ten steps ahead of you, and I'm increasing the lead every day."

Sprunt was a small man, not more than five-eight but he'd spent years in the gym bulking up until he probably weighed close to Sugarman who was half a foot taller. In the last few months, he'd grown a mustache, a bushy walrus style that hid his entire mouth. It was a look he apparently copied from Florida's current governor whose photo hung on the wall beside his desk. Though the governor's mustache had no specks of salsa adorning it.

"Why am I trying to intervene on Thorn's behalf?"

"Play dumb, okay, if that's your approach, fine. See how far that gets you."

Sugar watched the man neatly slice another morsel of fish and steer it carefully into his mouth. If his precision was meant to keep his mustache clean, the approach was sadly failing.

"We should hear later this afternoon," Sprunt said, stabbing a few French fries. "Soon as the girl decides, you'll be hearing from us. In the meantime, you should advise Thorn to start shopping for a good criminal attorney."

"Are we talking about Stetson Spottswood?"

"Mendoza," he said. "Stetson Mendoza. Daughter of Carlos Mendoza."

His eyes gleamed and his posture straightened ever so slightly, as if the mere mention of the man's name had a galvanizing effect on him.

"So that's the alias he's using? Good to know."

"I don't follow you."

"Never mind," Sugarman said. "So, what exactly is Stetson Mendoza going to decide?"

"If she's going to press charges. Or maybe try to find another way to achieve justice. Off the books, as it were."

Sugarman absorbed that for a moment. Watching an ugly glint appear in Sprunt's eyes.

"Charges about what?"

"As if you didn't already know."

"I'd love to hear your version."

"Ms. Mendoza was hitchhiking on US 1. Thorn picked her up. Took her against her will to his isolated home and molested her. She fought him off, managed to escape, ran out to the highway, and waved down one of our deputies who was driving past at that moment. He stopped and rescued the girl and returned her safely to her father."

"Deputy Minks."

"So, you do know the details?"

"And you spoke to the girl, Stetson? You interviewed her?"

"I spoke to her father."

"So, this was his version of events?"

"I have no reason to doubt the gentleman."

"Are you saying Stetson hasn't given a formal statement?"

"Sugarman, you can be forgiven for not understanding how these things work, having never risen beyond the shabby confines of your police cruiser, but in the case of someone of Mr. Mendoza's prominence in this community, requiring his daughter to come in to make a formal complaint, especially after suffering such a traumatic event, is simply not how it's done."

"I'd like to speak to Minks."

"Would you now?"

"Is he on duty today?"

"Minks is taking some vacation leave. A week, I believe. He's earned it."

"I'd like his address."

"Not going to happen, Sugarman."

Sugar rose to go.

"What's in the bag? Gift for me? Bribe perhaps?"

"Groceries."

Sugarman walked to the door, took a backward glance, and watched Sprunt using a metal comb to clear his mustache of debris, sending a shower onto his ink blotter.

Jinny was at her desk, eyes down.

"Good seeing you again," Sugar said.

She looked up at him, held out a folded slip of notepaper and gave him the defeated smile of a hostage with little hope of escape.

Sugar thanked her and took the note. He waited till he was back in his car to unfold it.

Minks address: 62 S. Blackwater Drive

TEN

THORN WAS JUST LEAVING THE bookstore when his pants pocket buzzed. Goddamn phone.

It was Sugar calling to say he'd gotten an address on Minks. Blackwater Drive, bayside, a few miles north of Thorn's place. They could meet at Thorn's, drive together to the address.

But first, he needed to tell Thorn about his meeting with Sheriff Sprunt. First, Osvaldo was going by the name of Carlos_Mendoza. And second, the story Osvaldo was peddling was that Thorn picked up Stetson hitchhiking, took her to his house, and molested her. She escaped, Minks happened to be driving by and rescued her. Sprunt was waiting for her to decide if she was going to press charges against Thorn.

"And Sprunt bought that?"

"Man would love nothing better than to nail your ass to the nearest coconut palm."

"You didn't show him the T-shirt?"

"Hell, no. We'd both be behind bars."

"Need to put it somewhere safe. Might need it later."

"Or burn it," Sugarman said.

"Who knows? It might come in handy. Stash it under my bed."

After Thorn clicked off, he was tempted to pitch the phone out into the middle of the highway, let the traffic decide its fate. But he took a deep breath and slid it back into his pocket.

They met up at Thorn's house and drove together to the address on Blackwater Drive. It was a standard white stucco house up on concrete pillars with an apartment below, a common arrangement throughout the Keys. On the east side of the building, a shirtless man in camouflage shorts and a yellow Caribbean Club T-shirt was watering a patch of grass with a garden hose.

He had a nest of unruly white hair and his flesh was sun-tortured to the shade of dark roast coffee. He'd probably once been over six feet but now with his slumped shoulders, he was in the fives. Last week, Thorn had encountered the same guy in Publix wearing that same outfit.

Thorn was stuck behind him at the checkout while the guy babbled to the weary clerk long after his groceries had been bagged and paid for, and he kept prattling on until a woman leaned over Thorn's shoulder and informed the old man that people were waiting.

As Sugar and Thorn approached, the man began to speak without looking their way.

"All the rain we had this summer, you think grass wouldn't need any watering. But you'd be wrong. It's only been one sunny day out of the last hundred, and this damn grass is already parched. See how it's yellowing around the edges. I know I should rip it all out and replace it with pea rock. It'd be the eco-hippie thing to do, slow down the global warming, do my part for the planet and everybody's grandchildren, but that grass is a memorial, I guess you could call it. The old lady planted it thirty oddball years ago, and I just keep it going to remind me of her. I'm a sentimental old fuck, I guess. But there it is. Cancer came out of nowhere and snatched her. Had her first twitch of pain in April, a month later she was in an urn on the mantel. Who'd have thought a pancreas was so damn important?"

When the man paused for breath, Thorn said, "We're looking for a man named Minks. He's a deputy with the sheriff's department."

The man kept watering.

"What'd he do, this Minks fella?"

"We just need to speak with him about a personal matter."

The man walked to the faucet and shut off the hose.

"Do I strike you as senile?"

Sugarman said, "No, sir. You seem pretty normal to me."

"People say I'm senile, or maybe it's dementia, I forget which. I know I dodder a little, I'm not the strapping stud I once was. I get it. Happens to everybody. But I think I'm pretty sharp still. Not sharp as a tack, but sharp. What's your reading, you two?"

Thorn said, "You're a talker, that's for sure."

"You got that right. Yes, sir, I do like to talk. Whether it's friends or enemies or complete strangers, or maybe I'm alone, I'll talk blue blazes. I got things to say, a lot on my mind. It relieves the pressure, talking does. Like opening the steam valve, a whole lot of hissing."

"This Minks fellow. We have an address for him. It's right here, 62 South Blackwater."

"Minks is his name all right." The man shot his thumb at the apartment below the house. "Man pays his rent like clockwork. Can't complain about him, can't complain about the noise he makes, women he brings home, a lot of hollering and swearing and carrying on with monkey business. Smoking dope or smelly cigars. Can't complain about any of that. Know why?"

"He's a quiet man?"

"It's because I never seen him but that once when he rented the place, stayed that first night and that was it for Mr. Minks. Since that day, he never returned. Gets some mail now and then. I don't snoop on him, open his letters or anything like that. I got my standards. But every month rent check arrives, check clears. Fine by me. I was kind of looking forward to having someone around I could talk to when I felt like talking. But Minks isn't that person. You friends of his?"

"I'm a private detective," Sugar said. "Minks might have some useful information in a case I'm working on."

"Private eye, are you? Like Sherlock, which makes your buddy here Doctor Watson if I remember my Conan Doyle. See, do I sound senile to you? Huh, answer me that, private eye."

"Sharper than any tack I've run into," Sugarman said. "Could we look at his apartment?"

"Don't know why not," the man said. "I won't even ask to see your badge or license or whatever it is. That's how much I trust you. I'm a damn good judge of people. Always have been. Sharp eye for con men and good for nothings."

The apartment was a one-room efficiency, minimally furnished. A breakfast nook with a microwave, a kitchen sink with a drying rack on the counter, a single bed, closet, bathroom the size of a phone booth. No paintings on the walls, no knickknacks, no rugs, nothing that would suggest anyone had lived in that space. Thorn opened drawers and cabinet doors. Stacks of plastic plates and glasses. A box of toothpicks, a corkscrew, a can opener. Flimsy silverware.

"How about that mail?" Thorn asked. "Do you store it somewhere?"

"He's got his own mailbox, just outside the door."

"Mind if I look?" Thorn asked.

"Don't see what it would hurt. What'd he do? One of them serial killers? A drug lord."

"We're not sure. But a young girl's life might depend on what we learn."

"Well, shitfire and piss down my leg. Why didn't you say that right off?"

His mail was mostly flyers with a single first-class letter from the Police Benevolent Association.

"Not many clues in that pile of paper, is there?"

"He only stayed one night," Thorn said. "Any visitors that night? Or maybe you noticed the kind of car he drove?"

"Don't remember his car. Guess he must've had one. Didn't have any visitors, no. Can't help you there either. Wish I could. You two seem like good fellas. You want to come upstairs, pop a Bud, chew the fat as they say, though I never knew why they called it that. Seems gross, you ask me."

"We can't stay," Sugarman said.

Sugarman was backing onto South Blackwater when the man came trotting out to the driveway and slapped a hand on the hood. Sugar stopped.

The man came around to Thorn's open window and stooped down.

"Old Minks did have a visitor that one night he was here. A pizza girl."

"Pizza girl," Thorn said.

"Goddamn if I couldn't smell it all the way upstairs, all the windows open. Got me hungry as hell, felt like ordering one myself but I didn't. I'd just finished a big bowl of chili, but damn that pizza smelled good."

"You remember what pizza shop delivered it?"

"Yeah, I remember."

"Well?"

"The good place. Wasn't Tower of Pizza or Dominos. It was the good place. Gourmet with those craft beers. Right on their sign. She was a cute girl, too, hair dyed purple, that's why I remember, and big old tits. I've always been a tits man, though you can't say any of that stuff out loud anymore or they'll take you away to jail. Did I just say that out loud?"

"Your secret's safe with us."

"Was it Upper Crust?" Sugarman asked. "The pizza place."

"That's it. Upper Crust. Yeah, see, sharp as a goddamn tack. Had to be almost a year ago and I still remember that girl, her hair, purple and oh, my, those breasts."

Thorn thanked the man, asked his name.

"I'd rather remain anonymous, if it's all the same to you."

Thorn assured him it was.

Sugar put the car in reverse again, and the man called out.

"That girl with the great tatas, her hair was green. Did I say purple? I meant green."

ELEVEN

THE GREEN-HAIRED GIRL WAS NAMED Clarice Martinson. The manager of Upper Crust Pizza, Artie Underwood, remembered her well. Last spring he'd fired her after one too many delivery customers complained Clarice had made lewd propositions, indicating she'd be willing to provide an extra topping for a bump in price.

"Sex is what she meant," Artie said. "I don't know how many customers took her up on it. She might've even increased our business, but that's not the PR I want. Small town like this, word gets around. Didn't want that. Calling me the Pizza Pimp or something of that sort."

The address he had for Clarice Martinson led them to a small concrete block house in the neighborhood near Buzzard's Roost where Thorn had taken Stetson for lunch. The shirtless man who opened the door was bleary-eyed and wobbled as he looked the two of them up and down. He had a straggly red beard that hung to his sunken sternum.

"We're looking for Clarice," Thorn told him.

"I kicked her out a month ago. Bitch was useless. Let herself get fat."

Sugarman asked if he knew where she was living now.

"Fuck Clarice. I got one twice as good and half her age." He turned, whistled loudly into the house, and called for someone named Julie.

A girl with stringy blonde hair staggered out of a back room wearing a slip and bra. She wasn't more than seventeen with a few dozen tattoos scrawled on her arms that looked like cave drawings from the Paleolithic era.

"What're you guys into? Julie's got skills. Lots of skills, don't you, Julie?"

Thorn reached out and gripped the man's beard and hauled him onto the porch. The man tipped forward and almost toppled onto Thorn.

Thorn yanked him upright and said, "Where's Clarice living now? Last chance, asshole."

"Hardy's Motel," he said. "Friends with the owner or some shit."

Thorn released the beard and nudged the fellow back into his sickening house.

"Stay right there, you motherfucking fuckers," the man said. "I'm getting my gun. Stay put. Going to shoot the both of you. Fuck if you can come in my house, strong-arm me. Stay right there."

He closed the door and locked it. Thorn didn't move.

A half minute later, Sugarman grabbed his arm and dragged him back to the car.

They drove in silence to Hardy's Motel. Sugar pulled in front of the office and parked.

"You're out of control, Thorn. It's not helpful."

"Sometimes, you scrape a fingernail across the skin of this island just deep enough to break the surface, the maggots come crawling out."

Sugar nodded and stared ahead at the wooden cottages huddled around a Tiki hut and shuffleboard court and a sandy expanse that was shaded by dozens of graceful coconut palms. Beyond the seawall was the turquoise glimmer of the Florida Bay.

"And sometimes," Sugar said, "there's this."

Clarice Martinson was staying in a cottage close to US 1 where the rumble of traffic was chattering the jalousie windows by the front door.

Her hair was cut short. Shorn of its purple and green past, it was now a mousey brown.

She planted herself in the doorway and sighed when Thorn asked her about Minks.

"Sure, I know him. What'd he do, beat up some girl?"

"Not as far as we know," Sugar said. "Just trying to find him to ask some questions."

She appraised them carefully and said, "You're not Johnny Law."

"Concerned citizens," Thorn said.

"I know you," Clarice said. "You're the dude lives in the woods, always stirring up shit."

"That's him," Sugar said. "Now, about Mr. Minks?"

"Okay, yeah. I screwed him a few times. Real asswipe. Liked it rough, too rough for me. Never a tip. Just threw a wad of bills at me and sent me on my way. Real charmer."

"We're looking for his address. He's a hard man to track down."

"Breezy Palms Trailer Park, second trailer past the gate, on the right."

They thanked her and were turning back to the car, when she said, "I guess I should be grateful for that fucker."

"Why's that?" Thorn said.

"Guys like him got me fired. Wouldn't be here otherwise, wouldn't be getting clean."

"Probably the only good thing Minks has ever done," Thorn said.

Breezy Palms was a few miles south with an unmanned guard gate that looked more decorative than functional. The second trailer on the right was pale blue with an attached carport built of flimsy aluminum sheeting. At the edge of the carport's concrete slab was a single pygmy date palm with withered fronds. The slab was cluttered with ice chests, bicycles, overflowing trash bins, and a golf cart with four flat tires. There were wooden steps leading up to the sliding glass doors that were cloaked with a dark curtain. A battered Subaru SUV was parked in the tiny gravel side yard, an iguana sunning on its hood, giving them the poison eye.

"Cheerful ambiance," Sugarman said.

Sugarman knocked on the sliding glass door, but no one answered.

The door was cracked open about four inches, and an edge of the black curtain had sneaked out and was rippling in the breeze.

Sugarman brought his face to the crack and called out for Minks.

A few seconds later, a black and white cat squeezed through the opening and looked up at the two of them and yowled.

"Blood," Thorn said.

The cat's paws were dark with it and a gluey red paste coated his muzzle.

They found Minks' body sprawled face down on the kitchen linoleum. Head twisted to the right exposing the slice on his throat. Blood spread around him in a three-foot-wide Rorschach inkblot. Butterfly or bat or the bloom of a rose.

Two crisp twenty-dollar bills were stuck to a tendril of blood that had wandered under the kitchen table.

Sugarman said, "We'll need to call this in."

"But look around first," said Thorn.

Sugarman nodded and said, "No touching. We were never here."

The trailer was a single wide. Chintzy wood paneling, a plaid couch and matching chair, no art or decorations, a TV crammed into a bookcase. In the bedroom, Thorn stopped in front of a shabby recliner. A tangle of fishing line was heaped on the seat, several strands looped around the headrest.

"What the hell?" Sugar asked.

"More blood," Thorn said. "On the seat, a few dabs."

Sugarman wandered into the hallway while Thorn examined the fishing line. Behind the chair he found a pair of faded jeans wadded up and lying atop two high-top basketball shoes.

"You need to see this," Sugarman called.

Thorn picked up Stetson's clothes and joined Sugarman in the cramped bathroom.

"Screen's gone."

Thorn said, "Could be missing for years."

"Look out the window, down below."

Lying in the grass a few feet away from the trailer was the screen's mangled remains. Around its aluminum frame, the patchy grass was trampled.

"Somebody was tied up with fishing line, got loose, jumped through that screen."

"Somebody like Stetson," Thorn said. "She was wearing these jeans and sneakers at my house. Minks got her from my place, brought her here."

"How does that square with what Osvaldo is claiming? The guy reappears after all these years and sells the sheriff on that story about you kidnapping her. Claims Minks brought her straight to him."

"Guy like Osvaldo, who the hell knows. But something set him off, now apparently he's trying to set me up."

"We need to get out of here. Sort this out later."

Thorn left Stetson's clothes where he found them. Exiting the trailer, he took a last glance at Minks' body and the Rorschach blot surrounding him. Not a butterfly, and not a bloom. At that grim moment the shape looked to Thorn like a throng of maggots.

Sugarman headed north for a half-mile and turned off the highway onto Seaside Avenue home of Snappers restaurant.

"Food, after that?"

Sugar said he hadn't eaten since yesterday. His headache was roaring.

"After all that blood," Thorn said. "My stomach is stone."

"Have a beer," Sugar said. "Watch me eat."

Sugar could've chosen a dozen other restaurants but given how Kathy Spottswood had resurfaced so dramatically in the past twenty-four hours, Snappers did seem a fitting choice.

The spot where Sugar had introduced Kathy to Thorn, where he'd first heard her sing and where they'd exchanged their first words. That night so long ago, still so vivid, still so charged with the coupling of pleasure and pain that would follow.

Sugar picked a table outside on the deck, close to where they'd sat that night.

Sugar ordered iced tea and a fish sandwich. Thorn had a black coffee. They sat in silence looking out at Rodriquez Key and the blue glaze of sunlight on the Atlantic beyond that small island.

"You still driving up to Delray, see this writer."

"That's the plan, yeah. And you?"

"Not sure. Maybe drop by your place, pick up more of Kathy's books, see what other intimate details of our lives she ripped off."

"Does it feel weird being here, this restaurant, this table?"

"I've been here a few hundred times since that night," Sugar said.

"So have I, and I think of her every time and that night."

"Yeah," Sugar said, his voice husky with emotion. "So do I."

"You think it's possible to change your memory of the past?"

"It's a little early in the day for metaphysics."

"I'm serious, Sugar. In that novel, Kathy told the story of my early years and you were in there too. But she changed things. The names, geography, a lot of subtle stuff. North isn't me, Berryman isn't you. Cape Cod is nothing like Key Largo. A long time ago I told her that story and now she's retold it, same melody, different lyrics. Now, after reading those words on a page, those pages inside a book, somehow her version of events seems more real than my memory of it."

"A palimpsest."

Sugarman was a lifelong vocabulary enthusiast. He loved words, their etymologies, the intricate stories of their evolution. He collected words as if they were rare coins, then spent them sparingly. Thorn, more of a one-syllable guy, often had to summon patience when Sugarman went on one of his word sprees.

"A palimpsest is a manuscript with multiple layers of writing. The original words on the manuscript are rubbed out, partially erased, but traces remain, so you can see the previous words down below the new writing like an object resting on the ocean floor. Memory is like that, it's a page that keeps getting overwritten, but the original never completely disappears. Kathy retold the story of our past, but the past you and I remember is still lurking down there. We still see it, still remember it, but it's changed by this new layer on top."

A moment earlier the waitress had appeared and stood listening at Sugar's shoulder.

"You guys," she said when Sugar finished. "I don't get a lot of fancy talk around here. Mostly it's football or fishing. Or women's bods. I feel smarter just from standing here."

"This is professor Sugarman," Thorn said. "He's always happy to be of service."

"I like it," the waitress said. "Kind of sexy."

Sugar smiled at her, and the waitress returned the smile with interest.

She took a gulp of air and asked if they needed anything else. Sugar kept on smiling.

When she was gone, Sugar said, "Plus, with memories, there's another variable. Because I have a very different recollection of that evening when you met Kathy than what you remember. It meant something different to me than it did to you. Same event, different memories."

"You lost her that night."

"Oh, hell no. She was never mine to lose."

Thorn didn't press him for more. It was an awkward subject between them. Always had been. Best friends loving the same woman in very different ways.

They were quiet for a while. Thorn was visualizing that evening, the first time he'd heard Kathy sing. Her dress, her face, the breeze toying with her hair. All that was still there. Still vivid and real. Maybe it was all on the ocean floor, but the water was crystal clear and not very deep.

"Look," Sugar said. "You need to make that call to 9-1-1, report the body. Use that cell I gave you. It's a burner, no way to trace it."

Thorn sighed and dragged the phone out of his pocket. The black disk from Stetson's bag tumbled onto the deck at his feet and spun like a coin. He leaned over and retrieved it.

Sugar got a glimpse of the disk and asked what it was.

Thorn held it up. Sugar squinted, leaned close.

"Where the hell did you get that thing?"

"What's the problem?"

Sugar said, "Make the call, let me take a closer look at this."

Thorn punched in 9-1-1, using a harsh whisper to disguise his voice with the operator, he described Minks' body, its location, dodged her questions about his identity and how he'd discovered the scene.

While the operator questioned him, Sugar carried the disk out into the direct sunlight and lay it on the railing, dug a coin from his pocket and lay it next to the disk. He used his phone to snap a photo of the two objects, then he typed, swiped, tapped, doing all the cell phone gymnastics Thorn had witnessed many times, though most remained a mystery to him.

Thorn hung up on the 9-1-1 operator and Sugar returned to the table.

Their meal arrived, the waitress smiled again at Sugar and left. Sugar waited till she was back inside the restaurant.

"Now tell me where you came across this thing, man?"

Thorn described the Ziploc bag hidden in a compartment inside Stetson's duffel, a few other disks just like it.

"And you just stole one."

"An impulse. I don't know why."

"You don't know what this is, do you?"

"I believe I'm about to find out."

"It's a bug. A listening device with a tiny camera. See that glass dot in the center?"

Thorn had to squint, but yeah, he made out a shiny speck the size of a pinhead.

Sugar said, "I've seen a lot of bugs, but nothing like this. I Googled it, found it on an image search. Turns out it's manufactured by an Israeli high-tech firm that does a lot of business with *Shin Bet*, the guys who handle Israeli internal security."

"Spy stuff."

"Right. But what's cutting-edge is the battery. The device recharges off a Wi-Fi signal. It's got an internal radio-wave harvesting antenna, a tiny hair-like thing that lets its battery continually refresh from whatever active Wi-Fi signal it can latch onto.

"It watches, it listens, and it broadcasts on the same Wi-Fi network it uses for energy. Sends a continuous signal over a hundred-yard radius. Extremely sophisticated device. Sci-fi level."

"So, Stetson was trying to plant listening devices in my house."

"Appears that way."

Thorn looked out at Rodriquez Key, at a windsurfer who was tilted back against the breeze, skidding across the slight chop.

"I mean, hey, you leave your door unlocked, you make it pretty easy."

"No," Thorn said. "She wasn't planting them. She was there to fucking replace the old ones with the new version."

Sugarman sighed and gave him a gloomy nod.

"Which is how Kathy writes so accurately about your life, long after she disappeared."

"And yours too. Sounds like you need to debug your office."

Sugarman shut his eyes and bowed his head in disgust. A detective who'd missed such a basic violation of his privacy.

"Okay, okay, let's say Stetson was there to switch the bugs. A low-level job in the family business, spying on you and me for material, but something went wrong. Minks shows up, takes her hostage. Who sent him and why?"

"Let me ask you, Thorn. Stetson was tied up in that chair and got loose, okay that seems clear enough. Question is, would she be capable of slicing Minks' throat?"

The image sent a harsh prickle across his shoulders.

"I was only around her for a couple of hours. If you mean, is she big enough, strong enough, quick enough? I don't think so. Does she have the nerve? Yeah, I think she does. But if she did manage to kill him, why'd she dive out the bathroom window?"

"Maybe someone was barging in the front."

"Are we spitballing now?"

"Spit away," Sugar said.

"Okay, those two twenties on the floor, they were crisp and new. Like maybe there was a payment of some kind, and a dispute broke out. What if Minks abducted Stetson? He'd been tracking her, knew who she was, and once he had her tied up, he called Osvaldo and proposed a ransom.

"Osvaldo's men arrive, they're carrying some cash to make it look real, but the scene blows up, Stetson is so frightened she flies out that window. Which would explain one other thing: why Osvaldo lied to Sprunt that his daughter was safely back home. He's trying to cover up the Minks killing, his part in it."

"Far-fetched, but maybe something like that's possible. A lot of loose ends. Like how's Minks wind up arriving at your house right after you call it in?"

"Don't know."

"It's a decent first draft, but it needs work."

"And there's another thing," Thorn said. "I don't have Wi-Fi."

"Maybe you do, and you don't know it."

"How could that be?

"Let me finish my lunch. When we get back to your place, I'll scan the area. There's a simple way to find out."

"What kind of way?"

"I'll show you when we get there."

Sugarman ate in silence. Thorn sipped his coffee and kept glancing at the small stage where Kathy Spottswood sang her enchanting songs. Nothing about that night had faded. Her voice, her manner, their conversation afterward, the untanned groove in her ring finger, and later that evening the shy touch of her lips and fingertips that awakened sensations in Thorn that had been slumbering for years.

When he finished eating, Sugar said, "We should roll. I want to take a look around your house, my office, too."

"Guess I need to get going if I'm going to make it to Delray Beach today."

"You think this Rocco guy is going to know where Kathy Spottswood lives."

"I think it's our only lead."

"You still have a thing for Kathy, all these years later?"

"Don't you?"

Sugarman looked at the Atlantic, at a squadron of pelicans skimming across the dazzle of sunlight on the light chop.

"Well," he said, "she's a hard woman to forget."

"I'm not looking to rekindle anything. I want to know her daughter is okay."

"And the Trickster stuff, you're just going to let that slide?"

"What do you think?"

"You have a plan, or you going to try to beat Kathy's address out of this writer guy?"

Thorn took a minute to sketch out what he had in mind.

When he was done, Sugarman shook his head in reluctant admiration.

"Just crazy enough it might work."

TWELVE

THORN DROVE BACK TO HIS house, showered off the stink from Minks' trailer, changed out of his shorts into black jeans and a faded blue work shirt—what passed for Thorn's dressy attire. Meeting an author was as close to a celebrity encounter as Thorn had ever had. The least he could do was look spiffy. His version.

Only by keeping the accelerator flat to the floorboard, could Thorn stay even with the slow lane traffic on the Turnpike and later on I-95. His ancient VW complained the whole way but managed to soldier on.

The drive was two and a half hours of NASCAR insanity, lane-hopping idiots on all sides, several screaming up behind, nearly crushing his back bumper before cutting into the next lane. Got so bad Thorn had to turn his rear-view mirror sideways to keep from breaking into an angry sweat every two minutes.

He was still staggered by the idea that he'd been spied on for years. After lunch, back at his house, Sugar used his cell phone to check for a Wi-Fi signal, and yes, there was one radiating around Thorn's house. After Thorn departed, Sugarman was going to prowl the property and poke through the house to locate the broadband modem or router or whatever it was that might be producing the signal.

They agreed not to tamper with any surveillance equipment Sugar found. Let them keep operating, spying on Thorn's comings and goings, and Sugarman would do the same at his office. Adjust their conversations accordingly.

At the Delray exit, Thorn took Atlantic Avenue east to the beach and headed south on Ocean Boulevard to a right turn onto Seacrest Drive, a stone's throw from the dunes and booming waves.

It was a short street of massive houses, their upper stories peeking above the sculptured hedges. Driveways blocked by gates of wrought iron or solid steel hid the festivities within. At least it was generally assumed that wealth translated to a high incidence of happiness. Though in Thorn's experience with rich folks, that was rarely the case.

On that manicured street, several lawn service trucks were parked at the curb, and a dozen shirtless men with weed eaters and leaf blowers were marching through the neighborhood making such a racket and kicking up so much dust, Thorn cranked his windows shut to keep from choking.

At Rocco Budd's address, the front gate was open, and as Thorn slowed to peer down the driveway of gray paving stones, the plan he'd devised earlier in the day, then refined on his journey up from the Keys, completely dissolved.

In the driveway was parked a blue and white vintage Rolls Royce with a Florida vanity plate: TRKSTR

With an ache in his hands from gripping the damn steering wheel so tight, Thorn drove past Rocco Budd's house and at the end of the block took a right to Ocean Boulevard, drawing in slow breaths to ease the clench in his shoulders. He found a parking spot behind a diner, shut off the engine, and sat for several minutes retracing the day's events.

After Stetson's driver dropped the girl off at Thorn's yesterday, he'd apparently driven to Delray and now was parked outside the house of the writer of Kathy Spottswood's novels. Stetson was attempting to plant surveillance devices inside Thorn's house but before she could pull it off, she'd been abducted by Minks who was now dead. It appeared that Stetson escaped from Minks' trailer through the bathroom window. Beyond those few bits of shaky evidence, the rest was such a tangle the more Thorn considered it, the more confused he became.

Sugar answered on the first ring and started speaking before Thorn had a chance.

"Found two bugs in your house," he said. "Two more in my office.

They're primitive compared to the ones Stetson had. Mine were just audio, but yours had crude motion-sensitive cameras, voice-activated audio, everything is internet-friendly. You twitch or make a peep, it's captured, sent to the cloud, and stored forever. Apparently, Osvaldo decided it was time to install an upgrade.

"All the bugs were well-concealed, very professional, one was up on the wall just above the mirror in your bedroom, camouflaged so well you could be staring right at it, never see the damn thing. I'm not surprised you never noticed them. But I'm pissed I didn't. Still haven't tracked down the source of the Wi-Fi signal. Best guess, there's a hotspot stashed in the woods nearby. Could be as small as a cell phone, up in the branches. No way you could find it down in all that foliage. By the way, good thing you're not home today, on the lot next door you got some bulldozers ripping up a few dozen hardwoods by the roots, native trees. And oh yeah, their radio's blasting Reggae, rattling your windows."

Thorn said, "Welcome to the neighborhood, Jimmy Buffett."

He told Sugar about the Rolls in Rocco Budd's driveway, the vanity license plate.

"I'll be damned. What the hell do you make of that?"

"I don't know."

"And what do you have in mind?"

"I'm scrapping Plan A."

"God help us all. You're improvising."

"I need to meet Mr. Budd, see what he has to say for himself."

"Just go up, knock on the door? Guy might be a badass. Not every writer is a pansy."

"I'll figure it out. Find a monkey wrench, throw it in the first gears I see."

"Look, buddy, do me a favor. Just wait for me, a couple of hours is all. Go have a beer and cool off. I can hear it in your voice, the strain."

Thorn gave him the address.

"You'll wait?"

"I'll give it my best shot," Thorn said and clicked off.

He waited five minutes. All he could manage.

Wired now, feeling the heat glow in his face. Thinking about the outrageous scope of the violation. Eavesdropping on Thorn and the women who'd come into his bedroom, listening to their private conversations, the hilarity, the moans, watching their naked bodies writhing in the sheets. Someone always listening, watching. The anger he felt was beyond anger. Those murmurs of affection, the first night fumblings, the frenzied yips and squeals, the laughter, the tears, the parting words. Intimate moments fanned through his mind like a filmstrip broken from its sprocket.

But far more damning were his talks with Sugar, their schemes to rescue victims, deliver justice, retaliate against the violent bastards who'd injured one friend or another. How many confessions had they made inside Thorn's house, how many unlawful acts had they plotted? Planning to do bad things for good reasons. Defend the innocent, right wrongs. But yes, sometimes what they'd done was undeniably criminal. All recorded.

All of it stolen simply to flesh out another of Kathy's novels.

He walked the five blocks back to Seacrest Drive. The lawn care drill teams were still blasting away. Thorn didn't try to conceal his approach and none of the workers took notice.

When he saw his chance, he ducked behind a white panel van with Lawn Ranger stenciled on the sides.

He inched behind the truck and raised the rear door just enough to peek inside. There was a weed eater and two blowers within arm's length. If this were Miami, that door would be triple-locked and even then, there was a high risk the van could be picked clean. But a couple of hours up the road apparently folks were more trusting. The plague hadn't spread that far north. Thank God for that.

He chose the weed eater, then helped himself to a Lawn Ranger baseball cap that lay on the floor of the truck. Nicely sweat-stained. He put it on, screwed it down tight so his sun-bleached hair was mostly hidden. He stripped off his shirt and wadded it into a ball and hid it beneath a ligustrum hedge. Not the greatest disguise, but it would do on short notice.

No one was mowing Rocco Budd's lawn today, but unless Rocco stayed abreast of the lawn maintenance schedule, it was unlikely he would object to having his grass trimmed.

Thorn cranked up the two-cycle engine, gunned it, and began to edge the grass along the base of the ligustrum hedge beside the street, working his way to the open driveway where the Rolls was parked. One of the Lawn Ranger's crew, an older Hispanic gentleman, gave Thorn a wary look, but Thorn shot him a conspirator's wink, and called out, "New hire."

The man shrugged and got back to blowing yard clippings into the street.

Thorn reached the end of the hedge and began to work at the base of a row of ficus bushes shaped into a high wall of privacy. He rounded the end of the ficus and stepped inside Rocco Budd's property and kept on trimming the edge of the St. Augustine grass.

With his back to the house, he worked toward a thick hedge of podocarpus that separated Rocco's property from the Spanish-style mansion next door. Working down that side of the yard, Thorn kept his head bowed, focused on his work. Twice he broke the trimmer line and had to rap the head against the hard pathway to release more length.

It took him several minutes to weed eat his way to the backyard.

As if taking a breather, he let the two-cycle idle, propped the weed eater against the stubby limb of a frangipani tree with gaudy pink blooms. He turned slowly to survey the backyard, the swimming pool with a raised hot tub adjoining it, a cascade of water falling over the lip of the hot tub into the pool.

On the pool deck, a tall man with wavy black hair that fell past his shoulders was speaking on a cell phone. His face was half-turned away from Thorn, showing only his sharp-angled profile. Enough of a view to spark a vague recognition followed by a very ugly memory.

Thorn picked up the weed eater and slipped a few feet to his right and pressed his back against the creamy stucco wall of the house.

The man's sturdy build had softened over the years, and these days his black mane was streaked with gray, though the style had remained unchanged. The same Fabio hairdo the other two badass gangsters had worn that night. Those strapping guys who piled on Thorn and kicked and pounded him unconscious.

Much of that evening was a blur, but there was enough moonlight filtering into Thorn's house for him to imprint the images of the three thugs, and the silvery hair of Osvaldo Baltazar Garcia spectating from the doorway.

The years had not dimmed his memory of that night, and time had not washed away the rage he felt as the men clubbed him to the ground and pounded him until he lay helpless and straining to breathe, choking on his blood and bits of broken teeth.

He revved the two-cycle and chewed up the edge of a flower bed as he worked his way toward the pool deck and the man on the phone. The man wore dark slacks and a white guayabera that fluttered in a light ocean breeze and revealed the chunky contour of a pistol at the small of his back.

Thorn pushed the little gas-powered motor as loud as it would go. And the man turned to look his way then spoke a quick phrase into the phone and slipped it into his pants pocket.

Thorn stepped onto the white limestone pool deck.

The man yelled at Thorn, but his words didn't penetrate the roar of the engine.

Thorn released the throttle trigger and the trimmer line stopped spinning.

"Who the fuck are you?"

The man took two steps toward Thorn.

Around his neck he wore a gold crucifix on a chain, the cross tangled deep in the mat of black hair on his chest. He was a couple inches taller than Thorn and heftier by at least twenty pounds. Thick shoulders, blocky hands, fingers too large for piano keys.

A man who was paid to crush bones and mangle limbs. On that night at Thorn's house, he'd traveled in a pack, but he had the look of a guy whose favorite sport was bar room brawling, taking on all-comers. A weight class above Thorn's and a man who played by no rules.

Thorn's ears were hot, his throat clutching. The rage from that long-ago beating had never completely boiled away. It was rising from some molten place in his gut. Laced with a new outrage—a former lover hijacking his darkest secrets as fodder for her potboilers.

"You hear me, fool? Who the fuck are you?"

"I'm the Lawn Ranger, sir," Thorn said. "I'm here to cut your grass and whip your ass."

"What'd you say to me?"

While he was off-balance, Thorn said, "Is this the home of Rocco Budd?"

The man blinked and shook his head as if to clear it.

"I'm a fan of his books. Have you read them? That guy, North, his hero, what a character, huh? Maybe a little cartoonish, but hey, what superhero isn't, right?"

The man's right hand drifted to his side, heading for the small of his back.

"Go ahead," Thorn said. "Let's see how fast you can draw that thing."

The man eyed the weed eater idling in Thorn's hands, a motorized club within easy striking distance. And his hand relaxed at his side, dangling uncertainly.

"What the fuck do you want, *gilipollas*?"

"Shithead? Is that what you think I am?"

The man had just opened his mouth to reply when a voice from above called out.

"Rafe, what's going on? Who is this man?"

A throaty voice. Thorn didn't try to track its source. But Rafe shifted his gaze upward, and that instant was the opening Thorn needed.

Gunning the weed-whacker, he swung the head from ground level straight up and caught Rafe dead center in the crotch, doubling him over. Thorn churned that heavy monofilament into his slacks, tearing them open, drawing blood. The big man howled.

With Rafe's head slumped forward, Thorn raised the weed eater high and cracked it against the back of his skull, a deep and satisfying chunk of dented bone. Rafe dropped to his knees, kept his balance for a few seconds as if in prayer, then tumbled forward at Thorn's feet.

His arms sprawled wide, right cheek flat against the deck, his lips blowing bubbles of blood as delicate as sea foam. Thorn kept the trimmer line spinning at full speed and brought it level to his face, Rafe's eyes opening wearily, watching the whir of cutting line.

Thorn looked off at the waterfall cascading from the hot tub into the pool. A luxurious setting, first class South Florida amenities, an empire financed in part by the exploits of Thorn and Sugarman, a writer profiting on the deadly risks the two of them had taken, the injuries and battle scars they'd acquired pursuing justice.

Thorn inched the whirling monofilament close to Rafe's face. The last fumes of Thorn's fury had burned away, leaving only a cold resolve. He intended to leave a brand on this man, just as Rafe had left his lasting mark on Thorn.

"Don't do it. Thorn, don't."

The speaker was close behind him, an unforgettable voice. He hesitated a moment, then released the trigger and turned to face her.

He studied her for a moment, then killed the engine and lay the machine on the ground.

She wore loose-fitting beige slacks and a sleeveless maroon top. No jewelry, no wedding ring, and the depression on her ring finger was gone.

Kathy Spottswood's hair was trimmed to a short Pixie, just long enough to comb. The lush cinnamon-brown had turned an iron-gray, decades premature. When he first met her, she'd been fit and shapely, but now she was so gaunt her knobby shoulder blades surfaced through her blouse and her bare arms were frail and laced with prominent veins.

But it was her face that was almost unrecognizable, weathered beyond her years. Her sunken cheeks and the seams etched around her mouth and across her forehead were a map of lost hope and private violations, suggesting a starvation of the spirit as well as the body. And those fiercely independent eyes that once gleamed with captured starlight were flat and dulled as if by drugs or an unspeakable melancholy.

"If you've come to save me, Thorn, it's way too late."

"I didn't know you were here. I came to speak to Rocco Budd. Is that you?"

Her nod was almost imperceptible.

"Why?"

"An extra layer of anonymity," she said.

"Osvaldo's idea?"

"Everything is."

Her eyes were briefly drawn to Thorn's bare chest, a flush darkening her cheeks.

She cut her gaze away, mumbled something to herself, then drew a long breath and blew it out through pursed lips as though extinguishing a flame.

She crouched beside Rafe and felt for a pulse at his throat.

After a moment, she looked up at Thorn.

"He'll survive," she said. "But you made an enemy for life. And there are two more who ambushed you that night, Facundo and Miguel. They're on an errand, picking up the week's provisions. They'll be back any moment. You need to leave now."

"Are you a hostage, Kathy?"

"To be honest," she said, fixing him with her dark eyes, "I don't know anymore."

"Let's go somewhere, talk, I'll bring you back if you want."

"Talk? What do we have to talk about?"

"Oh, I don't know. For instance, I'd like to hear about Berryman and North. Their adventures. How you've made them mirror Sugarman's and mine so accurately."

"You must already know the answer to that, or you wouldn't be here."

Her eyes flicked away from his and followed a butterfly's jittering flight across the hedge into the neighbor's yard.

"I'd like to hear it from you. All the details. And the Trickster stuff too. That's Osvaldo, isn't it? The guy messing with North."

She swallowed and a brief spark flared in her brown eyes. Her mouth twisted as though a bitter taste had burned her tongue. Maybe it was a flash of anger, maybe self-loathing. Thorn had lost the knack of reading her expressions.

"Talk to me, Kathy. I want to know all the ways you and your husband have been tampering with my life, and Sugar's. Changing our storylines. Tell me about that."

"You need to go. Facundo, Miguel, they're worse than Rafe. A weed eater won't cut it."

"Good one, Kath."

"Thorn, this isn't a joke."

"If you want to escape, I'll help you."

"If it were only that easy."

"Why isn't it?"

She moved to the edge of the pool, stared down into the still water with such intense concentration she might've been trying to peer back through the years, searching the distant past for some fortifying memory.

When she spoke again her voice was fragile and raspy as if perhaps the tissues in her throat were raw from sobbing.

"I have a daughter."

"Yeah, I know," he said. "Stetson."

She whirled around.

"How do you know that name?"

"Met her yesterday. She appeared at my house. As feisty as you used to be."

"I don't believe you."

"She's quite a girl. Wanted to recruit me for something but was disheartened I wasn't the caped crusader she was hoping for. Apparently, she had me mixed up with your guy North."

Kathy raked a hand through her hair.

"Recruit you for what?"

Thorn heard a car door slam. Then a second.

"That's them," Kathy said. "If they see you, you're dead and I will be too. They'll be coming through the house. Go the way you came, do it now, you'll make it."

"Is that how North would handle this? Would he run?"

"Go. Goddamn it. Go, you idiot."

THIRTEEN

SUGARMAN SLID IN AND OUT of the clogged lanes, trying to find the sweet spots between the laggards and the flat-out suicidal drivers. Making it from Key Largo to Delray in two hours was a minor miracle considering it was Friday afternoon and the roads were packed with folks getting the jump on the weekend.

There was a time not long ago when South Florida traffic slacked off between ten in the morning and three in the afternoon. Things got civil for those five hours. And on school nights after eleven, the roads were mostly clear.

Not anymore. Every minute of every day and every night it was like this. Twenty-four/seven rush hour.

Year after year with newcomers flooding the state, looking for their sliver of paradise, they'd turned traffic into a full-contact brawl. It had finally reached critical mass. If the hurricanes or sea level rise didn't sweep away South Florida first, then the accumulated tonnage of all those cars and trucks and SUVs might just fracture the limestone crust and send this whole mess sinking into the damn aquifer.

Like Thorn had been saying for years, it was time to move farther out to sea.

Exiting I-95, Sugar headed east until he crossed the Intracoastal then, as Thorn had instructed, he headed south on A1A to Atlantic Dunes Park and pulled into a public lot across the road from the beach. He took one of the sandy trails through the scrub and found Thorn standing half-naked just north of a lifeguard stand.

"Somebody stole my shirt," he said. "I liked that goddamn shirt."

"What?"

"I stole their weed-whacker, they stole my shirt. Fair enough, I guess."

"You can buy a new shirt, okay. Now let's go speak to this Rocco Budd."

"Things have changed. There is no Rocco Budd."

While rosy-skinned tourists and the nut-brown melanoma crowd paraded past in their skimpy suits, Thorn described his recent adventure impersonating the Lawn Ranger. When he was done Sugar blew out a pained breath.

"But Kathy's okay?"

"I think she's being held prisoner. Those three thugs who sent me to the hospital way back when, they're keeping watch on her."

"And you didn't help her escape?"

"She wouldn't have it. Said Stetson was the reason she couldn't go."

"I don't get it."

"Neither do I."

"You tell Kathy about Minks taking her away, his corpse in the trailer?"

"There wasn't time," Thorn said. "Goons arrived. Ended our conversation."

"So, we go back to the house, the two of us, try again."

"Are you packing?"

"Glock Nine. There's a .357 in the car if you're interested."

"I'd prefer grenades and a howitzer, but small arms will do."

Back on Seacrest, the lawn service trucks were gone. Neighborhood quiet except for a dog yapping nearby. Two women with bright white hair blew by in a souped-up golf cart. The Rolls was no longer in the driveway.

"Goddamn it," Thorn said. "They jumped ship."

"Could've moved the car into the garage. Hunkering down."

"Maybe," Thorn said.

Sugar circled the block and Thorn directed him to the café out on A1A where his VW was parked.

"Kathy's eyes," Thorn said. "They were different. Dulled."

Sugarman nodded, waiting for Thorn to finish.

"At first, I thought it was sadness, or, I don't know, like she was on something. Anti-depressants, something stronger. But the more I replay it the more that seems wrong. The way she was moving was edgy, she was bristling like a trapped animal.

"The Kathy we knew was willful, tough, a warrior. Submission wasn't on her dance card. And I don't think Osvaldo has her under his spell. I think she's full of rage, crazy to break free, but something about Stetson has her handcuffed."

"Let's go find out what."

Sugar opened the trunk and pulled out a soiled T-shirt and tossed it to Thorn.

"Jesus," Thorn said. "Stinks of motor oil."

Sugarman drew a leather bag from the trunk, unzipped it and, after checking to see no one was passing by, slipped Thorn a stainless-steel Smith and Wesson.

"That shirt's my car rag. Put it on, you need something to hide the gun in your belt."

Although the streets were empty between their parking spot and Seacrest, Thorn had the cold tingle of being captured on numerous security cams.

A black man wearing neatly pressed jeans, a white shirt, and a spiffy bolo tie keeping a brisk pace down that sidewalk alongside a raggedy white guy— in that fancy neighborhood it was a wonder the sirens weren't already wailing.

Thorn led Sugar to Kathy's driveway, nodded for him to follow, then slipped along the hedge, the path he'd used earlier to enter the backyard. A few houses away a gang of construction workers were hooting, and whistling tunes as they hammered and shrieked their saws through boards, no doubt building another monstrosity to squeeze in beside its brethren.

Sugarman touched a hand to Thorn's shoulder, halting him.

"How's this?" he whispered. "I go to the front door, do my Jehovah's Witness come-to-Jesus pitch. Get a quick idea of what's what. Usually works."

"Sometimes I forget your masterful investigative skills."

"I'll wait here for a minute, give you time to get around back. I see who comes to the door, who's backing them up. You do some window peeping. This is just reconnaissance, buddy. Lay of the land, that's all, afterward, we meet back at the car, huddle up, decide what's next."

"A judicious approach."

"Promise me, Thorn. I'm not in the mood for a shootout."

Thorn promised, though from Sugarman's skeptical sigh, it was clear he didn't buy it.

They separated and Thorn went further into the rear yard. No one was outside on the pool deck. No sounds except the construction workers hammering and a gull's hysterical squeals. Thorn hugged the back wall, inched to a window, peeked around the edge.

He could see a refrigerator, the edge of a microwave. And as he crept closer, he made out an island with a stovetop and a hood above. A messy array of pots and dirty dishes and half-filled food jars covered the countertops, stacks of pizza boxes, and a collection of fast-food sacks.

A crash pad for swine. Kathy's orderly presence was missing, as though she'd withdrawn into a gloomy upper chamber, out of the flow of the daily life of the house.

Beyond the kitchen was a vast living room that looked like it had been furnished by a band of speed freaks and vandals. Three leather recliners in gaudy shades huddled around a TV the size of a storefront window. The walls were crowded with paintings of Florida landscapes that might've been stolen from a dumpster behind a hot-sheets motel.

On one crimson recliner, Rafe was slumped, his head tilted to the side, cheek planted against his shoulder. At that moment, Sugarman rang the doorbell which resonated with the solemnity of a Buddhist temple gong.

Rafe didn't wake. Rafe didn't even twitch.

Sugar pressed the doorbell again, and again that sonorous chime failed to stir Rafe. With the late afternoon sun playing tricks with the reflection off the glass, Thorn had to move a step to his left for a clearer view. Pressing his nose against the plate glass, he saw with stark clarity that Rafe was long past twitching.

What earlier in the day had been Rafe's skull was now demolished. Damage so drastic only a large caliber weapon fired at close range could have caused it. Shards of bone and a gray pudding were sprayed across that tacky recliner.

Thorn budged the heavy sliding door, found it unlocked. Opening it further, he angled inside. The air had the acrid bite of gunpowder and the stomach-churning stench of fresh corpse.

A mere civilian, Thorn had never trained for war or so much as considered police work. So, he had not developed the emotional techniques, visceral hardness, or other skills of disengagement that he assumed the military or police force taught their new recruits.

Although he'd never tallied the number of violent deaths he'd had the misfortune to cause or encounter, such exposure had become so commonplace over his years of seeking justice for the harms done to his friends or lovers that Thorn should have grown a hide so thick that nothing could penetrate it and injure a vital organ.

But that was not true. Right now, as he entered the expansive living room his pulse jittered, clammy sweat coated his body, his breath tightened in his chest. He felt as dizzy and disoriented today after seeing Rafe's corpse, one of the assholes whose deaths he had pictured dozens of times with grim satisfaction, as he'd felt decades ago after encountering his first cadaver. All those years of exposure to murder and mayhem had not hardened him. His feelings were as ripe and defenseless as they'd been when he was a boy.

Thorn drew the .357 from his belt, aimed it with extended arms, and followed its sights through the spacious room, sweeping the aim left, right, and pivoting slowly to check the room behind him, all the while listening for floor creaks or the scuffing of shoe leather, but hearing nothing. He aimed his way to the front door and found it unlocked. He drew it open and shushed Sugar with a raised palm.

Whispering, "Downstairs is clear. One corpse. The guy I weed-whacked, Rafe."

Sugarman nodded and motioned for Thorn to follow him. Sugarman headed up the curved staircase, its steps carpeted with a deep pile.

At the head of the stairs, he signaled Thorn to take the left side rooms and he headed right. Thorn had no issue following Sugar's commands. His years of police training gave him indisputable seniority in such matters.

In the first room, Thorn nudged the door open and stepped clear. After several moments, he peeked around the edge. The room appeared empty. He went inside. The air reeked of body odor and cheap cologne and stale cigarette smoke. Two twin beds lined up side-by-side. All the mattresses were naked but for rumpled Army blankets and soiled pillows. Two feet inside the room, a loud whoosh sounded behind him and Thorn spun, aiming the revolver at the empty doorway.

A chilly blast blew on his neck as the air-conditioning cycled to full blast. He drew a breath and waited till his pulse eased back.

The bathroom was bare. Toilet seat covered in yellow spatters. Long hair clogging the shower drain. Nothing in the medicine chest. Closet empty except for a few wire hangers.

The next bedroom was Kathy's.

He knew it the instant he opened the door, inhaling her haunting scent. She wasn't one for perfumes or fragrant shampoos. But the aroma she radiated was as unique as her fingerprints. It was as if Thorn had stepped into a French bakery, buttery, flaky dough, a hint of toasted almonds, all of it bringing back a swirl of memories from those exuberant weeks long ago.

The woman who'd left behind this incense was not the same dour version he'd met poolside earlier. This was the old Kathy, the torch singer, capable of rhapsodies that transformed a ramshackle seafood joint into an enchanted wonderland for a few hours on a weekend night. Yes, she'd clearly languished since then, withered, lost her joy, turned fearful and anxious, but a crucial part of her essence remained the same. It permeated that room.

Her closet was empty. The bathroom bare of toiletries. He opened the medicine cabinet and found the shelves cleared out.

When he was shutting the cabinet door, something caught his eye.

He opened it again and examined the back of the door.

In a pale pink lipstick, two letters were printed in the lower corner of the aluminum. So well-concealed it was apparently missed by her watchdogs who, before they abandoned the house, must have inspected her room looking for just such an act of defiance as this.

KL

Sugar was waiting for him on the landing when Thorn exited Kathy's room.

"All clear," he said. "And you?"

"When I showed up this afternoon, I spooked them," Thorn said. "They know we're onto them. Osvaldo must have ordered them to abandon ship."

"And your friend in the La-Z-Boy?"

"Maybe the savages are turning on each other. Or Osvaldo ordered it for botching things with me."

"That's one hell of a harsh penalty," Sugar said, "for letting you escape."

Thorn nodded.

"What now? Any ideas?"

"Kathy left a message in her medicine chest. Printed in lipstick, KL."

"Key Largo?"

"That's my guess."

"You said she was being held prisoner."

"That much was clear," Thorn said. "But when I told her Stetson showed up at my house looking for some superhero, Kathy freaked. Maybe that pushed her to try what she's been afraid to do, break free."

"Has to be that," Sugar said. "But I don't get Stetson. Is she at your house to plant bugs or plead for help?"

"Thing is, she didn't plead or I would've helped. She shut me down before I knew who she was or what she wanted. She was playing it so goddamn coy. Like maybe she wasn't sure herself what she wanted."

"Only thing we can do is go back to Key Largo," Sugar said. "Wait to see if Kathy shows. She knows where to find us. That's all we've got."

"If you had to guess, could she have shot Rafe?"

Sugar shook his head.

"Not unless her life was in danger. And it's not. She's the golden goose, laying those novels, bringing in the bucks. No way Osvaldo is going to lose that."

"There's more to this," Thorn said. "More than just those books and money."

"Like what?"

"I don't know," Thorn said. "But I'm chewing on it."

He followed Sugarman down the stairway, halting in the foyer.

"Golden goose or not, we put Kathy in a lot more danger now than before," Sugar said. "And after today, these assholes are going to be on red alert. Which will make it very challenging for her to get loose."

"But she'll find a way."

"You sure of that?"

"Aren't you, Sugar?"

He gave his forehead a deep one-handed massage then his lips formed a cryptic smile as though he might be debating whether to reveal some long-held secret.

Buddies since grade school, Thorn and Sugar had always been open and frank with each other. No subject was off-limits, no personal issues out of bounds no matter how messy. But despite all that, he and Sugar had fundamental conflicts.

Thorn was impetuous and Sugarman temperate and thoughtful. Thorn's moral constraints were elastic. Act on impulse, sort out the consequences later. Sugar had a rule book embedded in his heart, a gift from the two black mothers who raised him, church ladies who took him into their home when he was abandoned by his foolish, unmarried parents.

That bible had guided him unerringly through numerous upheavals, Sugar always coping with composure and equanimity. Despite these differences, they'd risked their lives for each other repeatedly and forged an understanding and trust that was battle-tested, founded as it was on the flow of brutal honesty between them.

So that cryptic smile, which clearly hid some consequential secret, was a breach in their long-standing accord. Thorn was about to call him on it, but before he could speak, Sugarman sighed and the strain left his face and his usual good-natured countenance resurfaced. Whatever troubling admission he'd been about to make vanished into the balmy twilight air.

"If Kathy is anything like the woman we used to know, hell yes, she'll find a way to get free of those sons of bitches."

Back at the diner parking lot, they were about to head south in their separate cars when the phone in Sugarman's pants pocket burped.

Thorn opened his car door and was easing into the driver's seat when Sugar raised a hand, signaling him to wait.

"Thanks," he said into the phone. "I appreciate the call."

Sugar put the phone away and his gaze drifted up to the dusky sky and a purple haze of clouds. Thorn got out of the VW and walked over.

"Tell me," Thorn said.

"That was Jinny Strickland, old friend from the department."

"Yeah?"

"She's risking her job by calling, but she thought I should know. Osvaldo called Sheriff Sprunt, informed him that Stetson is pressing charges against you for rape."

"That fuckhead."

"It gets worse," Sugar said. "A couple of hours ago Sprunt got a search warrant, put together a team, and raided your house. Found Stetson's bloody T-shirt."

"Perfect."

"Stetson will identify it, blood will match hers. Along with her statement, it's all the evidence they'll need. Meantime, they're staking out your place. You show up, they'll arrest you, put the bail out of reach, it'll be months before a trial. All this to take you off the board."

"You know what this is, Sugar?"

"What?"

"Stetson's T-shirt hanging on my dock, you were right. That was the bait in the trap, and I went for it. This is a Trickster stunt, nudging the storyline in a new direction."

"This is a shitload more than a nudge."

"Yeah," Thorn said. "And now it's time to nudge back."

"Before we can do anything to Osvaldo, we've got to find the asshole."

"Sure," Thorn said. "That'll be second on the list, right after making sure Kathy's safe."

"Roger that."

"So, let's move."

"I know you want to barrel ahead, but look, the cops will be staking out your house, my office too. On the lookout for both our cars. Osvaldo might want to have some face time with you, too, showing up like you did at Kathy's hideaway."

"My last face time with Osvaldo didn't end well."

"So, we go to Homestead."

"What's in Homestead?"

"A guy who owes me a favor. Actually, a couple of favors."

"You're losing me."

"Joey Wasilewski, he's a car dealer. Specializes in luxury items, but he keeps a warehouse full of less conspicuous vehicles."

"Okay."

"A couple of years ago I tracked down an ex-girlfriend of Joey's who'd driven off in one of his Aston Martins without permission. She'd been gone a week when Joey called me. I tracked down the young lady through her credit card charges. She was in Savannah, trading on the image that fancy car conferred. I got Joey's car back, made sure the authorities had a talk with the girlfriend and the older gentleman she was stringing along.

"I'll call him as we drive down, see if he can set us up with something nondescript, maybe tinted windows. He should have a ride in his inventory that meets our needs."

"These are stolen cars?"

"Repossessed. Joey has a deal with a few local banks, buys them cheap, cleans them up, and off they go."

"Pretty smart, Sugar. I don't know what we'd do without your logic."

"If we were depending on your decision-making, we'd both be in jail by now."

Thorn patted Sugarman on his wide shoulders.

"Jail," Thorn said. "Or worse."

FOURTEEN

THURSDAY NIGHT STETSON SLEPT IN her own bed and continued to sleep most of Friday, knotting the sweat-damp sheets around her body as she thrashed and twisted, tormented by disjointed snippets of the day before. Thorn's house, kidnapped by Minks, tied to a chair in his shabby trailer, witnessing his murder as she escaped, and after running free for an hour, captured and dragged home by the three stooges, Pablo, Victor, and Jorge.

What brought her fully awake was a sharply-detailed memory. It was nighttime, Osvaldo and the stooges were on a beach. Osvaldo was tipsy. He wanted to try out a new purchase, a Glock with a laser sight and suppressor. Osvaldo ordered Victor to wade out into the water and take off his baseball cap and hold it out to one side. Stetson watched from the bushes just off the beach. Drawn by their voices, curious.

Victor obeyed. He walked out until he was ankle-deep in the water, ten yards, fifteen, and he held out the cap. Osvaldo raised the pistol, a green laser dot jiggling across Victor's chest, then settling on the cap and holding perfectly still for several seconds. Osvaldo blew the cap from Victor's hand.

"Now pick up the hat and go farther away. Deeper."

Without hesitation Victor waded out into the black water, waist-high.

"Farther."

Victor backed a few feet more, water up to his chest.

Osvaldo ordered him to lift the cap, hold it next to his face.

Victor hesitated.

"No confias en mi."

"I trust you, Trickster. I trust you."

"Next to your fucking face, the cap. Now!"

Victor touched the cap to his cheek.

The green dot wobbled for a second, then stilled.

The cap exploded, blew ten feet into the sea.

All his men applauded.

That's the image that woke Stetson in the afternoon on Friday, tired but wired. Panting from the memory. The utter loyalty of his men. Osvaldo's crazy need to dominate. His cold discipline, even while drunk.

From that memory, a plan began to emerge. She propped herself on the pillows and Googled on her iPhone for an hour. She made calculations and measured distances until she'd filled in every detail.

She climbed out of bed, slipped into her one-piece bathing suit and a quick-dry T-shirt that hung to her thighs. She laced up a pair of white sneakers, went out to the pool, stood for a moment looking into the water, set the timer on her watch, arranged her feet as if perched on a starter's block, then dove.

There were 880 yards in a half-mile.

Because the swimming pool was 25 yards long, she had to do 17 laps to cover that half-mile, which was the distance to the closest shoreline, Snapper Point in the Ocean Reef Club, a posh, private community that occupied the northernmost tip of Key Largo. There was a three-story mansion on Snapper Point whose golden dock lights blazed every night from dusk till dawn. Those golden lights would be her beacon as she swam.

Fifteen minutes was the female world record for a mile, held by an Olympic swimmer. Covering half that distance was all Stetson needed to do. Being a decent swimmer, she was pretty sure she could manage that half-mile, going flat out, in twenty minutes max.

Until the last few months, that span of water seemed too daunting to conquer. For years she'd been swimming laps half-heartedly, fantasizing an escape plan but too timid to activate it.

But after yesterday, everything changed. What she'd long suspected was true. With brutal clarity she'd seen the blade whisking across Minks' throat, Osvaldo killing a man as casually as swatting a mosquito.

Escaping at night would give her an edge. And if the diversion she had in mind worked, she'd have a few minutes head start, enough time, she believed, to stay ahead of the Zodiacs that would be combing the dark waters once her father realized she'd escaped *El Morro*.

Osvaldo had christened his island *El Morro* in honor of the fort that had guarded Havana harbor for centuries. Four hundred years old, the fortress was built to defend against pirates, buccaneers, and foreign navies trying to plunder the loot ripped off from the New World. Because it was a convenient layover for the convoys of Spanish treasure ships before making their long journey back to the motherland, Cuba was the juiciest target in the Caribbean.

Over the centuries the fortress survived sieges and assaults from all those marauders as well as every seafaring nation, and as far as her father was concerned its survival made *El Morro* a prime example of the unyielding tenacity of the Cuban people.

She'd heard the speech dozens of times at the dinner table after Osvaldo had warmed up with rum drinks. Usually, the fort speech was followed by a recounting of the grim details of his boyhood, the grueling street life of an orphan with no home or relatives, hundreds of fistfights with bigger boys, brawls that left scars on his chin and cheek and other parts of his body, scars he would pompously display as he repeated the hard-knocks sermon. Recounting the kill-or-be-killed horrors of poverty and near-starvation that forced him to pilfer garbage, and as he grew older and more daring, to mug American tourists for their fat billfolds. Later he learned the tricks of pickpocketing, then best of all, he'd mastered *las destrezas de chuchillos,* the devilish knife techniques he acquired from a virtuoso of the blade, an African goddess who Osvaldo claimed also taught him every bedroom secret a hot-blooded boy needed to know.

Probably Osvaldo would have died on the streets of Havana, dethroned by some back-stabbing rival, but as though he was the urchin-hero of a tale by Charles Dickens, at fifteen, tall for his age, Osvaldo was recruited by a wealthy nightclub owner to guard the doorway of one of his establishments and prevent the entry of anyone the owner deemed unworthy.

That doorway was where Osvaldo honed his knife skills and so impressed his boss that after only a year proving his valor and invincibility as a doorman and bouncer, Osvaldo was called into the office of his boss. In an act of disastrous lack of caution, Senor Mateo Garcia, who was childless and a recent widower, invited the boy into his own home and gave him a bedroom and a private bath for the first time in Osvaldo's life.

From that point on Osvaldo's boyhood tales always grew sketchy and riddled with ambiguities, and as Stetson came to see her father more clearly, it was evident that Senor Mateo Garcia had welcomed into his home his own usurper. Osvaldo had not simply stolen the Garcia name, he commandeered his benefactor's empire.

As Stetson swam her laps, her lungs on fire and her arms growing leaden, she summoned those stories of her father's youth to harden her resolve. In its own way, Stetson's childhood was as grim and loveless as her father's, and those deprivations had shaped her spirit, toughened her, made her contemptuous of the romantic fantasies that movies and books peddled to girls her age. Maybe Stetson didn't have Osvaldo's street smarts, but she believed she could be just as ruthless and unforgiving.

Aside from supervised visits with her mother in random Miami hotel rooms, and outings to the same half dozen eateries in the Ocean Reef Club, Stetson had spent her youth isolated in the stunted universe of *El Morro.*

The island was a neat oval, twenty-six acres of lush greenery with a sprawling five-bedroom house built only a few feet above mean high tide. From the water level, the house was hidden by dense mangroves. And the shoals that encircled the island were so shallow they warded off most passing boaters. Only a single meandering channel led through patches of brain coral and the deep sucking mud and sand, and that channel was only navigable by shallow draft skiffs, and then only at full high tide.

Stored in a camouflaged boathouse on the oceanside was a pair of twenty-foot Zodiacs, combat rubber raiding crafts, powered by 250 horsepower engines. The Zodiacs were used to ferry arriving and departing guests out to larger crafts anchored in deep waters or to take Osvaldo to his private dock in Ocean Reef for one business meeting or another. Stealing one of the inflatables to make her escape was out of the question. They were locked up, guarded day and night and alarmed.

Over the years a few passing boaters, foolhardy enough to attempt a landing on the island, were warned off by Osvaldo's enforcers. No weapons were necessary. One look at the badasses marshaled on the beach was all it took to intimidate the average nosy explorer.

As Stetson was touching the wall, about to push off to start the final lap of her workout, a hand seized her right wrist and yanked her upright, raised her high, and kept her suspended so only the soles of her shoes brushed the pool water. She gasped and wriggled against the grip but couldn't break free.

"I'll sit you down when you stop struggling."

After a moment's reluctance, Stetson relaxed her body and Osvaldo settled her on the lip of the pool.

"Dry off," he said. "We shall talk. There's much to discuss. *Ven a la sala del acuario*."

Osvaldo referred to it as "the aquarium room." But as far as Stetson was concerned it wasn't a room at all, but a watery tomb.

In her bedroom she stripped off the T-shirt and her one-piece, dried herself, then in the bathroom mirror she examined the cuts on her face. The saltwater in the pool had stung at first, but eventually it had a soothing effect. Tender to the touch, the wounds were no longer bloody, but her cheeks were swollen and her lips puffy and bruises had begun to appear.

She checked the timer on her watch. When her father interrupted her session on the final lap, sixteen minutes had elapsed. The sneakers and shirt slowed her down, but she would need them once she was ashore and traveling overland. Despite the soggy clothes, Stetson swam faster than she'd imagined, and more importantly, she'd almost completed the full half-mile with energy left for the next leg of her journey.

She'd need to do another training session to be certain, but she believed she was nearly there. Tomorrow night. Or the night after.

She felt a surge of hope. She'd track down Thorn, lay out the whole thing. Okay, so he wasn't the six-foot-five muscular superhero she'd pictured, but he was the best option she had. She'd find a way to convince him to help her locate her mother and free her from bondage as well. There was some connection between them. North, Thorn. From the way he'd reacted, she was certain the biographical details of her mother's fictional hero were based on Thorn. Her mother had known him once. There'd been a connection.

Friendship, maybe more.

Stetson didn't know what transgression her mother had committed against Osvaldo, but it must have been extreme to warrant a lifetime separation from her own daughter. Despite their monthly meetings, Stetson barely knew the woman, their every exchange harshly monitored. Always hovering, Osvaldo's men were quick to intervene if any exchange strayed into the personal or a hug lasted more than a few seconds. Inmates in Federal Prisons had more freedom.

A glancing touch, a soft yearning in her mother's eyes, a whispered "I love you," that was all Stetson had to go on. Their conversations followed the same pattern every time. Her mother asked about her studies, what books she was reading. She asked what Stetson was doing for fun, if she had friends? No, not one. How could she? Unless you counted the Mexican busboy with a secret smile and dazzling eyes who she only saw when she and Osvaldo visited The Burgee Bar, one of the restaurants at Ocean Reef.

She'd spent hours searching online for any biographical facts about Kathy Garcia or Katarina Mayfield, her mother's pen name, but found nothing that shed light on the woman Stetson met in a hotel room once a month. For that matter, even Osvaldo Baltazar Garcia produced no search results. None whatsoever. Stetson's parents were anonymous. They were cyber phantoms.

Stetson toweled her hair, then changed into khaki shorts and a black tee. No shoes were allowed in the aquarium room, so Stetson padded barefoot to the northeastern corner of the house, took a deep bracing breath, and tapped on the teak door.

Osvaldo swung it open, stepped aside, and motioned her in.

The entire room was encased by one continuous aquarium. Glass walls, glass ceiling, and glass floor. The tanks were decorated with elkhorn corals and sea fans, twisted limbs of driftwood, dragon stones, brain coral, spider wood, hideaway caves of natural rock, staghorn coral, and sea anemones.

Only one type of fish populated the six interconnected chambers. From the family *Scorpaenidae*, the genus *Dendrochirus*, a creature whose dorsal, pelvic, and anal fin spines were as sharp as hypodermic needles, and each spine was connected to a venom sac inside the dorsal musculature of the fish.

Lionfish swam above her, beneath her feet, before and behind her.

Maroon with white stripes covering their head and body, tentacles above their eyes and below their mouth, wispy pectoral fins that fluttered wildly as they swam.

Dark angels of the deep.

Stetson knew first-hand the power of their sting. Snorkeling with Osvaldo and a couple of his men on Molasses Reef several years earlier, a small school of lionfish engulfed her, and Stetson panicked and thrashed her limbs wildly, brushing her thigh against the dorsal fins of one of the larger fish. At first, the pain was no more stunning than a bee sting. But back on the deck of the dive boat, the venom began its serious work. In minutes she was flushed and feverish and half-delirious, a knot of excruciating pain tightened in her gut and didn't subside for hours.

That single prick wasn't lethal, but it produced suffering Stetson would not soon forget.

Lionfish were an invasive species that first appeared decades ago in small numbers on the coral reefs throughout the Keys. But with their voracious appetite, aggressive nature, and few natural predators, these scorpions of the sea were now dominating large patches of the ocean and spreading fast through Florida waters and the Caribbean, outcompeting the native fish, and reducing their numbers drastically. Another example, as far as Stetson was concerned, of the survival of the shittiest. A phrase she'd encountered in one of her mother's novels, uttered by the hero, North.

Since she was barely old enough to walk, Stetson had been tutored in the lionfish's prowess by Osvaldo, whose voice always assumed a reverential tone when describing the fish's lethal artistry. In honor of the fish he admired so deeply, Osvaldo had designed and constructed this watery tomb with his own hands. A marvel of engineering.

Stetson knew the reason for Osvaldo's obsession. An alien species who'd out-competed the vulnerable local population, a fish both beautiful and deadly to its foes—the similarity to his personal story was unmistakable.

Inside the all-encompassing aquarium, there was no furniture, and there were no seams where one wall was fused to another, just a continuous wrap of glass that contained several thousand lionfish swimming continuously in every direction.

Stetson always felt weightless and woozy in this room, which was certainly Osvaldo's intention in designing it the way he had. He exposed this secret chamber to only very special guests whose favor, influence, or money he wanted some part of. The sheer disorientation of standing inside that watery domain while hundreds of those beautiful and sinister fish swam relentlessly above, below, and before his guests, gave Osvaldo an advantage in any transaction taking place there.

"What do you want?" Stetson asked.

She kept her eyes on her father's face.

Long ago she'd found that if her gaze strayed to the walls or ceiling or floor, and settled on the incessant swirl of color, the dipping, dodging, churn of so many identical creatures, her initial giddiness soon became a nauseating vertigo. And any hope of rational thought was gone.

"Why are you swimming such distances?"

"What do you care?"

"I repeat, why were you swimming such a distance?"

"Because I was pissed off and wanted to burn off my anger."

"Anger about what?"

"You got to be kidding. You stationed Minks outside Thorn's house. He comes and grabs me, punches me, drags me to his place, ties me to a chair with fucking fishing line. I escape from that maniac then your macho morons track me down and manhandle the hell out of me and haul me back here. Why wouldn't I be angry?"

"They were all simply doing as instructed."

"By you."

"That is correct."

"So that's why I was swimming so hard. Satisfied? Can I go?"

"No," Osvaldo said. "Not until you've revealed what you desired from Mr. Thorn?"

"You know why I was there. It was a job."

"I consented to your wheedling and whining. You claimed you wanted to join the family business. Yes, I was hopeful you were being sincere, so I decided to test that truthfulness. Your mission was to replace surveillance devices with the advanced models. It was to be as simple as that, and yet, you chose to engage with Mr. Thorn more intimately."

"There was nothing intimate about it. I chatted him up, looking for the right time to put the plan in motion."

"That's not what I heard."

It must have been at Osvaldo's instruction that the feeding tubes opened at that precise moment. Dozens of hidden valves released into the tanks a collection of ghost shrimp, fiddler crabs, freshwater crawfish, guppies, mollies, and damselfish that drifted through the water from every direction.

The captive lionfish tore into their feed, a whirlwind of color that left behind clouds of shredded flesh, scales, fins, and unidentifiable scraps. There was no way Stetson could ignore the sight. Such carnage, such voracious savagery.

"Of course, I heard every word you spoke inside that man's house," Osvaldo said. "How could you be so ignorant, so senseless as not to know I was listening through the very devices you were there to update. You mocked his bonefish flies, you derided the type of fishing his customers engage in, you asked him for assistance which he refused, and you told him that his name is an anagram for North. Do you remember all that?"

"I remember."

"Exactly what kind of assistance did you want from him?"

"I'm not stupid," she said. "I knew you were listening to everything. I asked for his help as a ploy to gain his trust."

"No, that is not truthful. Now answer the question. What kind of help did you expect Thorn to provide?"

"And Minks, he was on the road waiting for your signal because you didn't trust me."

"That's correct. I did not trust you, I trust no one. It's one of the ways I've survived, indeed, how I've flourished in a treacherous world. And in your case, I was right to doubt your sincerity. Now answer my question, girl. What kind of help did you want from Thorn?"

"Thorn's a putz. I could see that right off. He couldn't help an old lady cross the street."

"But you wanted his help. You asked for it."

"I was playing him. Okay, yeah, maybe I also wanted to see what kind of asshole he was. I was curious. Is that illegal around here, being curious?"

"I don't believe anything you are saying is true. I think you wanted to enlist his aid to escape from my control. That is why you pleaded with me to allow you to go to his house. You wanted that man to be your savior. You imagined him to be more powerful than he is."

Stetson watched the lionfish circle, felt her legs grow heavy, her head begin to spin.

Osvaldo stepped close, reached out, and pressed a palm to her cheek, cupping it. Stetson steeled herself for the slap.

"But none of that matters," he said. "You are home now, back under my protection. And though it was not your intention, you succeeded in accomplishing one of my goals."

"I did, did I? What goal is that?"

"You made the fool aware of your mother's books. He's discovered his pitiful role in them. Until now the illiterate man had no idea his life was being appropriated. That he was being belittled, shamed, his secret activities publicly exposed.

"And more importantly, because you inadvertently steered him to the novels, soon, when he's had an opportunity to read them all, he will no longer be certain if anything he has accomplished in the last two decades was done of his own volition. He will discover his life was not his own but merely fodder for fiction. At this moment and forevermore, he will not be certain what decisions he made for himself and what choices were made for him. That uncertainty will haunt him, and ultimately it will undermine his self-confidence, emasculate him, reduce him to a pitiful shell of the man he believed himself to be."

"Quite a speech," she said. "Like you're maybe obsessed with Thorn."

"I find him amusing," Osvaldo said. "Amusing and pitiful."

Stetson wandered the room, her defenses breaking down, beginning to surrender to the trance of lionfish swirling left and right and up and down and beneath her bare feet as they devoured their feast. Schools like the one that besieged her that day on the reef surrounded her in every direction.

"Do you love me?" she asked.

Osvaldo was silent. She could feel him standing close behind her. She wanted to wound him, plunge a blade deep into his heartless core. She knew the answer to her question but wanted to hear him struggle to respond. It was the only weapon she had against him, to remind him of his soulless nature.

"I asked you, Osvaldo, do you love me?"

"What kind of question is this?"

"I'm your daughter, your flesh and blood. But I've never heard you say those words. To me, or for that matter, to anyone."

"I find you highly useful. Isn't that enough?"

"Useful? How the hell am I useful?"

"For keeping your mother under control. Without you, she would have revolted long ago. You serve a crucial function. For that I am grateful."

"You're a fucking monster."

"You are free to leave now, return to your activities. Swim in the pool all you want, burn away more of your petulance. I'm done with you."

"When I see Mother this weekend, I'll tell her what you said."

"There will be no such meeting. She has violated our agreement. I haven't decided yet if you will ever speak with that woman again."

"What did she do?"

"It's none of your concern."

"The hell it isn't. She's my mother."

"You have no voice in the matter."

"I saw what you did with Minks. I was outside the trailer. I was an eyewitness to a murder committed by my father."

That halted him for a few seconds. He drew a breath, closed his eyes, and nodded to himself as if his suspicions had been confirmed.

"And if you did see such a thing, why should I have a concern?"

"Oh, you should have a concern, plenty of concerns."

Osvaldo smiled.

"Are you making a threat against me? My own child?"

"I know your men call you 'Trickster.' Like the character in Mother's novels. But what I saw you do was no trick. Maybe your hands are quick. I'll grant you that. But it doesn't matter how quick you are, there's nothing magical about what you did. It was vile and barbaric. And it can put you in the electric chair."

Osvaldo held her gaze for what felt like a thousand heartbeats, smiling all the while.

Then he said, "Ah, yes. You are such *a duplicado exacto* of your mother. Treacherous, spiteful, faithless. And like her you are weak, you are impotent, you have no weapons, no power of any sort. You have nothing but words, words, words, words, words, words…"

He was still repeating that single syllable as she pushed open the door and left him.

FIFTEEN

"**PROBLEM IS,**" **SUGAR SAID,** "**IF** Kathy gets free of Osvaldo's lunkheads, goes to your house looking for us, cops will grab her, return her to Osvaldo. If she goes to my office or my house, which are the other possibilities, same outcome. Cops will be staking out those places too."

"I like this car," Thorn said. "Never driven a BMW before. Feels fast. Touch the accelerator, bam, your head smacks the headrest. Much better than the VW."

"Too flashy for my taste," Sugar said. "But I think Joey was right. Cops give more leeway to luxury cars. Long as a black man isn't driving. They don't want to pull the white guy over, guy could be a Miami lawyer, ready to sue their asses for harassment."

They were on the eighteen-mile stretch between Florida City and Key Largo, a single lane in each direction with a large concrete divider between the northbound and southbound lanes. Not as many head-ons as the old days when there was no barrier and drunks and impatient Miami assholes were crashing into each other every other day, triple figures killed each year on that stretch.

Expanses of Everglades spread out on both sides of the highway, a recently installed chain-link fence running alongside the highway, which frustrated the hell out of the wildlife roaming that ancient landscape.

Thorn was wearing a new T-shirt, one that Joey Wasilewski had provided. Printed in elaborate script across the chest: Joey's Lightly Used Cars, and below it, a phone number.

"I might have a solution to the issue you raised," Thorn said.

"Yeah? Let's hear it."

"Think of it as a treasure hunt."

"I'm listening."

"Shirley Sheeran still runs the Hairport, right?"

"She's the boss, yeah. There every day, snipping away."

The Hairport was the beauty parlor that shared a wall with Sugarman's PI office. A two-way mirror allowed Sugar to see into the salon and even listen to local gossip if he so chose. The mirror was a remnant from a previous owner of the salon. That owner's office was situated in what was now Sugar's place of business. All the beauticians and hairdressers knew the mirror on their wall was two-way, but they never knew when the previous boss lady was in her office snooping on them, or when she was home sleeping off another long night of barhopping. Which kept the decorum high but the morale low.

When Shirley Sheeran bought the shop and rented Sugar the space for his office, Sugar offered to paint over his side of the mirror. He had no real interest in spying on the theatrics of the salon. But before she had time to make up her mind, a jealous boyfriend showed up to harass one of her hairdressers, and Sugarman, seeing what was going down, ran over and showed the shithead out. So, the mirror stayed.

"Call Shirley," Thorn said.

"And tell her what?"

"She has that big sign out front, puts up funny sayings, 'Hair Today, Gone Tomorrow,' 'The Higher the Hair, the Closer to God.'"

"She does."

"Kathy will pass that sign miles before my house."

"Okay."

"Ask Shirley to take down whatever silly message is up there and put Rocco on it instead. Kathy drives up, sees Rocco on the sign, knows it's a signal for her. Cops see it, they wouldn't know what the hell it means."

"But Osvaldo would, or one of his goons, they'd know it's a signal."

"That's where the other two words come in."

"Two more words on the sign?"

"Words Osvaldo wouldn't understand, neither would his muscle. Nobody would understand but Kathy."

The two-lane road widened to four passing lanes, two north, two south, still divided by that concrete barrier. Thorn stayed in the slow lane, keeping to the speed limit, letting the crazies fly by.

"Okay, Thorn. I'll bite. What two words?"

"Ring finger."

"What the hell does that mean?"

"Something personal between Kathy and me. The night we met, the place we met."

"Snappers."

"I noticed her ring finger. The ring was gone, but the groove was still there. She saw me looking at it and we talked about it."

"And Kathy will remember that? A bit of conversation from twenty years ago?"

"I think she will, yeah. I think she will."

Sugar clenched his jaw, nodded twice, then looked out at the vastness of the Everglades.

"She sees that sign, she'll go to Snappers."

"And then what?" Sugar said. "You and me, we can't be hanging around Snappers, a public place, waiting for her to show up. Somebody's going to see us. An off-duty cop, friend of a cop, friend of Osvaldo's."

"We won't be there," Thorn said.

"All right, where will we be?"

"Across the highway, bayside motel run by a friend we can trust. She'll put us in a cabin down by the water. Stella Hardy."

"Kathy goes to Snappers, we go to Hardy's Motel. How's that work?"

"Like I said, it's a treasure hunt, Kathy follows the clues."

"What's the clue that gets her from Snappers to Hardy's?"

"Donnie Joe Weir works the Tiki bar at Snappers seven days a week, sees everybody coming in. Been there forever, she'll remember Kathy. I get Donnie Joe to tell Kathy to go across the road to Hardy's. Bingo, it's done."

"All right," Sugar said, grudgingly. "Could work."

"It'll work."

"And if Kathy doesn't notice the Hairport sign? There a backup plan?"

"She's not going to drive by your office without giving it a thorough look."

"Damn you, Thorn. I must be getting dumber in my old age, because I think you've finally come up with a decent idea."

He got out his cell, punched in a number, and asked to speak to Shirley. When she came on, he explained what he had in mind. Rocco on the sign out front, Ring Finger just below it.

"Go with the biggest letters you got."

Shirley knew Sugarman well enough that he didn't need to explain more than that. Just had to promise he'd give her the whole story later when it was safe to do so. Shirley loved to hear the sanitized versions of Sugarman and Thorn's adventures.

"I'll talk to Donnie Joe," Thorn said. "She's always had a crush on me."

"You know that how?"

"She tells me every time she serves me a beer."

Sugar dialed the number and handed the cell to Thorn.

Thorn asked Donnie Joe for a favor, a hush-hush situation. If Kathy Spottswood appeared, steer her across the road to Hardy's, but tell no one else, absolutely no one but Kathy. Donnie Joe wanted to know what was going on, so Thorn promised he'd take her to dinner soon as he could explain everything. Lobster at Cheeca Lodge or pizza, or anything in between. That did the trick.

"It's about damn time you asked me out. I been making eyes at you since grade school."

A half-hour later when they rolled through Key Largo, the Hairport sign was up.

Rocco

Ring Finger

"Got to buy Shirley an excellent bottle of wine."

"Rum's her thing," Sugar said. "I'll pick out a good one when this is finished."

"You think that day will ever come?"

"Better happen soon. Rape conviction in Florida for a victim between 12 and 18 has a maximum sentence of life in prison. If Sprunt has a say, which he will, they'll go for the max."

A few minutes later, approaching Thorn's driveway on the bayside, Sugar pointed out the unmarked car the Sheriff's Department used, a gray Saturn five or six years old. It was parked across the highway in a bait store parking lot, backed in, fifty yards north of Thorn's drive.

"Not the brainiest surveillance team."

They drove in silence for a while, passing through the cluster of dive shops, liquor stores, and restaurants at Mile Marker 100, what passed for downtown Key Largo.

"Hey," Thorn said, "tell me something. Why would Osvaldo want me thrown in jail anyway? If I'm out of action, he's fucked. Where does he get his plots?"

"Same thing occurred to me."

There was something ominous in Sugar's tone.

"Okay, what're you thinking? Go on, spill it."

"I don't know. It's just a guess."

"Come on, Sugar."

He released a long, dispirited sigh.

"Maybe Osvaldo's finished writing about you and me. He's made a bundle selling books, got bored with it all. It's over. He's ready to wipe that slate clean."

"Meaning he has no further use for Kathy."

"Yeah," Sugar said and drew a long breath. "Let's just hope to hell she sees that sign."

At Hardy's Motel, they went together into the office. Turned out Stella Hardy was visiting relatives in New England. She'd left her teenage daughter, Moira, in charge.

After texting her mom and getting a quick reply, Moira showed Sugar and Thorn to a room with two kings and a kitchenette on the edge of the sandy beach.

"Our premier accommodations," Moira said. "Like Mom instructed."

"Our gratitude will be undying," Thorn said.

"It's been a slow summer, all this rain," she said. "Mom says stay as long as you like. Fine by me. Place can get spooky when it's so empty. We got a family from Arizona supposed to be arriving later tonight. I'll put them away from you, give you plenty of privacy."

"Clarice Martinson still here?" Sugar asked.

"Girl with purple hair?"

"It was brown when we saw her yesterday."

"Brown when she checked in, purple this morning when I offered her fresh towels."

"Purple, well yeah, that would be Clarice."

"She's another friend of my mom's," Moira said. "Mom's got a lot of 'em. But this Clarice, she's a gloomy one. Gets two large pizzas delivered every night, never comes out of her room, won't let the cleaning lady in, turns down fresh towels. You know her?"

"Not really," Sugar said. "Just know she's had some serious traumas. Trying to work through them."

"She keeps eating those pizzas, I'll have to rent a damn forklift to get her out of there."

Thorn was silent during their exchange, surveying the room. Ancient jalousie windows, a musty smell, grit on the floor, water stains and peeling paint on the ceiling, a rusty stovetop. A half-century of hard use and the unremitting scouring of salt air.

The property it occupied was worth millions. Some day if Moira didn't inherit her mother's stubborn devotion to that spit of land and the shabby cabins, she'd sell to some wheeler-dealer who'd slap up swanky condos, paint them pink in honor of a past that never existed.

For years Key Largo had been moving ever closer to a trendy, upscale island where the wealthy played out their Hemingway fantasies behind the stucco walls of waterfront compounds with ten-million-dollar sunset views. With all that flash and cash flooding the island, the last of the hardscrabble pioneers who for centuries cleared the jungle undergrowth, battled mosquitoes to a draw, and did the grueling and perilous work of civilizing those limestone and coral rocks, those old salts were being bought out, taxed out, and squeezed out. Only a few of their descendants were hanging on, skilled workers who serviced the needs of this moneyed breed. High-class fishing guides and yacht technicians and a few flamboyant bartenders with tall tales about the good old days when the water was gin clear and the largest groupers and snappers ever seen on earth jumped directly into each and every boat.

Sugar offered to head down to Tavernier and pick up some drive-through fast food. Half hour later, he brought back cheeseburgers and fries and chocolate shakes, and they attacked their late dinners in the squeaky metal lawn chairs on their deck and watched the dark grow darker.

A third chair sat empty between them.

A light bulb on the wall above their door cast a ghostly halo on the deck. High in the gumbo limbo beside their cabin, a lone mockingbird longing for a mate was running through its song list. Trills and cheeps and five-note lyrics plagiarized from its local competition.

"That Hairport sign," Thorn said, "does it have lights? Could she see the message after dark?"

Sugar said that sign was very well lit. He paid a share of the electric bill.

"You're confident Kathy got away from those thugs?"

Sugar didn't answer for a while. He scuffed his shoe against the concrete slab.

After more scuffing, he said, "I'm pretty sure."

"You sound worried."

"Snappers shuts down at ten. It's almost ten-thirty."

"Well, don't worry about that. Donnie Joe closes up the place, Friday nights, she doesn't leave till after one. Takes that long to throw out the last drunk. I know because I've been that guy more than once."

Thorn finished his burger, wadded the paper, and stuffed it back in the paper sack. He sampled some of his fries, rocked in the squeaky chair, and listened to the incoming tide slap the dock pilings. A commercial fishing tub was chugging south about a mile out. Road noise competing with backcountry noise.

An iguana climbed onto the edge of the concrete deck, gave them a challenging stare.

"Watch out," Thorn said. "Those fuckers will kill for a French fry."

Thorn was watching the iguana when the voice came from the darkness behind them.

"You save any of those fries for me?"

Kathy stepped into the soft light on the deck.

Sugar and Thorn came to their feet. After a moment's hesitation, she opened her arms to both of them and Thorn and Sugar stepped into an awkward group embrace. Though her arms were frail, they clenched with a rock-hard intensity. A grip that finally relaxed as Kathy's arms trembled and fell away.

She stepped clear of them and wiped a hand across her damp eyes.

"Thank god," Thorn said. "You made it."

She scanned the darkness out on the water as if gathering herself.

"Pretty clever," she said. "Rocco. Ring finger."

"I was counting on you remembering."

"I remember. Oh, yeah. I remember all of it."

"Are you safe?" Sugar asked. "You got away from those two thugs."

She turned from the water, faced them.

"You have time for a couple of stories?"

"All the time in the damn world," Thorn said. "Now that you're here."

"Well, there's the story of today, what happened after you left the Delray house this afternoon. And there's the twenty-year story. All the crap since the night I was dragged away from your bedroom."

Thorn motioned to the chair between them and offered her his carton of fries. She took it and rattled it like a dice cup. She ate a couple and wiped her lips on her sleeve then settled into the middle chair.

"Which one do you want to hear?"

"Your call, Kathy. You're the storyteller. We're in your hands."

SIXTEEN

IT WAS LONG AFTER SUNSET, Stetson wasn't sure of the time. The golden dock lights were blazing at Snapper Point across that half-mile stretch of water. Toweling off on the pool deck after another strenuous workout, she was gazing out at the route she would take tomorrow on the first leg of her journey to freedom.

Once she'd crossed that dark span and waded ashore, one way or the other she'd work her way south to Thorn's house. If she was lucky, she might be able to snag a ride south with one of the delivery guys who supplied the restaurants at Ocean Reef. She knew the lots where they unloaded their goods.

But if that didn't work, hell, she'd walk the whole damn way if she had to.

She was heading back inside when a stunning sight halted her.

Both Zodiacs were at full throttle, racing toward the marina at Ocean Reef. The overhead console lights were on, revealing Pablo and Jorge in one, Victor manning the other. Stetson stared at their rippling wakes. She blinked to clear her eyes and peered after them as they disappeared into the darkness.

El Morro was unguarded. It was only Osvaldo and Stetson alone on the island.

Maybe such a thing had happened before, and she hadn't noticed because she'd never been on the brink of fleeing. Tonight, at least for a little while, there would be no one to pursue her. No Zodiacs, no one monitoring the coastline of *El Morro* for intruders or runaways.

The diversion she'd planned, igniting a small blaze in the pantry to set off the sprinklers, was no longer necessary.

And she didn't need to race to shore. A leisurely, steady pace would be enough. The only issue was her stamina. Could she manage two swims of a half-mile in the same night? Had she built her endurance up to that?

As she stood and pictured her swim, Stetson could feel the thrill of adrenaline rising in her veins. Breath coming deep and strong. A spike of resolve and its partner, a spike of energy.

She headed back to her room. She only needed two things for her journey. First was the cash she'd been squirreling away for years. Traveling money. Four thousand, two hundred, and sixty dollars. She kept it in a Ziplock bag tucked inside the foam of one of her pillows.

She drew it out, stuffed the plastic bag into her swimsuit, checked in her mirror to be sure the lump was hidden beneath her T-shirt, then she crept back through the house.

She had no idea how long before the Zodiacs returned. She suspected she had to move fast, seize this chance. Her heart was speeding, but Stetson kept a casual pace across the living room. Not sure where Osvaldo was lurking, where he might appear.

He had a gift for reading her body language and would surely spot the heat rising in her face. If he encountered her in her present state, with his suspicions so elevated, he might even be able to spot her quickened pulse.

She slipped through the kitchen and exited the back door and crossed the sandy patch that led to the guesthouse where Pablo, Victor, and Jorge bunked.

Years before when she was only twelve, Stetson had been wandering the island, bored and lonely, and eager for some fresh diversion. She'd long been curious about how her father's bodyguards lived, and that day, in the spirit of adventure, she'd pushed open the front door of the guesthouse and followed the clank of metal to the gym where Pablo and Victor were pumping iron. Across from the weights and bench press was a wall of weapons. Dozens of handguns and automatic rifles.

Victor dropped his barbells on the concrete floor and barked, "Go tell, *El Jefe*."

Pablo sprinted from the room.

For that innocent transgression, Osvaldo penalized Stetson with three months of no contact with her mother. A sentence Stetson served in a deepening depression. Never again had she crossed that sandy plot, and even now, though she knew the three men were no longer on *El Morro*, simply approaching their living quarters caused chills to flare across her back.

As she expected, their door was unlocked. The smell of garlic, booze, and male sweat choked the air in their living area. She passed quickly through the kitchen and stepped into the workout room. Dozens of long rifles and machine pistols were mounted on brackets fastened in place with braided steel cords. While the handguns lay in glass-topped wood cabinets filled with foam cut-outs that fit each pistol. All the cabinets had their own brass padlock.

"Shit."

Stetson had imagined the weapons would be unsecured. After all, it was an island sanctuary defended twenty-four hours a day by a troop of musclebound street soldiers. The entry doors to the main house didn't even have locks.

She didn't intend to shoot anyone. Her only objective was never to be kidnapped again, lashed to a chair, forced to dive through a window and run for her life. Once she was free of *El Morro*, she was going to stay free, with or without Thorn's help. And a gun might also be essential in achieving her next goal. Tracking down her mother and liberating her from her own imprisonment.

Stetson hurried back to the kitchen, pawed through drawers until she found the utensil she was looking for. Back in the gym, she surveyed the selection of handguns, chose the smallest one, easily transportable and a good fit for her hand. Based on a few hours of YouTube study, Stetson believed the pistol was a Glock nine-millimeter. Its magazine fit neatly into the foam cutout beside the pistol itself.

She picked a spot in the glass covering, raised the meat tenderizer above it, and smashed a ragged hole in the glass. She had to hammer twice more to widen the opening, chipping away a few stray pieces.

As she was sneaking a hand into the cabinet, a siren blared so loud the floor shook beneath her and more shards of glass broke loose, scratching her wrist.

"Fuck me, fuck me, fuck me."

She scooped up the pistol, popped in the magazine, tucked it between her breasts, and sprinted from the guesthouse. Outside in the darkness, the siren continued to whoop and screech. Spotlights clicked on, flooding the sandy area with blinding radiance.

Stetson froze as a robotic voice delivered its grim threat.

"Stop where you are, or you will be shot. Stop where you are."

Then repeated the warning in Spanish.

"*Detente donde estás o te matarán.*"

She hissed a curse and plunged out of the cone of light, hurdled a waist-high hedge, and took a sharp left onto a shadowy path that looped through the dense bay cedar and buttonwood bushes leading away from the main house toward the western shoreline of the island. She knew every turn by heart. A thousand times she'd covered this course. A blindfold wouldn't have slowed her down.

She raced to the narrow beach and halted, bent forward, hands on knees, panting hard. When she straightened, still huffing, she peered back toward the house and saw more floodlights had been switched on.

Osvaldo had discovered the broken gun case and was in pursuit. There would be no detention for this crime or anything as trifling as a withdrawal of visitation rights.

She had only two choices to escape his wrath. She could begin her swim on this side of the island, but it would add at least another half-mile to the total. She was already winded from her run and her legs and arms were sluggish from her earlier laps.

Or she could try to return to the closest spot to the shoreline of Ocean Reef. From her current position, she could take any one of a dozen separate trails that meandered back through the scrub, briars, and shrubbery that covered most of the island. All the paths led eventually to the main house.

Problem was, Osvaldo could position himself at one of two major junctions and have a fifty-fifty chance of catching her if she tried to work her way back to the opposite shore. Fifty-fifty weren't odds Stetson could chance.

She made her decision. She wriggled her hand inside the right leg of her one-piece and worked it upward across her butt and gripped the Ziploc bag of cash where it was lodged against the small of her back. She dragged it out, pulled the bundle of bills free. Years of hoarding twenties and fifties intended for new clothes, books, meals with her mother.

She looked out at Card Sound where the moon had paved a golden pathway north into the heart of Biscayne Bay toward the hazy glow of Miami.

Stetson dumped the bills and watched the restless tide take them away.

She wedged the Glock into the Ziploc bag, a tight fit, pressed the seal firmly, and tucked the grim device in the hollow between her breasts. Finally, her chest was good for something more than drawing hungry looks.

She took a deep breath and waded into the shallows and began a slow, silent stroke. Exhaustion be damned, she was determined to circle the island, get a fix on those golden dock lights, and escape *El Morro* forever.

As she rounded the northern tip of the island, she realized there was a hurdle she hadn't considered. The tide was going out, the heavy push of the current flowing against her, making every stroke far more difficult than her pool workouts. For a while, it felt as though she was swimming in place, making no headway at all.

Ten minutes, fifteen. She kept her focus on the golden dock lights, staying with the breaststroke for better visibility and to hear any approaching boat. So late at night, the traffic in this narrow passage was almost nil. But yes, there was the rare evening cruise returning to the club's marina that used this cut.

She was maybe fifty yards off the beach at *El Morro* when a spotlight found her.

Osvaldo shouted her name and demanded she return immediately.

She didn't look back, kept a steady stroke forward. Without the Zodiacs, he was helpless. Let him watch her swim away as long as he liked. If it tortured him, so much the better. What was he going to do, swim after her?

She pushed on against the current, ten yards, fifteen, then Osvaldo bellowed louder.

"One more stroke and I'll shoot. Do not defy me. Do not tempt me. Return now."

Stetson swung around, treading water, and saw a green laser dot dancing across the water.

A shot hissed into the water ten feet to her right. The green laser dot inched toward her. Another round splashed a yard directly in front of her. She had seen what a marksman he was. If he wanted to kill her, she was well within his range.

"Drop your pistol, girl. Drop it or this will be the end for you."

SEVENTEEN

KATHY CHOSE THE TWENTY-YEAR STORY, and told it without emotion, fast and simple, as if recounting the synopsis of some movie she'd watched long ago.

That she could report it all without a trace of bitterness or regret was for Thorn strangely unsettling. The events she described were freighted with so much horror and despair, it was a wonder Kathy hadn't perished under their weight.

To punish her for her betrayal, Osvaldo dragged her out of Thorn's bedroom, blindfolded her, bound her wrists, and transported her from Thorn's property, traveling by land and by water. During the journey, to further humiliate her, Osvaldo gave her nothing to cover her nakedness. When they arrived at their destination, he tore off her blindfold and shoved her into a bare room.

There she stayed in solitary confinement, a thin and lumpy mattress on the floor, a small bathroom devoid of soap or towels or even a toothbrush. No windows, an overhead light set on a muted twilight setting. The air vents blew cold for hours, hot the next few. She sweated, she shivered. Soon she began to cycle through periods of clarity and delirium.

For the duration of her imprisonment, one of Osvaldo's men delivered her meals wordlessly. Always the same canned beans dumped cold over rice. Plastic bowl, no spoon.

Day and night a single song whispered through the walls. *"Guantanamera,"* the legendary version sung by Maximo Francisco Muñoz.

A song clearly chosen by Osvaldo for its history and its relevance. Originally a song about infidelity, its lyrics evolved to become an anthem of Cuban national pride. Volume turned so low it was barely audible which made its effects somehow more ominous as it subtly invaded her thoughts. The song played continuously with only a second's gap between the end of one repetition and the beginning of the next.

She sang along with it, then tried to block it out, then sang along some more.

Kathy lost her sense of time. Weeks might have passed, or perhaps it was only days. She slept little, paced the room, wept, screamed curses, pounded the door, pleaded for forgiveness, raged at Osvaldo's villainy. She chewed her nails to the bloody quick. She shivered and sweated and wept. She talked to herself until she ran out of things to say. She huddled, mute, in a corner and stared at nothing.

Desperate to regain her composure, she tried to sing the tunes she'd written and performed a hundred times, for singing had always been her superpower, but, maddeningly, she could not summon the lyrics of her own songs or any others, not even a fragmentary passage. Only *"Guantanamera"* whispering again and again, infecting every thought.

One day the music ceased, the door swung open.

No one was there.

Full of dread, Kathy slipped into the hallway and edged warily through an enormous house, a place she didn't recognize. Elegantly furnished and decorated, understated tropical luxury. Nothing like the modern condo she and Osvaldo had shared during their two years of marriage.

She soon realized this house was on an island. Outside every window were blue waters, boats passing by, yachts, sleek powerboats, and sailing vessels. The island was positioned in a bay of some kind, the land to the west was indistinct, barren, several miles away. Eastward the coast was much closer. She could make out houses and docks.

She had no idea where she was or what came next.

Still speaking in a casual tone, Kathy didn't use the words rape or violation or anything hinting at the brutality of the abuse she suffered at Osvaldo's hands, but her euphemisms made it perfectly clear. The man hurt her badly, forced her into acts meant to degrade and terrify her. He broke what was left of her spirit.

"At first, I resisted, but ultimately there was nothing I could do. He used me any way he wished at any hour of the day or night."

Kathy was silent, staring out at the Florida Bay, the inky waters spattered with moonlight. A car pulled in the motel's gravel lot and stopped beside the office and shut off its headlights. The Arizona family Moira mentioned, checking in late.

Kathy handed the French fries back to Thorn and he set them on the deck.

She cleared her throat, said, "When I realized I was pregnant, I told Osvaldo and he stopped the torture. He no longer touched me, he was silent, avoided me. He turned his attention to a building project, an elaborate indoor aquarium. He became obsessed with every detail of its construction. His abandonment was nearly as frightening as his violence.

"Later that year after Stetson was born, I fell into such deep despair I was immobilized. I wanted nothing to do with the child. I stayed in my bedroom and couldn't eat or sleep. I had thoughts of harming Stetson, drowning her, strangling her. I confessed these feelings to Osvaldo and later I told the psychiatrist Osvaldo brought to the house.

"I was in such turmoil, so vulnerable, I signed papers Osvaldo's lawyers drew up. I knowingly surrendered my rights to the child. I wanted to die. I wanted to escape this world. It was months before I recovered even a small sense of identity, but by then Osvaldo's attorneys created a contract that stipulated that I would never be allowed to be with Stetson unsupervised. Osvaldo would determine the time and place and frequency of those meetings. I signed that paper. I would have signed whatever was put before me.

"And for years I've lived with the consequences of those agreements. Osvaldo uses them as leverage. If I want to see Stetson, I must perform as Osvaldo dictates. I must live where he decides, write the stories he orders me to write, fulfill his commands if I want to spend a few hours with my daughter.

"This is what I was trying to tell you today, Thorn, when you asked if I was a hostage."

"Does Stetson know she's being used? Just Osvaldo's pawn to keep you in line?"

"No, I've told her none of what I just told you. She is innocent. A victim. She's a smart girl and may have figured some things out herself, but…" She blinked back tears.

"Please stop, Kathy," Sugar said. "Spare yourself. We don't need to hear any more."

"Maybe you could tell us something upbeat," Thorn said. "Like today, how you escaped Osvaldo's men."

Kathy glanced over her shoulder into the darkness.

"I didn't," she said.

"You didn't what?"

"I didn't escape them. They're here."

Sugarman shot to his feet. Thorn remained seated, assumed Kathy was joking.

Kathy called over her shoulder: "Everyone arrive?"

A deep voice responded, "*Si, todos.*"

"Facundo and Miguel," she said. "They drove me down from Delray. They've been listening to my tale of woe, waiting for the others, Pablo, Victor, Jorge. Those are Osvaldo's bodyguards. After what you did to Rafe this afternoon, Facundo and Miguel weren't sure they could handle you unassisted."

A derisive chuckle came from beyond the circle of light. One by one the men emerged from the shadows, forming a loose circle around the deck. Thorn saw three handguns, an automatic rifle, and the dark glint of a machete.

"Your weapons, where are they?" Kathy said. "Don't make this more perilous than it already is."

"In the cabin," Sugarman said. "On the bed. Two pistols. That's all we have."

Thorn came to his feet and the circle of men tightened a half step.

"Why, Kathy?"

"It's the only way. This is best. Trust me, Thorn, this is best."

"*Buscarlos*, Facundo. *No confio en ellos.*"

It was machete-man giving the orders. Telling Facundo to search Sugar and Thorn, saying they were not trustworthy.

Sugarman raised his hands and submitted to the one-handed frisking.

Facundo wore a long ponytail and was dressed in dark trousers and a black polo shirt. He gripped his pistol in his right hand and used his left to pat down Sugar.

When Facundo finished, he sidled over to Thorn with a wolfish leer. He had a lanky build, but Thorn noted his wrists were thick and knobby, the kind of rawboned body that often masked impressive tensile strength.

The fact that Thorn and Sugar were so thoroughly outnumbered had given the men a sense of superiority, apparent in their slouching postures, their careless looks at one another, and whispered banter.

Sugar caught Thorn's attention and with a flick of his eyes warned him to cool it. Drop whatever crazy-ass idea was on his mind. Thorn returned a noncommittal nod.

One of the men went into the cabin to retrieve Thorn and Sugar's weapons. Improving their odds for the moment.

Facundo ran his free hand up and down Thorn's ribs, right side, left side. Then bent forward to work his palm down the inside of Thorn's thigh, turning his face up to smirk at Thorn's helplessness.

If these same jackals hadn't once beaten him unconscious and kidnapped and imprisoned Kathy in the hellish story she'd just told, maybe Thorn would have kept his composure and tried to reason his way out of this. But that wasn't an option.

While Facundo was still bent forward, sliding his hands along Thorn's pants leg, with all the muscle he could muster, Thorn kneed the asshole in the side of his head, snatched at the pistol, wrenched it free, used it to whack the back of Facundo's skull and send him sprawling.

The impact broke loose the handgun from Thorn's grip, and the damn thing spun away and skidded across the concrete slab and into the sand rimming the deck.

Sugar cursed at Thorn and flung an elbow at the man next to him and waded in.

Thorn launched himself across the tight circle at machete-man, *el jefe*.

"*Ven a mi, Papi*," machete-man said and lowered the blade, giving him an excellent angle to cleave Thorn at the knees.

El Jefe extended his free hand and waggled his fingers, beckoning Thorn closer.

"Don't do it, Victor!" Kathy screamed. "Don't hurt him."

"Come on, superman. What you waiting for? Come and get a taste of steel."

Thorn had never faced a machete, but the physics seemed tantalizingly simple. The kill zone was narrow. Inside the arc of the blade's swing, the weapon would be nullified, the fight would be hand-to-hand. If Thorn timed his lunge correctly, one good swipe was all machete-man got.

Behind him, Sugar yelped, maybe in pain, maybe a Karate "kiai."

Thorn flinched, shot a look at Sugar, long enough to miss Victor cocking the machete and starting his swing. An instant later, Thorn's reflexes woke, and he dropped to his knees, ducked below the blade's path, steel whisking through his hair, grazing the crown of his head, numbing it.

He thrust up from his squat, rammed Victor's mid-section. Shoulder versus gut. The blow got the big man stumbling backward, and Thorn reached down, seized Victor's calf, jerked up, and tumbled *El Jefe* onto his back. With a long grunt, the air thumped out of him.

Thorn stamped a foot on the wrist of his machete hand, bent down, and twisted the weapon from his grip. Before he could turn back to the others, a muscular arm looped around his throat, tightened, and jerked him upright. The barrel of a pistol dug into the hollow of his cheek and ground against his molars.

"Drop the blade. Do it, *puta*."

Thorn released the machete and it fell into the sand.

"Smart move, *cabrón*."

Duct tape sealing his mouth, wrists taped behind him, Thorn lay on his side in the cargo hold of a bulky SUV. He could feel a body lying behind him. He grunted twice and Sugar grunted back.

Somebody reached over the seat and cuffed Thorn on the back of the head.

"Shut the fuck up, the both of you. Last warning."

The gang of cretins had stupidly laid them back-to-back.

The SUV turned left onto the Overseas Highway and drove north, keeping to the speed limit. Because Thorn had traveled that same stretch of road all his life, he ticked off the miles, noted the traffic signals as they passed beneath them, and was able to keep track of their location

Thorn shifted his butt closer to Sugar and wriggled his fingers until he found Sugarman's hands. He pulled his shoulders back to gain another inch or two and touched the duct tape around his friend's wrists. It took some probing and fumbling, but finally, Thorn located the sliced end piece of the wrap and began a slow unwinding, the noise obscured by the rumble of the SUV and their captors' banter.

When they left the well-lit highway and headed onto a dark straightaway of rough pavement, Thorn pinpointed exactly where they were, and with some certainty where they were headed, and he calculated that he and Sugarman had about fifteen minutes left to free themselves.

It was slow and clumsy labor over the bouncy highway.

When Sugar's hands were loose, he went to work on Thorn's wrists and finished just as the SUV slowed and left the bumpy county road and crossed a short stretch of smooth asphalt. Thorn craned his head to the right to peer out the cargo window and saw the arm of a guard gate rising, confirming his suspicion.

With his hands free, Thorn made a quick loose wrap around Sugarman's wrists, and when it was done Sugarman trussed up Thorn in the same way, maintaining the illusion that they were both securely restrained.

They'd arrived at Ocean Reef Club on the northernmost tip of Key Largo. A swanky community where Miami nobility mingled with an international mix of hedge fund billionaires, movie stars, exiled despots, and big shots of every stripe.

The out-of-towners jetted in to the private airport to spend a week or two in the seaside residences and some of them devoted their days to trolling the Gulfstream, searching for the dwindling supply of billfish, while others golfed on one of the fastidiously maintained courses, and others just lay around in the sun sipping rum with their exotic paramours.

When Thorn was a kid, Ocean Reef was a rustic fishing camp, but little by little, like most everything else in the Keys, it had been discovered by the outside world, and exploited, monetized to the hilt, and was now off-limits to anyone without a quarter-million-dollar membership fee, which naturally excluded Thorn and his scruffy ilk.

A decade ago, he'd been hired on occasion as a fishing guide by various members of the club who were steered to Thorn by some local dockhand or mechanic attending to their yachts. And Thorn had taken those well-heeled folks to the nearby flats and creeks that only skiffs like his could navigate and led them to permit, tarpon, the occasional snook and bonefish. As rich and sophisticated as they were, when a big fish took their fly, most of them whooped and howled like ten-year-olds. Such was the power of gamefish.

Though it had been years since he was on the grounds of Ocean Reef, Thorn recalled the workings of the marina and knew that at this hour the dockmaster was off duty. Only the club's security team patrolled the area so late, and it was likely their numbers declined in these late summer doldrums when most of Ocean Reef's members were off in more refreshing climates. All in all, help was unlikely to be forthcoming.

Keeping to the shadows, Osvaldo's men prodded Thorn and Sugar out to the end of the nearest dock where two Zodiacs were moored, twenty-footers with big Yamahas, fast, efficient boats. Thorn kept his wrists locked together, Sugar doing the same. They exchanged a glance, Thorn shrugging the obvious question, "Now?" Sugarman returned a be patient headshake and nodded toward Kathy.

Never let your adversary move you to their chosen spot. That had long been the cardinal rule Thorn and Sugar followed. But Kathy's presence changed the calculus. Putting themselves in danger was one thing, but risking her life was unacceptable. Yeah, she'd drawn the two of them into an ambush, but there had to be a good reason. Thorn was certain of it.

Or almost certain.

In any case, they silently agreed to stay alert for their next best chance.

Victor caught the look passing between Thorn and Sugar and gave Thorn a knowing smile, touching the handle of the machete he wore in a hand-tooled scabbard on his left hip.

By now Thorn had picked up their names and assessed their danger potential. Victor was the boss, but Facundo headed the danger list. He clearly hadn't pardoned Thorn for kneeing him in the face back at Hardy's Motel. And his rangy body seemed coiled more tightly than Victor's husky frame. But it was Facundo's smile that truly tipped the balance. Cold and bitter. A lot of pent-up rage in those eyes, some childhood beatings or indelible humiliations along the way gave that cocky grin a merciless edge.

Pablo was third on the list, a short sturdy fellow with the simpering sneer of a guy daring you to make a crack about his size. Jorge and Miguel were interchangeable punks except for the man-bun perched atop Jorge's head and coming undone, a few oily strands leaking down his neck. Both Jorge and Miguel were so muscled up they'd lost whatever agility they once had. Good guys for breaking bones and hammering nails, but not going to win the limbo contest.

After a quick exchange, Victor and Facundo divvied the group between the two boats.

Sugar was put aboard with Kathy, Facundo, and Miguel. Facundo at the wheel. Which left Thorn with Victor, little Pablo, and Jorge with his failing hairdo.

Victor took the helm and led the way across the marina, handling the boat like a model citizen, leaving a negligible wake, only upping his speed a careful notch as they entered Dispatch Creek, a narrow waterway that emptied into the Atlantic.

Once out of the creek, having drawn no attention from security or late-night residents, Victor throttled up until they were on plane. He switched on the overhead console lights, better to keep a watch on Thorn. Their way ahead was lit by a handheld spotlight that little Pablo swept left and right in a tight arc, searching out obstructions.

With a shove to his chest, Jorge drove Thorn to the deck, cramming him into an awkward sprawl, back hunched against the transom, hands trapped behind him.

"Nice night for a boat ride," Thorn said. "Moonlight, soft breeze."

"*Pendejo* likes to talk," Jorge said. "Go on. Soon enough the pretty fishes will be feeding on your *cojones*. Enjoy the fucking moonlight. Last one you'll see."

"What exactly did I do to deserve this?"

Victor turned and told them both to shut up.

"You know what you did. You fucked with the boss man's wife. I was there, man."

"Oh, that," Thorn said. "Man's got a long memory. That was twenty years ago."

"Trickster don't let nothing go." Jorge grinned. "This going to be fun."

In the open water, Victor throttled all the way up and they raced across a light chop, heading north along the Atlantic side of Ocean Reef. On their starboard flank, Facundo kept the second Zodiac just beyond the slop of Victor's wake.

After a couple of miles, Victor slowed and steered into the mouth of Angelfish Creek. By that point, Thorn knew their destination. They were headed to the island from Kathy's story, the place where Osvaldo took her the night he tore her from Thorn's bed.

An oval of twenty acres or so, a half-mile off the western shore of Ocean Reef, the island had changed hands a few times over the years. Last Thorn heard, it sold for fifty, sixty million. On the nautical charts, it had long been labeled Pumpkin Key.

That island refuge was a perfect spot for a man with high society ambitions and criminal tendencies. With a club membership, he could park his cars and come and go through Ocean Reef, dine with the uber-rich, compare portfolios, then boat back to semi-seclusion a safe distance offshore and indulge in his current deviancies.

They snaked through the creek, skimmed past two mangrove islands that stood guard at its western mouth, and swung sharply into Card Sound, heading south toward Pumpkin Key.

Over the gunwale, Thorn saw dozens of security lights blazing throughout Ocean Reef, and in the distance the hump of the island where they were headed.

As they drew close, Jorge shouted at Victor.

"What the fuck? Something's going down."

Thorn had to crane past a cleat for a clear view.

Victor slowed the Zodiac and Facundo pulled alongside.

A hundred yards away, on the eastern shore of the island, someone stood on a narrow beach shining a high-powered spotlight out into the narrow pass between the Pumpkin Key and Ocean Reef. To the side of the spotlight, the man's arm was extended, aiming what appeared to be a handgun toward the illuminated patch of water.

"Boss in trouble," Jorge called. "Something's fucked up."

"Told you. Somebody should stay behind, too much bad shit going on."

"Fuck you, Facundo," Victor said.

He flattened the throttle and their Zodiac leapt ahead into the darkness. Facundo caught up quickly, shot Victor a bird, and the two boats raced side by side, their hulls brushing.

Running flat-out so close together was pure macho madness, a blunder for which they would all pay dearly.

EIGHTEEN

INCHES FROM HER FACE, THE green laser dot skittered across the surface of the bay.

Stetson ducked below the waterline and swam straight down, kicking hard to stay in place while she reached into the silt, groping left and right but finding nothing.

When she came up for air, the green dot wavered an arm's length away. Stetson heard the thump of another discharge of Osvaldo's silenced pistol, and the spatter of seawater stung her eyes.

She dropped below the surface, swam to her left, then dove to the bottom again, clawing through the loose muck and marl, lungs aching, running out of air. About to kick back to the top when her fingers scraped against a chunk of limestone rock. She dislodged it from the mud. About the size of a baseball. Not exactly right, but it would have to do.

She shot to the surface, gasped. The pistol in the Ziploc between her breasts wriggled to the brim of her cleavage, nearly spilled out. She caught it, tucked it back just as the spotlight caught her in its blinding glare.

Osvaldo shouted, "Come back, *mi hija*. I'm begging you. *Te amo tanto*."

It was a trick, of course. The man was incapable of love. But Osvaldo knew these were words she longed to hear. Anything to coax her back to shore.

"No way, old man! You won't kill me."

She wasn't sure he heard her. The distance and the breeze sapped her voice.

She swiveled around, turning her back on him, located the golden dock light that was her beacon. She was about to let go of the stone when she saw the two Zodiacs flying toward her. Heard the rumble of their outboards. The boats' spotlights crisscrossing the waters around her, the beams bouncing wildly.

Both of them bore down on her, their lights passing nearby but not stopping. They didn't see her, didn't slow.

She watched Osvaldo's green laser dot rise from the water and bounce across the console of one of the Zodiacs. Heard the thump of his pistol, saw the windshield shatter. Her father trying to save her from his own men. Not out of love, nothing he did was for love. Saving her because she was useful, nothing more than that.

There was no time to swim to safety, the Zodiacs were on her.

Stetson ducked, held to the chunk of limestone, and dove.

Thorn saw the laser dot jiggle on the windscreen, someone targeting them. He climbed to his feet, shook his hands free of the duct tape, lunged into Jorge's back, shouldering him into the leaning post, and slammed a forearm into the big man's head, crumpling him against the starboard gunwale, Jorge windmilling to keep from going overboard. With a one-handed push, Thorn sent him over the side.

As Victor turned to the commotion, behind him the Plexiglas windshield exploded and a slug caught Victor's jawbone and bounced him into the leaning post.

Half his face blown away, his hand still on the wheel, Victor sagged, and Thorn saw the catastrophe about to unfold. He surged around the leaning post to grab Victor before he went down. But he was a half-second late, got only a swatch of Victor's sleeve that tore from Thorn's grasp as Victor slumped, his arm hooking a spoke in the wheel, yanking it as he fell.

The Zodiac cut hard to starboard, rammed Facundo's boat and the impact flipped both vessels and catapulted Thorn through the darkness. He sailed fifteen, twenty yards, splashing feet first into the warm bath of Card Sound. Got a gulp of air as he hit the water, plunging all the way to the soft marly bottom before kicking back to the surface.

Spitting seawater, he felt a cold numbness in his left arm. He patted the flesh, searching for a wound but found nothing. Probably a stinger, simple nerve damage from a blow against something unyielding, metal, fiberglass.

He heard the others thrashing nearby, and in the radiance from Pumpkin Key's outdoor lighting, he saw both capsized boats coasting away.

Treading water maybe a hundred yards off Pumpkin Key, Thorn called out for Sugar.

"Over here, man. Kathy's cut bad, got to get her ashore."

With his good arm, he pulled himself toward Sugar's voice, made only two strokes when his right hand bumped a body.

In the dusky light, he saw Victor floating face up, left cheek gone.

Thorn pushed past the body and managed only one more stroke before someone climbed onto his back and forced his head underwater. Powerful arms locked him in place.

From a lifetime of freediving the reefs, tickling lobsters from their hidey holes, chasing them across the sandy bottom, snatching at them as they scooted backward toward safety, Thorn's lungs had built extra capacity. He'd never bothered to count how many minutes he could stay down, but at that moment, by god, he'd hold his breath as long as it took to fake out the beast riding his back.

He remained limp. Relaxed his chest. Felt the stubble on the man's cheek grind against the back of his neck. Thorn blew out a string of bubbles. More fakery.

But the guy atop him wasn't buying and tightened his grip.

Thorn waited, working to still the rising uneasiness, knowing stress would eat his oxygen supply twice as fast. He imagined himself a pearl diver on an effortless descent to a hundred feet to retrieve a precious gemstone from the sea floor. Imagined himself a Buddhist monk quieting his pulse to thirty beats a minute.

Thorn blew out more bubbles.

And this time the thug on his back fell for it and pushed him away. Thorn floated face down, continuing his drowned man act.

His head bumped Victor's lifeless body.

As Thorn was about to turn his head to draw a breath, the beast climbed onto his back again, squeezing him in a bear hug. Either to make sure Thorn was gone, or for some final sadistic thrill.

Thorn waited until his lungs ached and his mind began to fog, until he could wait no longer. He took hold of the man's hands that were locked together around his chest, gripped a thumb, twisted it backward against the joint, and when the man's grip loosened, Thorn wrenched loose from his embrace, got a glimpse of Facundo's hellish grin, sucked down a breath, and thrashed free of the man's grasping hands.

On his back, he flutter-kicked away from Facundo, until he bumped Victor's body.

He ducked below the water, fumbled and groped his good hand down Victor's torso, located the fancy scabbard, found the handle of the machete, drew it.

He spun onto his back, more flutter-kicking till he was upright, head and shoulders out of the water, Facundo closing in with sloppy strokes. Thorn cocked the machete to warn him off, but the lanky man kept splashing forward. When he was an arm's length away, Thorn slashed at his upper body but the blade twisted and the flat side glanced off Facundo's rigid arm muscles.

"Motherfucker." Facundo pitched forward, his fist slamming Thorn's sternum.

Gasping, Thorn raised the blade again and hacked at the base of Facundo's neck then chopped a second time and was lifting the weapon for a third blow when he saw the smirk fade and the hatred drain from Facundo's face and his head slumped to the side.

A second later, Facundo lost his traction in the world of the living and disappeared below the quiet waters of Card Sound.

Panting hard, Thorn released the machete. The weapon drifting to the floor of the bay to join the other lost treasures down there. In the distance he spotted Sugar side-stroking toward shore, right arm pulling through the water while his left was looped around Kathy's upper body.

With a one-armed crawl, Thorn made his way to Sugar's side, both of them silent for several strokes.

Then Thorn asked how badly Kathy was hurt.

"Just a scratch," she said.

"She'll need stitches, a lot of them," said Sugar. "Where are the others?"

"Victor and Facundo are down for the count. I've lost touch with the rest."

"I saw Miguel drown," Kathy said. "All that muscle, couldn't stay afloat. Jorge tried to save him but Miguel grabbed onto him and dragged him under. Neither of them resurfaced."

"Which leaves who?" Sugar said.

"Up ahead, the little guy," said Thorn. "Pablo, not much of a swimmer."

"Who was shooting?" Sugar said. "And why?"

"Has to be Osvaldo," Kathy said. "God knows why."

"So we're swimming to the island, into the gunfire," Thorn said. "Not Ocean Reef?"

"I don't know about you," said Sugar. "At this point, I'll take my chances with whichever's closer."

"I should've held on to that machete."

Sugarman took another stroke.

"I'm not even going to ask what happened," Sugar said.

"Self-defense," said Thorn.

"Listen," Kathy said, "from here on, everything we do is self-defense."

Stetson stopped swimming and let her legs drift down. Toes of her shoes brushing bottom. Two more strokes toward shore, then another two and she stopped. Let herself settle, testing the bottom. Soft. Sinking to her ankles, holding there.

Osvaldo shut off the spotlight, tossed it aside, and moved to intercept her.

"Give me the pistol. Give it to me, girl. I know you have it."

"Fuck you."

Stetson swung around and hurled the rock out into deep water where it skipped once and splashed. She turned back to him, not sure he was fooled, waiting, dreading the worst.

Osvaldo said, "Okay, come to me. Get out of the water. Are you hurt?"

"What do you care?"

She staggered through the shallows and stepped onto the beach.

"Aren't you going to call for help? Some of them are drowning."

"Let the weaklings drown," Osvaldo said. "We'll see who survives."

"You're one evil fuck, you know that?"

"Oh, yes," he said. "I've known since I was younger than you. An evil evil fuck."

Osvaldo pocketed his pistol and drew out a cell phone.

"Who are you calling, reinforcements?"

"No," said Osvaldo. "Someone to clean up this mess."

NINETEEN

IN THE PAST, STETSON HAD heard Osvaldo shout curses into his phone more times than she could count. Bullying, ranting, screaming death threats, all that was routine for him. But she'd never heard his voice drop to the crooning whisper he was using now as if lulling a newborn to sleep.

Stetson watched Pablo slosh through the shallows, stumble onto the beach, and flop on his back, lie there, heaving and gasping.

Osvaldo ended the call with a quiet, "Yes, sir. Two boats should be sufficient."

Then he shoved the phone back into his pocket and glared at Pablo.

"Where are the others?"

"Victor, shot in his face, dead. Miguel, Facundo, not sure. No good swimmers."

"Do you have a weapon?"

Pablo shook his head mournfully.

"Get up," Osvaldo said. "Go to the barracks and arm yourself. And bring me another pistol. Do it now."

Pablo sat up, struggled to his feet, and marched up the low dune.

"Run, little man," Osvaldo shouted at him. "*Tenga prisa.*"

Pablo broke into an unsteady trot.

"You shot at me," Stetson said. "You only missed by inches."

"If I'd wanted to hit you, I would have hit you. I was urging you to return."

"By shooting at me?"

"You are here beside me, are you not?"

She watched Thorn and another man she didn't know, steady her mother between them as they slogged through the ankle-deep mud and sand.

Osvaldo raised his pistol and aimed at them.

"What're you doing?" Stetson said. "Don't shoot, goddamn you. Don't."

"I'm not going to shoot them, darling." Osvaldo had raised his voice, loud enough for the new arrivals to hear. "I have more entertaining plans for these people."

Blood seeped from a long gash on her mother's upper arm.

"Oh, my god. Mother!"

"Help her to the house, girl, take care of the wound. Do you hear me? Do something constructive for once."

"That looks bad," Stetson said. "She needs a doctor. She needs stitches."

"Do what I say. Do it now."

* * *

"So now we're the entertainment," Sugar said.

"I have the feeling," Thorn said, "we've been this guy's entertainment for years."

"She needs immediate medical attention," Sugar said, as they stepped onto the beach.

"The young lady will handle first aid," said Osvaldo. "Won't you, Stetson?"

"I'm okay," Kathy said, but the wooziness in her voice suggested otherwise. "I can manage. Just give me a hand, sweetheart. We'll do this together."

Kathy slung her arm across Stetson's shoulders and the two of them hobbled up the dune to a walkway that led to the house.

With a pistol in each hand, Pablo trotted past them and halted beside Osvaldo.

"Welcome, gentlemen, to *El Morro*, my island citadel."

"You mean Pumpkin Key?" Thorn said.

"No, Mr. Thorn. These are the shores of *El Morro*."

"Call it what you want," said Thorn. "You can't change its real name."

"How naïve, Mr. Thorn. He who owns, names as he sees fit."

Osvaldo smiled coolly.

"Now, gentlemen, here's what is about to unfold," Osvaldo said. "We are going to make ourselves comfortable for a while and wait for the clean-up crew to arrive. We can't have corpses washing ashore in Ocean Reef, now can we?"

In a short burst of snarling Spanish, Osvaldo ordered Pablo to follow the females to the house and keep a close watch on them. Neither of them could be trusted. He said more than that, but it was so encoded in slang Thorn couldn't translate.

Osvaldo took one of the handguns Pablo had been carrying. Before he departed, Pablo glowered at Thorn and spit at the sand between them.

Sugar and Thorn followed Osvaldo's orders and sat on the lower edge of the dune.

"I have no interest in adding to the body count this evening," Osvaldo said. "However, if I sense even the slightest hint of aggression from either of you, I will end your lives instantly. Do you understand?"

"Where's your blade? Leave it in your other trousers?"

"You think of yourself as a humorist, Mr. Thorn?"

"It's a simple question. A blade is what you used on Minx. Poor sap probably never saw it coming, trusted you right to the last second, let you get too close."

"If you think you can provoke me, induce me to make an imprudent move, you are sadly mistaken. I know you better than you know yourself. I know cockiness is a strategy you employ to tip your opponents off-balance. You fancy yourself more savvy than your foes. You prod and poke like an insolent child hoping your opponent will lash out, making themselves vulnerable."

"So, no blade tonight? That what you're saying? Left it on the dresser?"

"My blade never leaves me. It is my constant companion."

"So the Glock, that's not your first choice. Apparently, you're a good shot cause you blew Victor's face off. Assuming Victor was what you were aiming for."

"My daughter was about to be run down. I saved her life. Traded Victor for her."

"A few others got lost in that transaction," Sugarman said.

"Ah, the sidekick speaks. The gladiator's understudy."

"Let me ask you something, Oz? Can I call you Oz, is that your nickname? Or just Trickster?"

Osvaldo stiffened ever so slightly, and his gaze shifted to the moonlit water as if he couldn't bear to set eyes on Thorn for a second longer.

Osvaldo was wearing a black T-shirt, faded blue jeans, and running shoes. There was a tattoo on his right forearm. A fish of some kind done in the Polynesian style, lacey, fragile. Like some prehistoric creature's skeleton imprinted in stone.

"So you bugged my house, you bugged Sugar's office. You listened to our comings and goings, our conversations, my bedroom antics. You gave all that to Kathy and she wrote the novels that pretty much paralleled what actually happened. Have I got that right?"

"What's your question? Ask it, go on, share whatever is tormenting you."

"It's flattering, actually. The things Sugar and I did, they're sexy enough to make good novels. Sell a bunch of books. Although, if it were me, I think I'd have a hard time plagiarizing somebody else's story, ripping off adventures I'm too lily-livered to have myself."

Osvaldo chuckled. He paced the waterline, keeping a cautious ten-foot cushion between them.

"It's not possible to steal someone's story, Mr. Thorn. There is nothing original under the sun. Everything is a copy of something that came before. It's either improved upon or diminished."

"Wow," Thorn said. "What is that, Aristotle, Plato, Dr. Suess?"

"Cool it, Thorn." Sugar shifted his butt in the sand. "No point bickering with the asshole."

"Listen to your friend, Mr. Thorn. His African wisdom is charming."

"All these years, you never let go. The cuckolded husband getting his revenge, one book at a time. Rubbing Kathy's nose in my escapades. You're just as pissed off tonight as you were that night in my bedroom. You never got over it."

"All true," Osvaldo said. "I deny nothing you say. Although you must give me credit for finding such a lucrative way to vent my rage."

Thorn was about to try a different tack, mention something even more intimate about Kathy, see if he could piss him off enough to drop his guard, but before he could speak, two center console boats roared into the bay. Twenty-five footers, dual outboards. Big bruisers.

They followed one another into Card Sound and cut their speed, sweeping just offshore of Pumpkin Key as if presenting themselves for inspection.

Osvaldo's cell phone dinged and he drew it from his pants pocket.

He listened for a moment, then said, "Three bodies and any other flotsam you find. And if you could tow the boats back to the docks, that would be quite helpful."

He listened again and said, "Burials at sea would be appropriate, I believe. Yes, thank you for your assistance. I am deeply in your debt."

"Jesus H. fucking Christ," Sugar said.

"Does it really surprise you?" said Thorn.

A gold star was emblazoned on the hull of each boat. Next to the star, in large gold letters: SHERIFF.

Below that single word, in a smaller font was "Monroe County."

"No," Sugar said. "Doesn't surprise me. But this shit just got a whole lot shittier."

With searchlights blazing, the two boats began a methodical reconnoiter of the bay.

"Now, gentlemen," Osvaldo said. "We will be joining the ladies in the house. Mr. Sugarman will lead the way, then Mr. Thorn, and I shall bring up the rear. My finger remains firmly on the trigger."

Sugar got to his feet, sent another of his "cool-it" looks to Thorn.

"Now you, Mr. Thorn, up the dune, to the walkway."

Thorn rose, turned to face Osvaldo.

"You wouldn't slit my throat from behind, would you, Trickster?"

Osvaldo smiled, as smug as a house cat with a cornered mouse.

"If I kill you, Mr. Thorn, I give my word, you'll have time to see it coming."

Thorn was only halfway up the dune when he heard a grunt of effort behind him, and this time there were stars. It wasn't always that way when he'd been knocked unconscious. Sometimes it was a simple blackout shade pulled down across the window of the world. Sometimes there was nothing at all. One moment there. The next moment somewhere else. This time there were stars. A galaxy of them, a swirling Milky Way that sent Thorn back to that night with Kathy on the Chris Craft in the islands, the sky unzipped and spilling out blazing pinpoints of light. That night when he'd claimed everything was luck and accident. Nothing more than that. No heavenly hand controlling events. No God with Thorn's itinerary written in stone. But he'd been wrong. There was someone controlling events. Trickster. Someone who'd been there behind him, just out of sight, raising the butt of his revolver high above Thorn's skull and bringing it down with crushing finality. A sky full of glitter. Red and yellow pricks of light. Traveling through limitless space.

Thorn was not quite unconscious, but paralyzed, with a faint awareness.

He heard Osvaldo command Sugarman to carry Thorn into the house.

Felt his friend's strong arms cradle him. He heard Sugar grunt as he lifted.

He heard Sugar whispering, "You'll be okay, you'll be okay, everything's fine."

He heard Osvaldo direct Sugar, left, right, right again, down that hall, left, open the door. Yes. That's right. Now lay him on the floor. On the floor right there. Take off his shoes, and then remove your own. That's perfect, thank you, Mr. Sugarman. You've done well so far.

He heard the door close.

He heard the lock set.

He heard the sound of bubbles, bubbles. Not fizz, but bubbles the size of dimes, tiny globes of air tumbling up through water. Bubbles and starlight.

After that, he heard nothing. Nothing at all.

TWENTY

IN THE KITCHEN, STETSON LOCATED the first aid kit, sterilized the wound with hydrogen peroxide, then smeared Neosporin over its length. Her mother didn't cringe or moan. Didn't even draw a deep breath as if such pain hardly registered on her scale.

The bleeding slowed and though the cut looked deep, to Stetson's untrained eye, she was pretty sure it wasn't life-threatening.

From a few feet away, Pablo kept watch, his head and body swaying as if the floor rocked beneath him.

"Mother and I need to clean up," Stetson told him. "And change into dry clothes. Are you required to watch us strip and shower?"

"You make a lot of trouble," Pablo said. "You have been like this always."

Once the wound was firmly bandaged, Stetson announced that they were going to her bedroom now.

"I'll be near," Pablo said. "Be quick about it, *tu perra*."

"Yeah, and you're a little bitch too," Stetson said.

She led the way down the corridor to her room.

Pablo halted a few feet from the door and braced himself against the wall.

Stetson shut the bedroom door. There was no lock, but she moved a chair away from her desk and cocked it against the doorknob. Not going to stop Pablo or Osvaldo if they wanted to invade. But it would slow them down, give her extra seconds if she needed them.

"What happened to your face?"

Her mother stepped close and reached out to her cheek.

"Fishing line," Stetson said. "Long story. Gory details later."

"Did Osvaldo do this to you?"

"Indirectly, yes."

The bandage on her arm was already showing a stripe of blood seeping through.

Stetson went to her closet and tore a plastic dry cleaner bag off a sweater.

"We need to wrap that bandage," she said, "before you shower."

Her mother nodded, gave her a faint smile of gratitude.

"I have some clothes that will fit you. You need to get out of those wet ones."

"We both do," her mother said.

Stetson used a roll of packing tape to seal the plastic around the bandage. When it was secure, she told her mother to go ahead and shower first.

"You have a lot of books," her mother said. "Have you read all those?"

Floor-to-ceiling shelves covered three of the four walls. It was how Stetson had passed the years, what she'd had instead of friends, instead of school, instead of contact with anyone outside her father and his thugs. When she wasn't reading, she spent hours wandering the island, collecting shells and bits of sea glass that washed ashore, watching the flights of birds, the streaming clouds.

But books were where she truly lost herself. Where she learned about heroism, cowardice, about dreams and hopes, and love, its many faces, its deceits, its trials, its ecstatic flights. Where she learned history and geography and about as much of the human condition as was possible to glean from ink and paper.

"I see you've got my complete set. The adventures of Mr. North."

"You're a good writer," she said. "They're fun."

"Fun? Really? Not silly? Not melodramatic?"

"A little silly, sure. And there's nothing wrong with a dash of melodrama."

Her mother laughed.

"You need to get out of those wet clothes, Mother."

Her wounded arm made undressing so difficult, Stetson had to help her unbutton her blouse and peel out of her clothes.

When her outfit was a damp heap on the rug, Stetson stepped back.

"I've never seen you naked," she said. "Is that normal for mother and daughter?"

"With us," her mother said, "nothing's ever been normal."

With artless serenity, she stood before Stetson, arms at her side as if to let her daughter fully absorb her body. Her mother was skinny, not quite gaunt, but close. Her breasts were firm, but bones were showing where bones had no business showing. All her hair was silvery gray. Stetson could remember a time not long ago when it was long, dark, and lustrous. She could remember when her mother was shapely, well-proportioned. Never as buxom as Stetson, but ample.

"You're a beautiful woman," Stetson said.

"I'm old. I'm shriveling away."

Stetson put a hand on her mother's shoulder and turned her gently toward the bathroom, guiding her forward.

"You're a long way from old, but okay, yeah, I see a little shriveling."

Her mother laughed again, a husky chuckle.

As far as Stetson could recall, these were the first times she'd heard her mother laugh. Also the only time they'd truly been alone together, not monitored by one of Osvaldo's goons standing within earshot.

Their hotel room meetings had been brief, with awkward conversations about trivia. Like strangers thrust into adjoining seats for a few hours, struggling to connect. Over the years, their talks had become so stilted, their embraces so bumbling, Stetson had all but abandoned hope they would ever bridge the distance between them.

Her mother showered. Steam filled the bathroom.

Stetson slipped out of her soggy clothes, peeled open the Ziploc bag and removed the pistol and tucked it beneath a bed pillow. She put on an old terrycloth bathrobe and found a fresh one for her mother and when she came out of the bathroom wrapped in a towel, Stetson held up the bathrobe and her mother slipped into it.

"Now I want to show you something, but don't make any noise, okay? Pablo is just outside."

"Sounds dire."

Stetson drew the pistol from beneath the pillow, careful to keep the barrel pointing toward the far wall.

"Is that loaded?"

"It is."

She held out the Glock and after a brief hesitation, her mother took it and seemed to weigh it before wrapping her hand around the grip. She aimed it at the far wall, keeping her finger outside the trigger guard.

"My god," her mother said. "How did you manage it?"

Stetson told her about the rock she'd thrown to hoodwink Osvaldo.

"I'm a clever and daring girl. I must get it from you."

"Where's Thorn? And Sugarman? Do you know?"

"I'm not sure. They stayed on the beach when we left. Who is Sugarman?"

"Old friend from way back. Close friend. He and Thorn are like brothers."

"Thorn is North, isn't he? The model."

She nodded.

"Which means Sugarman is Berryman, the private detective."

Another nod.

"Thorn's a puny substitute for North."

"Thorn's real, North's a fantasy."

"So give me the quick version. Who these people are, why they're in the novels."

"We were close once, the three of us," she said.

"How close?"

"Very close, Thorn and I, especially."

"Lovers, you mean."

She nodded again. Eyes losing focus, clouding.

"Did you love him? Thorn?"

"I loved both of them. In different ways. Yes, I loved them. I still do."

"I know about the bugs in Thorn's house. Osvaldo was spying on him, passing on his secret life to you. And the novels came from that."

"Yes, they're based on Thorn, loosely. Osvaldo couldn't find a way to spy on him twenty-four hours a day. So imagination was required. A lot of it sometimes."

"I still don't get it. Why him? Why the bugs?"

"Before you were born, Osvaldo and I were separated. I'd filed for divorce. I met Thorn and Sugar during that time and it wasn't long before Osvaldo discovered Thorn and I were lovers. The books are part of his revenge."

"He punished you by rubbing Thorn in your face all these years."

"He considered it a very personal payback, yes. A way of mocking Thorn, making him larger than life was a way of belittling the real Thorn. And yes, at first it was painful. But gradually I found it was a way to stay in touch with him, and Sugarman, too, a world I'd been exiled from. Of course I never let Osvaldo know that part. Two men I cared about. Two men I respected and adored. I've spent the last twenty years with them, living their adventures vicariously."

"And me? My job was to keep you in line, that's what Osvaldo told me. I'm his leverage over you."

"He said that?"

"He did, yes."

"A rare moment of honesty. Yes, years and years ago, back when you were born, he made me sign documents, legal agreements. I was vulnerable, trapped with a man I hated and feared. And you, I didn't have the emotional capacity to deal with what your arrival meant. This sweet, innocent child entering this hideous situation."

"Post-partum depression."

"The phrase makes it sound simple, but it wasn't. I totally lost my way. There was torture, deprivation, imprisonment, things I can't even describe, all of it happened right here in this house."

"Osvaldo tortured you."

Her eyes filled with cold silence. A small nod was all the confirmation she managed.

"And he held the threat over me that I would never see you again if I didn't keep producing the books."

Stetson tucked the pistol back beneath the pillow.

"And you went along with it. Couldn't you fight it legally? Escape somehow."

Her head slumped forward and she shook her head at the floor.

"Oh, I tried. I was so worried about you, tormented imagining what Osvaldo might do to you. I got away two or three times, not far. They caught me, and as punishment, he refused to let me visit you for months. You were so young, you don't remember."

"Oh, yeah, long stretches without seeing you. I didn't understand, but I remember."

"Local police, FBI, I tried everything I could think of. A couple even came to the door, but I could never convince anyone I was in danger. They'd look around. See the house, the furniture, the neighborhood. I wasn't locked up, I wasn't bruised or hurt. They suggested I contact an attorney or a therapist.

"I wrote to lawyers, emails, letters, I phoned, detailed the situation. But Osvaldo always knew what I was up to. He moved me from house to house all over south Florida, properties he owned. To keep me off-balance, make it harder for Thorn or Sugarman or anyone else to track me down. Every house I occupied was filled with cameras and audio bugs. Victor, Facundo, the others, they were always snooping.

"All the lawyers I contacted, each backed out. I assumed they were roughed up, threatened, or bought off. Osvaldo had me trapped. My only pleasures were the books, the tapes of Thorn and Sugar, their escapades, their love affairs. Hearing their voices, their silly jokes, their conversations about the weather, the fishing, Sugarman's latest case. But what truly kept me afloat was you. Our monthly get-togethers."

Stetson sighed and circled the room, looking at the bookshelves, gathering herself to say a hurtful truth.

"For me, Mother, our meetings were always awkward. The two of us never alone. I didn't really get to know you. Never felt at ease. After a while, I dreaded going."

"It's okay," her mother said. "Same for me, some of that. But just seeing you, watching you grow, develop, become the savvy, healthy young woman you are, that kept me going."

"Did he visit you in those houses where you were trapped?"

"Visit me? Oh, no. No, after you came along he never touched me again."

"Well, I'm glad to have played a part in that."

Her mother fashioned a smile.

Stetson sighed, opened her arms, and her mother stepped into an embrace. Inhaling the scent of her hair, feeling the rise and fall of her chest, her sinewy body, so strong, Stetson felt the burn of tears she'd withheld for years begin to well, a rising rush of sobs. She blinked the tears away, swallowed back the acid burn of sorrow. No time for that. Not now. Not yet.

When they parted, her mother said, "Do you know how to shoot that thing?"

"I've never done it. But I think I can manage."

"This is the end," her mother said.

"The end?"

"I've refused to write another book. I knew you were old enough, independent enough to make it on your own. So I told Osvaldo I was done. No more. He hired a ghostwriter to finish this last one. I suppose that's what set this off, Thorn showing up in Delray, the men taking him and Sugar hostage, I don't know."

"I set it off," Stetson said. "Not you."

"What?"

"Look, I'll explain later. I'm going to shower. Those clothes I laid out on the bed, something there should fit you. I'll be quick then we can make a plan."

"It's only Pablo and Osvaldo left. The others, they didn't survive the crash."

Her hands were clenched and her eyes drained of light.

"So four against two," Stetson said. "Unless you think Osvaldo did something to…"

"No, no. The man's been consumed by Thorn and Sugar for years, burning with hatred, he's a ruthless, merciless man, but he wouldn't kill them. That's too easy. He'll want to toy with them, something slow and excruciating. Milk it for every last poisonous drop. Make me watch, maybe you too."

"The aquarium room," Stetson said.

"What?"

"You know about it, right? Floor to ceiling lionfish?"

"Sure, sure, he built that monstrosity when you were just a baby."

"That's his dungeon," Stetson said. "He's thrown me in there for entire days when I disobeyed him or broke some rule."

"He did the same to me."

"So you know what a sickening place it is," Stetson said. "Five minutes, those goddamn fish swirling everywhere, I'm seasick, ready to barf. That's where he'd lock up Thorn and Sugarman. Heavy door, big locks. It's worse than solitary confinement. Those fucking fish under your feet, overhead."

"I'd forgotten about it," her mother said. "But you're right. That's where they are."

"Mother, look. Even if something happened to Thorn and Sugarman, and it's just the two of us, we'll make it. I'm clever and daring, right? And you're tougher than titanium nails."

"Am I?"

"Oh, yeah. Much tougher. All the shit you've endured, but look at you."

"Scrawny, withering. That what you mean?"

"Tough," Stetson said. "You survived. We both did."

"Tough," her mother repeated, as if trying to convince herself it was true.

Stetson showered and after toweling off, she chose a pair of shorts, no bra, and a loose peasant blouse with a scooped neckline. Showing lots of skin.

Sitting in Stetson's reading chair, her mother watched her with a frown.

"Of course, it's your call, Stetson, you must have a good reason to dress like that."

Stetson drew the pistol from beneath the pillow and tucked it in the front waistband of her shorts, fluffed out the shirttail to be sure the pistol butt was hidden.

"A distraction," Stetson said. "Men can't help themselves, even Osvaldo steals a look now and then."

Her mother smiled then a second later the smile curdled on her lips.

"But he's never touched you," she said. "He or his men?"

"Never. But his eyes can't hide what his cock is craving."

"The bastard."

"Showing skin, it's just a way to unbalance them. Gender jiu-jitsu."

"Where'd you pick up that bit of wisdom?"

"Read it in a book," Stetson said. "One of yours."

Her mother lowered her voice.

"Do you have zip ties, rope, anything like that?"

Stetson shook her head. Then thought a moment and picked up the lamp from the bedside table, unplugged it. Dug a pair of scissors from her desk and snipped the cord off at the base.

"Good," her mother said quietly. "Anything we can use other than the pistol?"

"These?" She held up the scissors.

"No, no. We need something quick and quiet. This could get messy fast."

"Osvaldo searches my room almost once a week. Anything I might use as a weapon, it disappears. He's paranoid. And for good reason."

Her mother looked around the room, went over to the bedside table. Removed the lamp, a clock, a ceramic dolphin. Flipped the small table over.

"What're you doing?" Stetson whispered.

Her mother used both hands to grip one of the tapered legs of the table and twisted. She twisted more until the leg was unscrewed from the base of the table.

She held it up by the narrow end. A well-shaped club, a few inches short of a bat.

"You want one?" her mother asked.

"Damn right."

Stetson twisted the second one loose and gave her mother a tentative smile.

"Now what?"

They kept their voices low and made a plan. Take them one at a time. Starting with Pablo

TWENTY-ONE

THORN HEARD THE BUBBLES RISING inside his gut, heard them streaming upward from his depths like tiny helium balloons set loose one after the other, rising in a column toward the bright sky. The bubbles jostling one another in their hurry to rise.

When he opened his eyes, he saw them, the real bubbles, saw them streaming to his left and right, above him and beneath him inside the floor itself. A dizzy space that clarified slowly as he came awake in stages, eyes open but unseeing, eyes open but blurry, eyes open with the bubbles coming into focus, and eyes opening fully, and there was Sugar sitting on a liquid floor with a book open on his lap, bubbles behind him, above him, to his left and right and overhead.

Thorn clenched his eyes to clear the bleariness, then opened them again. Sugarman was still there with his book. The bubbles still bubbling.

Thorn reached up and ran his fingers through his hair, approaching with caution the throbbing lump at the back of his skull. The parietal bone. He knew the name because this was not the first golf ball erupting in that area of Thorn's skull. Not even the second or third.

"How long have I been gone?"

"Maybe an hour," Sugar said. "Putting out a healthy snore the whole time, so I knew you were still in there somewhere."

"Jesus, that long."

"You must've been short on your REM quota."

Thorn sat up, gazed around the room. Studying each of the four walls and the ceiling. Last he stared between his spread legs, dumbstruck.

"What the ever-loving fuck?"

"Don't look too long," Sugar said. "You'll get queasy. I sure as hell did."

"Lionfish everywhere," said Thorn. "What the hell is this place?"

Sugarman closed the book and set it on the floor. He stood up and padded barefoot over to the far wall. He tapped on what appeared to be a wood door stained a deep mahogany.

"Based on the thickness of the portal, I'd say we're in some kind of cell."

Thorn rapped his knuckles against the floor beside his legs.

"Glass is an inch thick."

"At least that," Sugar said.

"Lionfish. Fucking lionfish. There must be thousands."

"At least."

"Like the tattoo on his arm. A lionfish fetish."

"Picked a hell of fish to obsess over. Those fuckers are evil."

"That's probably the point."

Thorn stared at the bubbles inside the glass of the far wall. His effervescent vision was simply an aeration system to keep the fish alive, the hum of pumps forcing air into saltwater.

"Hey, Osvaldo," Thorn called. "I'm awake. In case you're ready to chat."

"Don't believe the man's in a hurry. Wants to watch us squirm."

Thorn eased back and leaned against one of the glass walls. His numb arm was awake again. His sternum throbbed from Facundo's punch. There were tremors in his wrist, and aches deep in the joints of his elbow and shoulder, vibrations lingering from his machete blows. That heavy blade hammering bone, meat, tendon.

Facundo hadn't screamed. Or had he?

Those moments were erased, lost like the machete itself beneath the night waters. But he knew that scene with Facundo was inescapable. In the coming days, the images would resurface, invading a dream, or set off by some unrelated sound like the slap of the tide against his rocky shoreline.

"What's with the book?"

Sugar sighed, walked back and picked it up, and handed it to Thorn.

A crimson cover with embossed gold letters. *North Exposed*, Katarina Mayfield.

The cover art was simple, a photographic rendering of a dock with a flats boat moored on one side, an antique Chris Craft secured on the other. In the distance was a string of mangrove islands with a notch in the center. He knew those boats, that dock.

That notch in the mangroves was a channel leading out of Blackwater Sound into the Florida Bay. He boated through there yesterday, or was it the day before, on his way to snag that monster bonefish? That channel was called The Boggies. It had been a constant in Thorn's field of vision for as long as he could remember. 315 degrees due northwest from the end of his dock.

"That's my house, my place."

"Sure as hell is," Sugar said.

"Where'd the book come from?"

"Sitting on the floor when Osvaldo shoved me in here."

"You read any of it?"

"While you were snoozing, yeah. Fifty, sixty pages, enough to get the picture."

"And?"

"Like the others, it's you and me. Last year. Our trip to Arizona, the girl, Dulce, the militia guys ambushing the truckload of immigrants. I skipped ahead, read some of the ending. Whoever wrote it got most of that right. The stuff in Bad Axe, the landmines with VX nerve gas."

"What do you mean, 'whoever wrote it?' It wasn't Kathy?"

"It doesn't sound like the others. Sloppy, full of clichés, fourth-grade level. But it'll still sell a ton because her name's on the cover."

"What I want to know," Thorn said, "how the hell could anyone know about what went down in Bad Axe?"

"Yeah, I wondered the same thing. If it's only those bugs eavesdropping on your house and my office, how's it's possible? But there it is. Pretty much as it happened. You and me taking down those clowns in that Michigan barn, saving Dulce a second time."

"Trickster's in it?"

Sugar nodded.

"Tell me."

"You won't like it."

"Tell me, Sugar."

"He tipped off the TV people in Phoenix about Dulce hiding out with the nuns."

"You're shitting me."

Just after crossing the border into the U.S., Dulce had witnessed the militia guys murdering the migrants she'd been traveling with. When the killers discovered an eyewitness to their massacre had survived, they tracked Dulce down, were about to grab her when Thorn and Sugar whisked her away and secured her with a Phoenix nun who Dulce met years earlier in Honduras.

When the local TV news station in Phoenix broadcast the story about Dulce, celebrating the nun's good works, the killers swooped in and abducted the girl. Back when it all happened, Thorn and Sugar believed someone in the archdiocese had alerted the news people without realizing they were putting Dulce in danger. An innocent mistake. But there was nothing innocent about what Trickster did.

"Wait a minute," Thorn said. "Only way that could've happened, Trickster had to tail us from Key Largo to Arizona without us knowing. No way in hell."

"I don't know how Osvaldo did it, Thorn. I'm just telling you what I read in the book."

Thorn riffled the pages, the words a blur.

"Anyway, forget all that," Sugar said. "The back cover, that's the true gut punch."

Thorn turned the book over and read the brief paragraphs, then read them a second time to fully grasp their meaning.

North Exposed, the finale of Katarina Mayfield's bestselling North series.

For two decades North Danielson was portrayed as a vigilante crusader, a colorful antihero who hunted down very bad people and served them rough justice.

Often flouting the law, North frequently caused collateral damage in his quests. Innocent bystanders, friends and lovers were badly injured or left dead in his wake. But despite all that, his ends always seemed to justify his means. He was a decent man, forced to do bad things for very good reasons.

*But in this concluding episode of the series, **North Exposed**, the reader learns the man we believed was merely a tainted hero is actually a villain of the worst kind, a man who regularly kidnaps and forces himself on underage girls. A sickening compulsion North managed to keep hidden until now.*

Given this horrific revelation, Mayfield can no longer in good conscience continue the series.

*For in **North Exposed**, readers will discover that these fifteen novels were not make-believe after all. But a series of true crime stories chronicling the exploits of a particular man living in the Florida Keys whose escapades formed the basis of all the novels—a man whose identity Mayfield can no longer shield.*

Though her extensive research and sources must remain confidential for legal reasons, in the final novel in the series, North is unmasked. Because of his heinous acts, his real name must be revealed for the world to know.

It is the author's fervent wish that law enforcement will act swiftly and decisively to capture this man. And rest assured, Ms. Mayfield will provide all essential documentation and any other assistance to send this barbaric fiend to his new permanent residence, a federal prison cell.

Thorn lay the book aside and gazed at the far wall, watching the lionfish swirl and pirouette and brush their long feathery fins against the glass walls.

"You and me, Thorn, we're about to get famous. For all the wrong reasons."

"And Sprunt will be only too happy to make the rape case."

"The deck is seriously stacked against you."

Thorn shook his head, took a deep swallow.

"What about the little things?"

Sugarman gave him a puzzled frown and asked what he meant.

"In the books," Thorn said. "Day to day stuff. You said nudge. Does Trickster nudge small things in daily life? Not just the life or death situations, other stuff."

"We still talking about the North books?"

"I'm talking about Osvaldo, the obsessive fucker. What if he's been there all the time, ever since that night at my house, just out of view, prodding, poking, tripping me up? Sabotaging relationships, poisoning things."

"You looking for someone to blame for things not always going right?"

"Is that in the North books, little things, nudges?"

"I've only read that second book, and part of this new one, but yeah," Sugar said. "Bits of sabotage, a punctured tire, boat lines cut. Just to needle North, irritate him, make him waste his time and effort on bullshit."

Thorn considered that for a moment.

"That rock through my front window, remember that? It was a couple of years ago? Took all day to clean up the glass, put in a new one."

"Yeah, thought it was some drunken punks passing by in a boat, a prank."

"Maybe it was drunken punks," Thorn said. "And maybe not."

When Osvaldo spoke, his sonorous voice sounded from within the walls, coming from every direction at once.

"It wasn't drunken punks," Osvaldo said. "It was me, it has been me all along. If you found so much as a sandspur in your Jockey shorts, it was I who put it there. Do you understand now, Mr. Thorn? Your life has not been your own. You have been mine for every minute of the last twenty years. Do you understand?"

Thorn looked into the stillness of Sugarman's eyes.

Beneath Thorn's bare feet, a spew of fish food flooded the aquarium and the lionfish erupted, attacking the bits of flesh and gristle, skirmishing among themselves for dominant positions, and inside the far wall another discharge set off a similar flurry of gorging.

Behind them, Osvaldo cleared his throat and Thorn spun around. While they'd been preoccupied with the fish, he'd entered the room soundlessly. And that throat-clearing was his mocking show of superiority.

He'd changed into fresh clothes, baggy white trousers and a white guayabera with long sleeves and strips of embroidery down the front. In such shapeless attire, it was hard to make out the definition of his body. On the beach earlier, in the shadows, Osvaldo seemed rangy and rawboned, but Thorn had been dazed from the boat wreck, the struggle with Facundo, and the swim to shore. So he wasn't confident of his appraisal.

Here in the brightly lit aquarium room, it should have been easy to size up Osvaldo's muscularity. But the light radiated from all sides, above and below, and it filtered through the bubbling water and the churn of fish, making it flutter and pulse-like disco lights in a second-rate nightclub.

Clearly, Osvaldo was at home with the lighting but for Thorn it was disorienting. He shot a look at Sugar who was squinting at Osvaldo, seeming as flustered and off-balance by the jittery light and the frenzied fish as Thorn was.

Osvaldo kept circling, arms loose at his sides, hands brushing the bottom edge of his shirttail. Barefoot, he was perhaps an inch taller than Thorn and lighter by ten pounds or so. He had to be in his early fifties, but he navigated the room with the supple ease of a much younger man.

Osvaldo studied the fish, his back to them as he circled the room as though taunting Thorn and Sugar, inviting them to attack. While he ambled, the fingers of his left hand fluttered oddly like he was practicing the scales on a piano, limbering them up for a concerto.

Was Osvaldo left-handed and this a nervous twitch before he drew his blade? Or was he right-handed and this fiddling was nothing more than misdirection?

From numerous fistfights, Thorn had sized up more than his share of opponents. Inevitably most were right-handed and when they angled in to land a first blow, they led with their left shoulder. That was an easy read. But squared off, face to face, the best reveal Thorn had picked up was the slight dip of the shoulder.

The dominant arm was more developed, stronger, heavier, sometimes even a bit longer, so that shoulder slump was a giveaway. It was Osvaldo's right shoulder that was an inch or two lower than the left, so by Thorn's calculus, that finger waggle was trickery, a diversion.

He had to stay tightly focused on the right hand.

Twice tonight Thorn's vigilance failed him. Once at Hardy's Motel when he'd faced Facundo with his machete and shot a look toward Sugar, nearly losing his life in that instant of distraction. And second, when Osvaldo struck him on the skull with his gun. Thorn heard the grunt of effort and should have reacted instantly, dodging the blow. Both times his focus had strayed, he'd gotten sloppy and it could have cost his life.

This time, it was clear that if Thorn fell for any sleight of hand, any magician's patter, or head fake, he would end the evening like Deputy Minks, bleeding out on the glass floor of this unearthly room.

TWENTY-TWO

STETSON TUGGED HER SCOOPED NECKLINE down an inch, bringing more cleavage into view.

Her mother shook her head and gave her an admiring smile.

"Gender jiu-jitsu," she said. "Those were just words in a book, a felicitous phrase."

"Time to test them out in the real world," Stetson said. "Don't worry, Mom. It's going to be fine. Just don't hold back, okay? A good solid crack."

Her mother hefted the table leg, took a fresh grip on the tapered end. She raised it to her shoulder and stepped back from the doorway into the position they'd decided would work best. She nodded that she was ready.

"Break a leg, Stetson."

"You too."

Stetson took several deep breaths in a row until she was almost panting. An actress trick she'd read about, feigning panic. She turned the doorknob, took a few more deep breaths, then threw open the door.

"Pablo! It's Mother, she's fallen. I can't lift her."

He swung around, peered at her.

"*Vamos, vamos.*"

Pablo looked down the hallway toward the family room and kitchen. Deciding if he needed to alert Osvaldo.

"We need to get her up now."

Pablo cursed and trotted to the doorway.

Stetson stepped aside, tipping forward to the exact angle that exposed her breasts almost completely.

As Pablo stepped into the room, his gaze slipped down her blouse and held for a second or two, just long enough for her mother to step into range and crack the table leg against his skull and send Pablo sprawling into Stetson.

She shoved him away and Pablo sunk to his knees but managed to stay erect, wavering.

"Another one, Mom."

She winced and drew back from the helpless man.

Stetson held out her hand for the table leg.

"Let me," Stetson said.

"No, this is mine to do."

She raised the table leg above her head and hammered Pablo's skull a second time and a third which sent him flat onto his belly.

"Good work. The asshole couldn't help himself, had to look. That was more than a felicitous phrase. You knew what you were talking about."

"Every woman knows," she said.

They bound him up. Hands behind his back with the electrical cord. Clear packing tape around his head a dozen wraps to seal his mouth. More wraps of tape around his ankles

When he was secure, they lugged him to the bed, lay him out, rolled him inside the bedspread, and used another roll of packing tape to seal up the spread.

"Good enough," Stetson said. "Poor guy looks like a corndog."

She drew the pistol from beneath the pillow.

"Now comes the hard part," her mother said. "You sure about this?"

"What choice is there?"

"Then let's go get free of this bastard once and for all."

"Makes me a little dizzy," Sugarman said. "But I've got to admit, this room is an architectural marvel."

Osvaldo turned and gave Sugar his full attention.

"Stay in here long enough," Osvaldo said, "the dizziness passes."

"You designed it?"

"Designed it, built it, stocked it."

"Those lionfish are badasses. But then you know that. Got that tattoo on your arm. Collected a few thousand specimens. You're seriously into these fish."

"You called it a fetish," Osvaldo said. "You meant that as a pejorative, but I'm fine with the label."

Thorn was quiet, stepping away from the two of them, watching Sugarman work. His buddy was trying to use flattery to steal past Osvaldo's cold-blooded defenses.

"If lionfish outperform their rivals, is it fair to cast them as malevolent?"

Thorn took a deep breath and stifled his response.

Sugar said, "In my experience, nothing in nature is malevolent. Rattlesnakes, scorpions, or lionfish, they all have their roles, their places. Cram too many rattlesnakes in a confined area, that's when there could be trouble."

"And this is your philosophical worldview as well, Mr. Thorn?"

"They're pretty fish," Thorn said. "Problem is, they eat the natives that keep the algae from killing the reefs. Reefs die, the Keys die. So yeah, I'd call that malevolent, just like a virus that kills its host is malevolent."

So much for flattery.

"Like we Cubans, you mean?"

"What?" Thorn shook his head. "Where the hell did you get Cubans?"

"Outcompeting, invasive, overwhelming the native population."

"Is that what this room's about? Cubans? What're you, nuts?"

"I know you, Thorn. And I know Sugarman, too. You want to preserve the Florida of olden days. Anything moving into your territory, changing it, that threatens you. You're stuck in the past, a past that's crumbling before your eyes and you can't accept the inevitability of it."

"Yeah, okay, guilty as charged," Thorn said. "Except for the Cuban part. I admit I like the past better than the present. The good old days. Damn right."

"Not to change the subject," Sugar said, "I'm curious about your intelligence gathering on Thorn and me. I mean, it's very impressive. I have some expertise in this area myself and I have to say I was awed by all the intimate detail you were able to publish about the two of us."

"What's in the books," Osvaldo said, "is only a fraction of what I harvested from the two of you."

"We know about the high-tech bugs you were about to install at Thorn's place. Very cool. Get their power from the internet signal. Super advanced technology. But there's more, isn't there? More than just those listening devices."

"I have an Israeli source who has been most helpful. In your line of work, I suppose you're familiar with spyware."

"Oh, yeah. Of course, you hacked my phone too."

"Not only your phone. Every keystroke on your computer, every mile in your car. Every word you uttered for years and years and years. I've been perched on your shoulder, I've been invading your reef, outcompeting you. I am the lionfish, demolishing the very ground you stand on."

"Wow," Thorn said. "All that because Kathy and I spent some blissful hours together."

"You hacked my computer?" Sugar asked.

"Oh, yes," said Osvaldo. "And the password for your journal was no challenge. A child could have figured it out. Ah, what a treasure trove that journal proved to be. Such a thorough accounting of your days and your adventures. Even bits of dialogue between you and Mr. Thorn. I found that journal most useful, most enlightening."

There was a fresh tremor in Osvaldo's right hand. Thorn inched closer to him, moving into range, presenting himself, more than ready to test his reflexes against this twisted fuck.

But Osvaldo glided away from Thorn at such a leisurely, unthreatening pace at first it seemed he'd not moved at all. Sugar didn't see it coming and neither did Thorn, a blinding slash, a glitter of blade lost in the background flurry of feeding lionfish, a stroke that was barely a blur, starting at Osvaldo's shirttail and sweeping upwards to Sugarman's throat.

The door to the aquarium blew open and Stetson stepped into the room, a pistol in her hand. Kathy followed, and the two of them halted just inside the doorway and stared at the grim tableau before them.

A wide bloody streak swiped across the floor. Two fingers from Sugar's left hand lay side by side a foot from where he'd landed on the glass floor. Stunned, staring at his mutilated hand, blood pouring from the finger stubs.

Quicker and more alert than Thorn thought, Sugar had seen Osvaldo's blade arcing toward his throat and blocked it with his left hand. The blade gashed through the little finger and the one next to it, and sent Sugar sprawling.

Thorn lunged at Osvaldo, but he slipped away and slashed the bloody blade at Thorn's extended arm, nicking his forearm. Thorn side-stepped out of range and shot a look at Sugar. From the heavy pooling on the floor, it looked like he might bleed out in minutes if his wound wasn't staunched.

Osvaldo's eyes ticked back and forth between Sugar and Thorn. He reset his feet, poised to attack, a yard from Thorn, two from Sugarman. Sugar clamped his wounded hand between his right biceps and his chest. He was swallowing back the pain, and was blinking as if he might be barely clinging to consciousness.

That's when the door flew open and Thorn, seeing the pistol in Stetson's hand, stepped back to give her a clear shot at Osvaldo.

Kathy edged up beside the girl and asked Sugar how bad he was hurt. Then she noticed the amputated fingers lying on the glass floor nearby him and gasped.

"We need to get you to the hospital right now."

"Ice," Thorn said. "Go get ice."

"I'm okay," Sugar said. "Deal with Osvaldo."

"That gun," Osvaldo said. "Put it down, *mi hija*, do it now."

"She fooled you," Kathy said. "A seventeen-year-old girl."

"What?"

"She dived to the bottom, found a rock, threw it, and when it splashed you thought it was the gun she stole. She tricked you. A seventeen-year-old tricked the Trickster."

"You've been neglecting your medications, woman. Is that what's going on here?"

"Hand me the pistol, Stetson." Thorn edged away from Osvaldo. "You don't want to do this, and live with it forever."

"I don't need you, Thorn. I thought I did, but look at me. This is the way it will end. It's the only way it can go. It's my story, I'll finish it how I want."

"You can't shoot your father," Osvaldo said. "Not your own flesh and blood."

"You're not her father," Kathy said. "Not by blood, not in any way whatsoever."

"Oh, dear, you are unhinged. Flailing within the madness that consumes you."

"Mother?" Stetson glanced at Kathy, but kept the pistol steady on Osvaldo.

"Don't listen to her, Stetson." Osvaldo was inching closer to mother and daughter. He cut quick looks toward Thorn, his blade held waist-high, warning him off.

Thorn glanced at Sugar's severed fingers, at Stetson and Kathy. He lunged at Trickster. But didn't make it.

In that small room, the gunshot was so loud it rattled the glass walls and the fish erupted in panic, a churning tempest in every direction. Stetson fired once, twice, three times, then a fourth. Not at Osvaldo but at the glass floor beneath him.

As the floor cracked and gave way beneath Osvaldo, Thorn jumped to solid glass.

Osvaldo sunk to his chest in the water, feet disappearing into the sandy bottom. He pawed wildly at the splintered glass around him, trying to boost himself up. The knife in his hand broke loose and skidded across the floor, bumped Sugarman's severed fingers, and halted.

While Osvaldo thrashed and floundered, a shrill, faint-hearted wail came from deep inside him. The more he kicked, the more the spines of the inflamed lionfish stung his ankles and calves, and in the tumult, some of them bumped his groin, fluttering between his legs as though they'd been watching this man, their captor, through the clear glass floor, watching him for years and now were free to retaliate and inflict their revenge in an orgy of venom.

Of course, that was silly. Fish were primeval creatures. They operated on instinct, nothing more. But if there was a cosmic Trickster, a god of irony, he'd found a fitting end to Osvaldo's malevolent stay on Earth.

As he tried and failed to pull himself from the tank, Osvaldo lacerated his arms, ripped open his shirt, contaminated the tank with his blood, darkening it more with every attempt to free himself. His cries growing weaker, his eyes wide with some last revelation.

When Osvaldo's head slumped forward and he slid below the waterline, the first few lionfish began to peck tentatively at his earlobes, his lips, the folds of his neck. Carnivores tasting this new exotic food source.

Thorn went to Stetson, peeled the pistol from her rigid hand, wiped the grip with the tail of his T-shirt, edged back over to Osvaldo, stepping carefully around the fissures in the glass.

He kneeled beside the fractured hole, reached down into the bloody water, and grasped Osvaldo's limp right hand. He wrapped the man's fingers around the pistol grip, squeezing hard against Osvaldo's hand so the fingerprints would be clear, then stepped away as Osvaldo slumped back into the water and the pistol drifted from his hand.

Thorn took one long breath and let it go.

"He's done," Thorn said. "Now we need ice and two Ziploc bags, and we need it quick."

"And gauze," Sugar said, his voice frail. "And whiskey, if you have it."

TWENTY-THREE

SUGARMAN TALKED THEM THROUGH THE first aid, relying on the training he'd acquired in his days with the sheriff's department.

Gauze moistened with saline solution wrapped around each severed finger. Each digit was inserted into a fresh Ziploc bag and placed in a cooler filled with ice. A clean washcloth atop the ice so the severed fingers didn't make direct contact.

Sugar sipped Maker's Mark while he rattled off the step-by-step process. Awake, alert, rocked back in a leather recliner, his hand elevated. Two blankets lying atop him to stave off the shock. They were assembled in the family room that opened off the kitchen.

As Sugar instructed her, Kathy cleaned the finger stubs with saline solution, used more gauze to dress the open wounds, and added light pressure with a strip of surgical adhesive to slow the bleeding. It was a grim and messy job, but Kathy managed it with only an initial flinch.

Reattachment wasn't possible after 12 hours, Sugar told them, so they had to move fast. Thorn recalled the name of a hand surgeon in Miami, Michelle Miller. He'd guided her husband, Mickey Miller, a few dozen times flats fishing on Nine Mile Bank off Islamorada. They'd caught some beauties.

Stetson used her phone to track down Mickey Miller's cell, called him, handed the phone to Thorn. Unfortunately, his wife, Dr. Michelle Miller, was out of town at a conference, but Mickey gave Thorn the name of her partner in the surgical practice.

Dr. Zubin Romero listened to Thorn's description of the severed fingers and asked if proper steps had been taken to preserve them.

Thorn assured Romero that all the correct medical procedures were followed.

"And exactly how did these fingers come to be separated from the hand?"

"A very sharp knife."

Romero paused for a long moment.

"Will this be a police matter?"

"It was an accident," Thorn said.

"I'm not on-call for such a procedure and would refer you to a colleague, but my partner's husband, Mickey Miller texted and vouched for you and your injured friend, so yes, I will agree to perform the surgery, but I can promise nothing. Replantations can be quite tricky."

Romero arranged to meet Sugar at Baptist Hospital in Kendall. He would call ahead to organize the OR. Have Emergency Room nurses waiting for Mr. Sugarman's arrival.

When he hung up, Thorn said to Sugar, "I've got a new word for your vocabulary list."

"The boats are adrift," Stetson said. "How do we get ashore to the car?"

Thorn told them about Sheriff Sprunt's arrival after Kathy and Stetson left the beach, how Sprunt took orders from Osvaldo to recover the bodies and return the boats to the dock.

"The Sheriff is on Osvaldo's payroll?" Kathy said.

"Appears so," Thorn said.

"I'll go check on the boats," Stetson said.

When she was gone, Thorn said, "Osvaldo's not her father?"

"I don't know what Osvaldo believed. Maybe he suspected the truth, but was too cowardly to address it with me."

Kathy poured herself a shot of Maker's Mark, offered the bottle to Thorn. He made himself a full glass and gulped half of it down.

"Who's her father, Kathy?"

"You can't tell? Look in her eyes, those chestnut brown eyes. Who do you see?"

"I'll explain, Kathy," Sugar said.

"I'll do it," she said.

Thorn shook his head and watched Kathy struggle to find the words.

"Those nights when I went to Snappers to do my gigs…"

She took another sip of bourbon.

"You asked me not to come because I'd make you self-conscious."

"Some of those nights I didn't have a gig."

"But you left anyway," Thorn said. "Sugar, you have something to add?"

"I'm sorry, Thorn. It just happened."

Kathy said, "Most of those nights I was singing at Snappers. It was just a few times Sugar and I were together. We both felt guilty as hell. The guilt became too much, we were about to end it, that's when Osvaldo and his men came and hauled me away."

Thorn poured himself another generous hit, sloshed it in his glass, the honey brown of Stetson's eyes. The color of Sugarman's. How could he not have seen it?

"I knew something was strange," Thorn said. "These last few days, Sugar, you've been wanting to confess, haven't you? I saw something odd in your face."

"Look, back then, seventeen years ago, after Osvaldo's guys beat the shit out of you and Kathy disappeared and we couldn't find her, I felt it was best I didn't tell you. Add more pain on top of all the rest of it. I'm sorry, Thorn. I should have been honest. It was a shitty thing."

"All right, all right," Thorn said. "The good news is, you two created a smart, courageous daughter. So, okay, it's done. You're forgiven."

"You sure about that, Thorn? Let it go so easily?"

"Hell, yes," Thorn said. "Lot of water under the bridge. We're friends. Nothing's going to change that." Then he looked at Kathy for several seconds and managed a smile, "You're absolutely sure she's Sugar's?"

"Eyes, hair, body, bone structure. Come on, Thorn. It's right in front of you. No DNA test required. Osvaldo never met Sugar or he would've seen it right away."

Thorn nodded and rested a hand on Sugarman's shoulder, and Kathy crossed the room and fit herself against Thorn's body and lay a hand on Sugar's other shoulder, completing the circuit. The three of them united by deceit, by horror, but most of all by love.

"One of the boats is missing," Stetson announced from the doorway. "When I saw it wasn't there, I checked my bedroom and Pablo escaped. He must have taken the second boat."

Thorn peeled away from Kathy's embrace.

"It's okay, Stetson. Don't worry about it. That slimeball will ooze back into the sewer where he came from. Now we have to roll. Get our boy's fingers replanted where they belong."

Stetson shifted her gaze from Thorn to Sugarman and then to her mother.

"I didn't kill him, right? The fish killed him."

"It's going to be all right, honey," Kathy said.

She moved to Stetson's side and drew her close.

"I've thought about doing it for so long, but when I tried to shoot him, I couldn't."

"What you did was perfect," Sugar said. "Absolutely flawless. The universe is a far better place than it was an hour ago."

While Sugarman was in surgery, Thorn and Kathy sat in the Baptist Hospital waiting room, elegant and sterile. A Hispanic family occupied the chairs in the far end of the room, the mother and father were grimly silent while their two adolescent boys played some rapid-fire games on their phones. A TV was set to a cable news channel, the sound muted. Images of wars and street violence and politics.

Across the room, sleek wood shelves were filled with books and board games, and on the walls, a dozen landscape paintings of the tranquil Everglades tempered the somber atmosphere.

Fidgeting and grumbling to herself, Stetson had gotten up and wandered outside and was pacing on the sidewalk just beyond the bank of windows. She checked her phone every few minutes, then tucked it into the pocket of her shorts. A minute later she drew it out again and repeated the routine.

"She'll be okay," Thorn said.

"Will she?"

"From what I've seen, she's a tough young lady."

"I hope you're right."

They'd been sitting silently for half an hour when Thorn said, "This Trickster bullshit, was it all a lie? Or was Osvaldo fucking with me for real? Like that thing with Dulce, did he do that or just imagine it and feed it to you?"

"All I know is what he gave me," she said. "Was he doing those Trickster things in real life? I wondered that myself, but I don't know. Maybe it was all a mirage, just Osvaldo's fantasy. He cashed in on your escapades, but kept his distance from you in real life."

"But you're not sure?"

Thorn watched her working out what she meant to say. Living with those street punks for so long, she probably hadn't had a real conversation in years and had fallen out of practice.

"The details he gave me, Thorn, I made as believable as you can in a novel. But was all of it based on real events? I have no way of knowing if he was tampering with your life, or if it was just wishful thinking. Wanting to play a starring role in the books, the black-hearted villain."

She stared down at her lap.

"Maybe there's a third alternative," said Thorn.

"Which is what?"

"Planting the seeds of doubt. I'll never be sure if the guy was fucking with me or not."

"Well, okay, then there's also a fourth," she said. "You'll never know for sure, so simply let it go. Whatever he was doing, he'll never do it anymore."

"Just forget it all? Erase my memory? Is that possible?"

"You can try."

Thorn nodded that she was right. He wasn't great at letting things go, but this time it made sense. No way should he let Osvaldo fuck with his head long after the guy was dead. But he remembered Sugarman's vocabulary lesson at Snappers. Palimpsest. No matter how you might try, nothing from the past is ever quite erased.

"What I do know for sure is this, Thorn. The last twenty years, even if it was all vicarious and second hand, spending time with you, witnessing your romantic adventures, your various exploits, it was a wonderful escape from my imprisonment. Writing about you and Sugar, I felt like the three of us never parted. We were still together, still friends, lovers."

She sighed, rose to her feet, walked to the end of the row of chairs, took a breath and let it go, then returned. She sat down and stared into his eyes, her gaze steady, her chin lifted slightly as if ready to deliver a difficult admission.

"I loved you a great deal, Thorn, and in the midst of that love affair, I was unfaithful. I've never forgiven myself for that."

"Hey, it's a night for forgiveness. We all survived, that's what matters."

She leaned across the arm of the chair to kiss his cheek. More than a peck, less than a smooch.

"Now," he said. "That book in the aquarium room, *North Exposed*. Tell me about that."

"What book?"

"It had your name on the cover. You're the author, *North Exposed*."

"The last book I wrote was a year ago, *Desertion in the Desert,* about you and Sugar in Arizona, Dulce, all that. I've written nothing since. Osvaldo stopped sending me details. I was starving for anything about you and Sugar, but he gave me nothing for the last year."

Thorn considered that, watching the TV news unfold, lifeless bodies heaped in the street. With the sound off, it was impossible to tell if it was a foreign war or a Saturday night in Miami.

"Well, Sugar read some of *North Exposed* in the aquarium room while I was unconscious, and said it didn't sound like your prose."

She fanned a hand in front of her face as if clearing smoke.

"I'm baffled," she said. "Totally mystified."

Thorn told her about the back cover. Katrina Mayfield had discovered her long-time hero was actually a child rapist. And furthermore, North had all along been based on a real person living in Key Largo, Florida. The man's name was exposed in that book. And the author was going to turn over evidence of his crimes to authorities."

"Oh, my ever-loving god," she said. "Osvaldo was going to nuke you."

"It could still happen, between that book and Sheriff Sprunt. Even with Osvaldo dead."

For several moments her eyes went blind with thought, then they cleared and she asked if the book had a paper cover or hard.

"Paper, I think. Yeah, it was paper, embossed lettering, photographic image of my dock and my boats and Blackwater Sound."

"If it's paper," she said, "that's an ARC, Advanced Reader's Copy."

"Which means what?"

"It's early in the publishing process."

"So?"

"So there's time to stop it."

"Can you do that?"

"All the money I've made those people, damn right I can stop it."

Stetson came back inside and sat down in the chair beside Thorn.

"I'm okay," she said. "I'm going to be fine."

"Give yourself some time," Thorn said. "Tonight was a lot to absorb."

Dr. Zubin Romero appeared in the doorway across from them. Thorn rose and Kathy and Stetson did as well.

Kathy asked if Sugar was going to be all right.

"These operations are never without complications," Romero said. "But all in all, this one proceeded with only minor difficulties. It'll be a few months before Mr. Sugarman is playing Chopin or Ravel's *Gaspard de la Nuit*. But with some physical therapy, I believe he will regain full function in his hand. Some numbness might persist, but beyond that, I believe the long-term nerve damage will be minimal."

Stetson asked about *Gaspard de la Nuit* and the doctor smiled and said, "The final movement, Scarbo, is fearsomely difficult. I've heard it said that playing that piece is like solving endless quadratic equations in one's head."

"Can we see him now?" Thorn asked.

"One at a time," the doctor said. "No more than five minutes each."

Kathy went first.

Alone with Stetson, Thorn said, "Do you want to stay at my place tonight. You and your mom can have the bed. I've got a hammock I can string up on the porch."

Stetson's voice was strained, her face oddly soft and empty as if she'd just awakened from a drugged sleep.

"Don't lie to me, Thorn."

He promised he wouldn't, then immediately regretted it.

"Is he my father? Sugarman?"

Thorn said nothing, but Stetson read the answer in his face.

"Thank god," she said. "Since I was a little kid, I've been dreaming there was a Sugarman out there somewhere. A father I could be proud of."

TWENTY-FOUR

A MONTH LATER, THE FOUR of them had planned a fishing trip. They were going to poke around the backcountry, try a few of Thorn's most productive spots, a few of Sugar's, maybe work their way north to Flamingo and look for tarpon.

The weather had cleared and was in the high eighties with humidity so dense you could write a haiku in the air with your fingertip. No storms brewing. Hurricane season would last a couple more months, but so far, to everyone's great relief, this storm season was a bust.

Thorn assembled his gear, setting some spinning rods by the front door, a couple of fly-rods, his smallest tackle box, sunscreen, sandwiches, and beer.

Sugar was boating down from Pumpkin Key in his twenty-foot Mako. For the last month, he'd been recuperating on the island, nursed by Stetson and Kathy Spottswood. Gradually regaining feeling and movement in his fingers. With his twins off at college in Tallahassee, Sugar was settling in with his new family, more content than Thorn had ever seen him.

As luck would have it, Sheriff Sprunt and the deputies who'd helped retrieve the bodies of Osvaldo's thugs had been recorded on half a dozen infrared security cameras based at homes and docks in Ocean Reef. The videos were murky, but they clearly showed Sheriff Sprunt and his men dragging dead bodies aboard their boats, then taking them away.

The head of security for the club alerted authorities and later on, he passed the videos to the Monroe County State Attorney. It wasn't long after that before two of the deputies who'd accompanied Sprunt that night cut a deal to testify against their boss.

The trickiest part was explaining Osvaldo's death. Kathy, the professional storyteller, took charge of that part. Staying as close to the truth as possible, she kept it simple. What she called "the fifty word elevator pitch."

In a freak accident, a close friend of hers in Key Largo severed two fingers, and Kathy and her daughter rushed her friend to a hospital in Miami and were gone all night while their friend was in emergency surgery. If there were any doubts about this story, Baptist Hospital records would substantiate it.

Since she was not present that night on the island, she could only guess what went down. She believed the most likely scenario was that a business rival's gang attacked Osvaldo's men as they were returning to the island. They rammed the boat with Osvaldo's guys which caused both vessels to capsize. Osvaldo, who had been darkly depressed for months over some business setbacks, was now terrified his island would be overrun by his foes. In a fit of desperation, he took his own life.

"And who would this business rival be?" Captain Terry Miller wanted to know.

Probably had something to do with real estate, but beyond that Kathy had no idea. Osvaldo was secretive about his business affairs, and Kathy had learned not to pry.

All she could add was that when she returned home from the hospital, she discovered Osvaldo's lifeless body in the aquarium room in what looked like a suicide.

"A bizarre manner of suicide," Miller said.

"That aquarium was my husband's pride and joy. I believe he may have wanted to destroy it before his enemies could."

"I repeat," Captain Miller said, "bizarre."

In the following days, when Kathy was questioned further, she repeated the story word for word, tying up every loose end and explaining away each discrepancy the investigators threw at her. The poor quality of the various night-time security videos failed to contradict anything she said. And indeed, there were numerous videos showing Kathy and her daughter and another man with a heavily bandaged left hand returning to the island the next afternoon. Shortly after making it home, she discovered Osvaldo's body, and made a panicked call to 9-1-1. More substantiation of her story.

"I guess writing crime novels for twenty years taught me something," she told Thorn.

Sheriff Sprunt was put under house arrest in his Islamorada home, forced to surrender his passport, an electronic bracelet locked to his ankle. A Captain from the Key West sheriff's office was chosen to fill in for Sprunt until his trial for criminal conspiracy was complete.

And to add to Sprunt's woes, Jinny Strickland came forward with more information for the State Attorney about other legal violations Sprunt had committed during his time in office. She had evidence of a dozen instances of bribery that Sprunt extorted from local businesses in the Upper Keys. Cash payments ranging from a few hundred dollars to one for ten thousand to cover up acts of child molestation perpetrated by the owner of a biker bar in Lower Matecumbe.

Next, with a single phone call, Kathy managed to halt the publication of *North Exposed*. Her editor was grateful she'd withdrawn the book which he was certain would have caused irreparable damage to her literary reputation. Despite this awkward episode, the editor was eager to read her next novel, and hoped she would return to her series character, North. She assured the gentleman that she had no such intention. She believed she and Mr. North had parted ways for good.

Sugarman handled the removal of the listening devices and the video cams concealed inside Thorn's house. He hired a computer hacker from Miami to scrub all traces of audio and video records on Osvaldo's cloud account.

Because there was no last will and testament, Osvaldo's estate, including Pumpkin Key and all of his financial and real estate assets, passed to his wife and daughter. Buried in the paperwork, Kathy discovered a partnership agreement with Sunshine Productions which was building the bar and restaurant on the property adjoining Thorn's land. That establishment was meant to be one more act of torment directed at the man who cuckolded Osvaldo years earlier.

As the new controlling partner in that LLC, Kathy exercised the option to buy out Sunshine Productions' shares, then proceeded to cancel further construction work. She signed over the ownership of the property to Thorn to use as he saw fit, which doubled his total land to almost ten acres along the banks of Blackwater Sound. Enough cushion for Thorn to take a long deep breath, after which he resolved to stay put in Key Largo till he'd lived out his allotted days.

That warm September morning, out of one of his south-facing windows, Thorn watched Sugarman's distinctive blue-hulled Mako exit Adams Cut and enter Blackwater Sound. With rods in hand, Thorn headed out to meet them.

He pushed open the screen door and stepped onto the deck. And halted.

A man was sitting in one of the Adirondack chairs. He wore a baseball cap and his long hair was held in a ponytail.

"Going somewhere, *pendejo*?"

Pablo stood up, turned slowly, and trained the chrome automatic on Thorn's chest. He was wearing a black tactical vest, ribbed Kevlar.

"Thought by now you'd be dead meat, Pablo."

"Why'd you think that?"

"Law of the jungle."

"What the fuck, man. What law?"

"Kill or be killed. Weak little shit like you, it's a miracle some big lion didn't gobble you up without Victor, Jorge, and Facundo watching your back every minute."

"You about to see some law of the jungle, fuckface."

A couple of the rods in Thorn's hands were antiques. He'd inherited them from his father, Dr. Bill Truman, ageless beauties made from split bamboo with cork handles. When Dr. Bill died, the rods were in mint condition, and Thorn tried to preserve them that way. Only fished with them on special occasions like today. So he hated like hell to risk damaging them, but maybe Pablo was the reason he'd kept the rods all these years. The higher purpose they were destined to serve.

Thorn slung the rods at him, dodged to the left as the little guy fired twice into the chaos of bamboo shafts and reels.

Thorn waded in, hammered Pablo's wrist, knocked the pistol loose, drove the guy backward into the rot-weakened railing, kept driving him until the wood splintered and gave way. Pablo snatched at Thorn's shirt, trying to drag him along for the ride, but Thorn chopped his hand away, and Pablo plunged the twenty feet, doing a half-flip before he slammed on his back on the brick pathway.

He was still breathing when Thorn reached him. Eyes straining to open.

Thorn lifted him up, hauled him out to the dock. Grabbed him in the armpits and hoisted him up to the fish hook, making sure the steel barb penetrated the body armor but not the flesh. He didn't want to hurt the little fellow, even if he had intended to murder Thorn. Wouldn't look good when the stand-in sheriff came to take Pablo away.

By the time Sugarman's Mako pulled up to the dock, Pablo had regained consciousness and was squirming and kicking on the big steel hook. Not going anywhere.

Sugar tied off his lines and the three of them climbed onto the dock.

"Our diminutive friend came by for a last house call."

While Kathy called 9-1-1, Stetson walked over to look up at Pablo.

He wriggled his legs and slapped his arms at the piling, trying to tear loose.

"You had to sneak a look down my shirt," she said. "Trying to get a peek at my breasts, that's how you wound up on that hook. You just couldn't help your stupid self. Hoisted by your own pecker."

They waited for the cops in Sugarman's Mako, lounging in the seats, watching Pablo.

"I don't know, Kathy," Thorn said. "You sure you're finished writing? This could make a pretty good North story. A bad guy hanging on a hook. A happy ending and everything."

"All these years, doing the same thing over and over. It's gotten old."

"Try writing something different," Sugar said. "I hear taking a different approach can rejuvenate a person. Like having a second chance. Get it right this time."

Kathy gazed out at Blackwater Sound, at the silver shimmer, the distant strands of pink clouds rimming the horizon, a squadron of pelicans skimming by.

"You know," she said, "I might do that. Try a different kind of story. See how it feels."

Thorn excused himself and walked back to the house and retrieved his antique rods. He checked them over inch by inch. A couple of minor nicks, but nothing serious. He carried them out the dock and climbed back into the Mako, fit the rods in the holders.

"Here you go, Uncle Thorn."

Stetson scooted over and tapped the bench seat next to her. He sat, gave her knee a chummy pat, and she patted his knee back and showed him an impish smile.

"You know, Thorn," Stetson said. "You're definitely no North, but I have to admit you're not nearly as pathetic as my first impression."

"High praise," said Sugar.

"High indeed." Kathy leaned back and took Sugar's hand in hers and winked at Thorn.

Yeah, one of those rare happy endings.

Other Books By James W. Hall

Thorn Series

Under Cover of Daylight
Tropical Freeze
Mean High Tide
Gone Wild
Buzz Cut
Red Sky at Night
Blackwater Sound
Off the Chart
Magic City
Hell's Bay
Silencer
Dead Last
Going Dark
The Big Finish
Bad Axe
Trickster

Harper McDaniel Series

When They Come For You
When You Can't Stop

Standalones:

Hard Aground
Bones of Coral
Rough Draft
Body Language
Forests of the Night

Short Stories:
Paper Products
Over Exposure

About James W. Hall

James W. Hall is the author of 21 novels, four volumes of poetry, two
collections of short stories, and two works of non-fiction. He lives with his
wife, Evelyn, in the mountains of North Carolina. They share their home
with Hazel and Hank, two Cavalier King Charles Spaniels.

Made in the USA
Monee, IL
15 August 2022